Shifting Sands

Moraa Gitaa

Nsemia

First Edition April 2012

Edited by Charles Phebih-Agyekum
Cover Design Concept: Abel Murumba:
Cover Design: Danielle Pitt
Author photo by Simon Cox, courtesy of *True Love Magazine East Africa*

Published by Nsemia Inc. Publishers
Oakville, Ontario, Canada
www.nsemia.com

Note for Librarians:
A cataloguing record for this book is available from Library and Archives Canada

ISBN: 978-1-926906-04-1 paperback

"African women in general need to know that it's OK for them to be the way they are – to see the way they are as a strength, and to be liberated from fear and from silence."
Wangari Maathai

TABLE OF CONTENTS

PART ONE
SWIMMING AGAINST THE TIDE

PART TWO
KEEPING MY HEAD ABOVE WATER

PART THREE
STRIKING FOR SHORE

DEDICATION

Dedicated to all women and our girlfriends; the ones who hold our souls and are always there for us. The ones who recognise our struggles and achievements, our strengths and weaknesses – the whole bouquet that is the human experience on this adventure called life.

* * * *

Thank you Jesus, my Lord, for the strength to keep writing despite many hardships. May I always remember that in the book of James 1:17 you remind me that every good and perfect gift comes from Jehovah my God who does not change like shifting shadows. I pray that I will continue utilizing this gift and talent of writing that You have endowed me with to tell stories that need to be told. I will try my level best to furnish readers with profound insights into the human condition, while at the same time promoting and affirming positive and universal values.

* * * *

ABOUT THE AUTHOR

Moraa Gitaa is a Kenyan author living in Nairobi with her seventeen-year-old daughter Tracy. Moraa is currently in the process of registering the **Moraa Gitaa Foundation** (MGF), which ill consist of a Dyslexia (a writing disorder that challenged her daughter in her formative years) awareness unit, incorporate a Social Organization arm which will sensitise the community on HIV and AIDS, while sourcing for support for orphans and destitute young women affected by the endemic resident in informal settlements. The organization will also operate as a vocational training centre for the same group of persons and will have a community resource centre cum library. Moraa is also the Deputy Chair of International PEN Kenya Chapter Women Writers' Committee and Coordinator of PAN (PEN African Network). The Pan African grouping of African writers consists of members of African regional PEN centres. Moraa is pro-children/youth and pro-women and sets out to reflect this in her various treatises. For more information please visit her website at: www.moraagitaa.com

Crucible for Silver & Furnace for Gold (Nsemia Inc. Publishers, 2008) was her first full-length novel. She is currently working on other titles including *Indecent Proposal* (Crime Fiction Novella), *Shark Attack!* (Teen Novella), and *The Deepest Cut* (Inspirational).

Other future works include *Devil in the Detail* (Novel), *Katsanga Kenye – An Anthology* (Moraa's collection of short stories).

She has been featured in anthologies including *Author-Me Author Africa Anthology* (2011), *Kwani? Project Soma* (2012), *Author-Me Author Africa Anthology* (2008), and

G21 The World's Magazine – Africa Fresh! New Voices from the First Continent (2007) among others.

She has published a number of short stories that include *Searching Me, Katsanga Kenye, The Devil is in the Detail, To Serenity via Perdition, Diplomatic Immunity* and *From Shifting Sands to Deeper Dimensions.*

An excerpt chapter from this book won first prize in Adult Fiction from the National Book Development Council of Kenya (NBDCK) in 2008. Moraa was also nominated for the 2010 Penguin Prize for African Writing.

* * * *

Website: www.moraagitaa.com

Email: moraagitaa@moraagitaa.com

ACKNOWLEDGEMENTS

I take this opportunity to thank the National Book Development Council of Kenya (NBDCK) for recognizing the worth of an earlier form of this manuscript by awarding it first prize during the National Book Week of September 2008. The award was for an excerpt chapter from this book titled *From Shifting Sands to Deeper Dimensions*. This recognition provided a powerful impetus for me to complete the full length novel which you are now holding in your hands. My profound gratitude goes to Professor Wanjiku Kabira for her encouragement and deeming it worthwhile to pen such an incisive and enlightening foreword for this book.

Ahsante sana to all my girlfriends – you know yourselves, especially the ones who always knew when my daughter and I did not have any *unga* for *ugali* in my house as I struggled to write. I express my deep and sincere gratitude for our candid conversations, your timely calls, text messages, emails, and sometimes dispassionate opinions, which I treasured as I wrote this book.

I am thankful to my readers who took time to critique this novel in all its various raw forms since I started working on it back in 1999. You all offered invaluable insights and brazenly pointed out flaws, inconsistencies and the good parts too, peppered with encouragement, to ensure that I finished writing it. And to all fellow writers, much more ink to all our pens or as we would say in the twenty-first century, more power to our keyboards! Much love, Moraa.

* Note -- Credit is given to reproduction of 'The Serenity Prayer' by Reinhold Niebuhr.

FOREWORD

Moraa Gitaa, in Shifting Sands, is a companion of writers such as Margaret Ogola (Kenya), Mariama Ba (Senegal), Elieshi Lema (Tanzania), Chimamanda Adichie (Nigeria) and many other women writers who have added their voice by reflecting and sharing their thoughts about the lives and experiences of African people and women in their various societies. Through this growing body of literature, we are able to access women's perspectives on the social, political and economic experiences of the African people. Women continue to speak for themselves and name the world. The story told by Moraa is intense and captures the daily lives of the people from Mombasa, where it is set, and explores the experiences of four women, who have grown up together, and have their own dreams, which are never realised. It is the story of multiple oppression where the experiences of institutions of governance, religion, culture and other factors conspire against the girls. It is only the refusal to die and resilience of girls like Kemunto that keep the women and the poor in the African society going.

The story is captivatingly told utilizing the women's space, in the kitchen for instance, as the girls listen to the harrowing story of Latifah's experience with anti-terror agents. In between the story told by Latifah, she trails off to discuss the meal being prepared. What a creative way of utilizing women's space. It is in the kitchen as the girls prepare the delicacies, that one associates with Mombasa and the Waswahili community, that the shocking story of Latifah and her son is told. In utilizing the women's space, the girls introduce us to the complex, detailed, artistic and creative way of preparing meals. One gets to appreciate the role of women in this space and the kind of technical skills and knowledge required to prepare a meal which tradition has often made a mockery of and which contributes to the unpaid labour that society takes for granted. Moraa redefines the women's space.

The story is also told through liberal utilization of African terms including proverbs from the Abagusii community, Gikuyu community and Meru community. This is in addition to the use of words and names such as Magokoro, traditional foods and rituals. The novel also liberally uses Kiswahili words. It is indeed a drink brewed in an African pot. The detailed description of places such as the Old Town, Likoni, Mama Ngina Drive, the coastal strip of Kenya and others makes one walk with the author and experience the smell, the taste, the beauty and the warmth of Mombasa. Moraa has also used repetition of phrases such as the advice to Kemunto by her father "*kila mtu atabeba msalaba wake*" to create cohesion and a consistent reminder of the fact that you have your own individual life and will carry your own cross. Her use of flashbacks, such as telling the story of Latifah and Myra and her communion with those who have passed on and addressing them directly creates elasticity for the story. Her style is compelling, captivating, and very rich. The use of the narrative voice makes the story have a personal touch and the reader is able to empathise with the experiences of the narrator and her friends.

This is the story of four young women from different cultural and racial/ethnic backgrounds. Kemunto (from the Abagusii community) whose father is a former district commissioner and the mother a former senior state counsel, like the other three girls', lives in Mombasa. She goes through the harrowing experiences of FGM, experiences an abusive relationship with Maxi, the father of her daughter Nehema, and deals with sexual harassment at the work place. She is a victim of corruption, where the fat cats, as she says, who are involved in corporate fraud and money laundering walk in court corridors with big grins knowing they will be set free. In all these experiences she refuses to compromise, even when she almost contemplates suicide. She holds on to her upbringing, which was shaped by her father's influence and that of her Magokoro (the paternal grandmother). Her culture, belief in truth, honesty, integrity and dignity are her hallmark. Through her, we learn a lot about Abagusii culture and other ethnic cultures, the poverty of the people in Kenya, the status of women in society, corruption and injustices in Kenyan institutions and the survival strategies to keep afloat. Her dream to become a writer lives on even as the novel ends. On the other hand, from Shilpa, we learn about the Indian culture, racial discrimination as well as the status of girls in the Asian community. Her papaji and mamadi are conservative parents who prevent her from realizing her dream of becoming an architect by shipping her to India because she has fallen in love with Victor, a Kenyan of African origin. She is separated from the other girls for life as the parents hope that they will find an Indian man whose generation they will investigate and who would be appropriate for their daughter.

Through Latifah, the girl of the Arab origin, we learn about the status of women and girls in the Muslim community. Latifah was being taught to be submissive, unlike other girls, and threatened with hell fire at the slightest sign of deviating from the holy teachings. Her Ma and Shaghazis taught her that girls are supposed to get married and have babies. She shares with other girls the fact that all women in her life hid their emotions behind their veils and that they were dressed appropriately to social conventions and Muslim doctrine. As in many other cultures, the girls in this culture were meant to be seen and not to be heard. It was men who chose when to notice them and when not to. Her dream of becoming a dentist was shattered too. Later, Latifah is arrested by anti-terror detectives and taken to Nairobi with her four-year-old son. The harrowing experience that she goes through with a bullet in her spine and continuous snooping of detectives and the investigations by ATPU, FBI, MI and MOSSAD, leads her to seclusion.

It is Myra, the fourth girl, whose story is devastating. She became a Marine Biologist and decided to pursue the pleasures of life through associations and partnering with Germans and Italians at the Coast who were involved in drug dealings and money laundering, among other vices. In the end, Kemunto, the narrator, reflects on the lives of her three friends and others who have gone and "left me alone to my grief," and wonders, "Am I going to be able to move from shifting sands of doubt and insecurity to deeper dimensions of Kenyan's known incredible resilience?"

Moraa has told a story that many African girls and women must read. It is both inspiring and captivating. It is a true reflection of experiences of many women of Africa. She walks on the path of all those women writers who are redefining the women's space, naming the world for themselves and their societies and bringing the experiences and perspectives of women to the fore. It is a must-read for literature students and a major contribution from Kenya and East Africa.

-Wanjiku Mukabi Kabira, *Chair of Department of Literature, Professor of Literature & Convenor of African Women's Studies Centre, University of Nairobi, Kenya*

PART ONE

SWIMMING AGAINST THE TIDE

THE SERENITY PRAYER

God grant me the serenity to...

Mungu nipashe utulivu wa...

Magokoro

Paternal *Magokoro*[i] roared like a lion. When she spoke, everyone, including all my uncles, stood to attention. She despised lazy people and never wanted to see idlers in her *boma*[ii].

Magokoro believed that all young people should rise with the cows when they went to the grazing fields and come back with them when the sun had gone to rest. Magokoro's word was final. It was law and no one ever dared to defy or question her. Not even our army officer uncle or police sergeant cousin!

Sometimes I think Magokoro became strong and tough when patriarchal and paternal *sokoro*[iii] died and left her alone to look after the tea and coffee plantations. Even when we would be taken to our rural home by papa and mama during the holidays to visit her, we never rested. We were always made to work in the fields.

Despite Magokoro being so strict on how we spent our time during the day, in the evenings she would always have a folk tale for us. Her ogre story-telling sessions by her fireside would start with, *'mogano ngochande*[iv],*'* and the children gathered around would reply in anticipation, *'mogano inchwo*[v].*'*

Magokoro also had her foibles. I remember how in particular she would refuse to use mirrors saying that these were strange things brought to Africa by

---

i Kisii for grandmother

ii Kisii for homestead

iii Kisii for grandfather

iv Kisii -traditional way of asking permission to narrate a folk tale; transliterated it means loosely "Folk tale I am coming"

v Kisii -traditional way of inviting oral narration of a folk tale; transliterated it means loosely "Folk tale come"

Europeans. She would insist that looking at your face in the mirror at night would turn you into a thief just like the *wazungus* who had come and stolen our land while pretending to teach us about the Bible. She would then promptly put all mirrors face down in the entire house, especially when visiting us in the city!

Magokoro was a hard worker and she made sure she taught us 'town babies,' as she called us, how to fetch water from the river. She showed us how to balance the earthen pots on our heads and delicately traverse slippery ridges. Once at her *boma* we would gracefully shift the pot from head to knee, steady it there for a couple of seconds and bring it down onto the earthen floor, all in one swift sweeping graceful motion. We practiced many times until we were able to do it without spilling even a drop!

Magokoro was very enterprising. She said she would not spend unnecessary money to buy stuff when we could make it ourselves. She thus taught us girls how to expertly place our milk gourds on our thighs and coax *ghee* out of curdled milk to get cholesterol-rich cooking fat and homemade body lotions. She taught me how to till the *shamba*[i] and hoe out weeds from in between rows of sweet potatoes, arrowroots and bean stalks. She told me to shut up about blisters on my hands! She even taught me how to make hideous scarecrows from waste paper and blue gum tree sticks to scare away the birds which would feed on the millet. She also made me adept at expertly spinning huge mounds of *ugali* using the wooden cooking stick on the three-stone fireplace.

Though Magokoro is now a hundred-years-old, she is very healthy. I have never seen her add salt to her food or sugar to her tea. She never uses any additives to her cooking. Everything she eats, she boils herself and never wants to see cooking oil or fat in her house!

---

i Kiswahili -- farm, garden

I guess that is why she hardly has any wrinkles, is upright and is yet to use a walking stick. She still tills her farm like she is seventy years young. She has never bothered to use the cows to plough. I remember how she once scoffed and sucked her teeth in disdain when one of my younger uncles bought a combine harvester for his wheat fields. She reminded him of the time she was a young girl and they used to harvest the wheat and rice using their hands. She says young people have become lazy.

She taught me how to milk the cows using my hands. She never wanted to hear our papa telling her about milking machines! She taught me how to winnow. She made sure that I learned to correctly hold the traditional tray we called *oroteru* in Kisii, as I swirled it round and round to separate the chaff from the grains of rice, beans or pigeon peas. She made me do it over and over again until I ensured that only my arms swayed and not my whole body as I twirled the hyacinth reed tablets towards the direction of the wind.

Magokoro was a perfectionist. As a result, she hardly ever praised one for work well done or acknowledged excellence. She would entirely focus almost all her energies on the bad and would repeatedly talk about one's mistake, even up to thrice a day! She would say that she did this because if good deeds are given too much attention or prominence, then the good doers would tend to grow proud. While on the other hand, if a bad deed is tolerated and not shunned, the mistake would definitely occur time and again!

Magokoro also had strict rules like the spittle one. She would spit on the ground and before the blob of spittle dried in the sun we were supposed to be back from the millers, or whatever errand we had been sent on. If we broke the rule we would be punished. It was

7

her ingenious way of ensuring that we did not stray or get into mischief on the way.

I remember our song of the field that she taught me to scare away the birds.

> *Oobori bwa babaa, Oobori bwa babaa*
> *Egesingerero, ekebarara*
> *Getarikwaa, getarikorema*
> *Ekio gochi rogoro, ekio gochi maate*
> *Enyoni boronge, enyoni boronge, obe babaa, obe babaa.*

Just like in the Bible, we would sing of the lazy birds that do not till the land but want to reap where they have not sown.

I do not remember maternal Magokoro who passed on when I was a baby, but I learned fast that paternal Magokoro is the real and only matriarch and patriarch of our clan combined! That was why in hindsight, I came to realise that even her word on my circumcision was law. How will she ever take it if I were to write about my people's traditional rite and share it with the whole wide world?

THE SERENITY PRAYER

...accept the things I cannot change...

...kukubali vitu vyenye nisio na uwezo wa kubadilisha...

Papa and Mama

No quote beats our papa's mantra as we grew up. '*Kila mtu atabeba msalaba wake*[i].' It was a maxim I was to carry in my persona like my heart. It was his favourite comeback and line when lecturing us on dangers of premarital sex. He would never come out with it in so many words, but like talking drums going 'kabum, kadum, kabum,' he would always repeat himself.

We never saw papa cry, not even when we were in mourning after losing a relative. No one was ever sure of how he would react in any one given situation. Papa always told my brothers that men were not supposed to cry and that it was a show of weakness. I can still remember him in his colonial-style khaki trousers and matching shirt and colonial-style helmet.

Papa was a District Commissioner (DC). Though very tall, authoritative and strong looking in stature, he always had a soft and unique way of answering our questions or expressing himself. Like the instance when he declared, via mum of course, my favourite garlic was a banned substance in our home. He said that the onion fuelled sexual libidos. Not in so many words when I pushed him, but true to tradition he would say in Kiswahili '*Kila mtu atabeba msalaba wake.*'

The words stuck with me, and I would always remember them later in life when in catch-22 situations. Another time (if I remember correctly, I was twelve-years-old or thereabouts), I asked again what the garlic did to someone if he or she ingested too much of it. He replied in his usual veiled style, '*Si mnafundishwa Sayansi na*

---

i Kiswahili -- Every person will carry his/her own cross

Home Science? Uliza walimu wenu hiyo kitunguu saumu inafanya nini!'

I had just fidgeted in front of him and wondered why the old man never came out in straight talk, but had to use parables every time!

Later, I got a tongue lashing from mom as if I had broken all the Ten Commandments at one go! She reprimanded me for having such a discussion with dad. From then on, at home I referred to topics that touched on sexuality as 'The Garlic Talk.'

I remember those times in papa's car. Years back. Eons actually. I was only but a baby. I got to learn a lot about life through strains of music from the car stereo... Hugh Masekela, Fadhili William, Miriam Makeba, Franco, Beethoven, Manu Dibango, Bob Marley & the Wailers, Fundi Konde, Isaac Hayes, Tabu Ley, Frank Sinatra, Bruce Springsteen and Jim Reeves. If not these songs, then it was entirely Kenyan Benga, and Rumba or Congolese Lingala.

From his travels as a DC, papa always brought back presents. Like one time he went to Zambia and brought all of us copper plates and cups. When my siblings and I were small, papa and mama were, what older people who came to our home called 'career civil servants.' Our parents had met on official duty. Mama was a lawyer by profession and worked as a senior state counsel for the government. Papa and mama were in the civil service when it was for the very select few, and they tried to make sure that we never lacked for anything.

Papa would take us everywhere with him, including the army barracks at Nyali and the naval base at Mtongwe. Once we got out of the car, I would run alongside him clutching his hand, running to keep up with his long strides. I remember how excited I was on my first day at school. When it was my younger brother's turn he had not been too enthusiastic and thought he was being punished. He had cried while running after papa's Fiat.

Papa would take us with him to the Mombasa Municipal Stadium on all national holidays. We loved to watch the colourful passing parade by the Kenya Army, Kenya Navy and the Kenya Air Force. The music was always by the Kenya Prisons Band. I loved watching the leader of the band twirl his long silver mace without dropping it, the clang of cymbals, variety of sounds from the saxophonist and beating of the drums! We never missed to accompany papa to the ASK[i] annual trade fair at the Jomo Kenyatta grounds. We would sit proudly near him with mama at the podium. Sometimes we would be just a few metres away from the president.

Other times papa would be taken on transfer to another town and we would miss him terribly. When the transfers became too frequent, papa decided to quit the civil service and settle down as a businessman. I worshipped papa and he was my hero. That was until the other woman came into our lives and destroyed papa and mama's perfect love, or so I thought.

* * * * * *

"*Moja, mbili, tatu, nne, tano, sita, saba!*" That was our mama in Kiswahili. She would then ask us to repeat after her in English.

"One, two, three, four, five, six, seven!" I, together with my six siblings -- three brothers and three sisters -- lined ramrod straight in front of her, would oblige and intone.

She would continue: "Those are seven mouths to feed. Plus mine and your dad's that makes nine. We do not have extra money to feed any extra mouths, so we do not want you bringing us any extra babies." Sometimes she would tell us that she did not want us to be washing nappies and buying diapers with our first salaries as that was what happened to her and papa.

---

i Agricultural Society of Kenya

That was mama's way of introducing sex education, if you may call it that, to us, from our oldest brother turning thirteen to our last born sister barely a year old.

Mama had shut down her private legal practice and had been working as a civil servant for some years. Papa said she was head-hunted by the government to work as a senior state counsel. I was only eleven and did not understand what head-hunting meant but as I grew older I came to learn.

Mama always took us to the beach and treated us to dinner at a fancy restaurant, especially when papa was on transfer and she knew that we missed him. I loved to touch and play with mama's permed hair that reached past her shoulders and fell down her back. She always smelt like our baby sister's Johnson's talcum powder. Sometimes mama smelt of her *Binti el Sudan* perfume and Lady Gay body lotion. Her bathing soap was always Lux. She said it was the soap for international stars because she had seen the advert on TV say so! A waft of one or the other always drifted after her. Mama was petite and beautiful. She was always smart in African wear of *Kitenge*. But that was before she started fighting with papa.

THE SERENITY PRAYER

... courage to change the things I can...

...ujasiri kubadilisha vyenye nina uwezo wa kubadilisha...

Daring to Dream

Circa early 1980s

I hugged my knees tightly to my chest, curled into a ball and huddled into the dark corner of Magokoro's hut. My shoulders shaking due to the suppressed sobs and the tears flowing down my cheeks. I could hear the crickets chirping in competition with the croaking of the frogs in the night. I stared at the fireplace, the traditional cooking place with three stones dark with soot and at the glowing embers of the dying fire, the burning coals disintegrating and rolling away on the earthen floor. The hearth was warm beneath my bare feet. The flames cast shadows on the mud walls festooned with calabashes, shields and horns as decorations.

The trumpeting and blaring of cow horns brought wind of the news that the women of the ridge had come for me. The drum beats at Magokoro's doorstep heralded their arrival. I could hear the women dancing and singing outside amidst laughter and jokes. It sounded like dirges at my wake to my troubled mind. Ululations rented the air. It had been the order of the day for almost a week now. It was almost two in the morning. "God," I silently prayed, beseeching "please do not let them come for me." I did not want to go through this. I had no choice though I had begged my mama not to make me. She had stoically refused, saying that I had to go through it to become a woman, an upright one, and that the rite would help me maintain my chastity. I really did not understand any of it. She also said that I would not be called *egesagane*[i] anymore. What she did not seem to understand was that

---

[i] Kisii -- uncircumcised girl; often used in a derogatory and insulting manner.

it really did not matter to me what I was called. After all, I rarely heard any such talk in the coastal town where we lived and were brought up. Nor did any of my friends at school, Myra, Shilpa or Latifah, talk about it. My parents were 'modern' and I certainly did not understand where all this was coming from, but I had an idea at the back of my mind that it all had to do with traditional pressure bearing down on them – especially from Magokoro. Still, the rite would not change me now, or would it? My tiny mind struggled to understand the implications. Even before we had come from Mombasa to the shags or *bundus*, as we town kids referred to our rural highland homes, my mum and aunts in Mombasa had kept on hammering away into my head that I had to *kogenda bware kwaroka*[i], that is, go for the initiation. Why? My mind had screamed. I had refused, but mama kept on insisting that I must. I had laid awake in bed many nights for two months crying myself to sleep.

....Suddenly my reminiscing was shattered mid-stream as the wooden door was forced open. "Kemu! *Bwango! Bwango!*" paternal Magokoro's hoarse voice called out telling me to hurry. "*Tenena togende, chinsa chiaikire*[ii] she rasped further. Kemu is the short form of my name, Kemunto. Magokoro gave me the name. It means a petite or tiny person. She always looked at my ankles and elbows when I was a baby and would say that I would always be tiny because my bones are small. She had even given me a nickname when I was a baby, *ontururu*, which means five cents, because of my small stature. Even now she would use the nickname when in a happier mood, or when she had drunk lots of *amarwa*, the traditional booze she fermented and brewed herself from barley, sorghum and millet. But today she scared me. I thought of climbing onto the *irongo*, the traditional

---

i Kisii -- go for initiation, which included circumcision
ii Kisii -- "Stand up, Let us go. It is time."

ceiling which also doubled as a storage place built by laying rafters across the roof, but it looked impossible. I huddled further into the corner of the hut.

She tried to lift me up with her calloused, rough hands, which had turned so because of the constant use of the *jembe*[i] in her *shamba*, but I resisted. Magokoro then sucked at her teeth twice and clicked her tongue in anger. She called out to my mum, wondering if this granddaughter of hers was a coward. She asked if I was not aware that I was supposed to be circumcised before the naked sun rose. I also heard the other women inquiring over the same, wondering if I had not been listening to the wise counsel of my aunts and mama.

My mother had to save face. She came in and dragged me from the *riyo*, the cow hide, on which I had been resting, as any would-be initiate and the fresh initiate always did. I started whimpering again, begging her not to let me go through this, but she kept talking about respect in the community. For Heaven's sake didn't these people care and understand that I was only ten years old? I knew my cousin, who was a year older than I, had undergone the same ritual a few days before. When we reached *shags*, I found her already in seclusion. From the look of things, it seemed like I was going to join her soon. But then, she had been brought up here and had this zeal for tradition and all the taboos that go with it.

A celebratory mood was hanging over the *boma*. Two initiates! That was a cause for celebration in any *boma*! I always thought that only boys were circumcised. My brothers were so that they could be called *omosacha*[ii], a man, and not *omoisia*[iii], a mere boy.

---

i Kiswahili -- hoe

ii Kisii -- man

iii Kisii -- an uncircumcised boy, often used in a derogatory manner

Wasn't this rite on girls what the government through the local chiefs had been warning against at the *barazas*[i]?

Maybe that was why it was done in the dark of night – tradition dies hard. It is very difficult to eliminate. Even the chiefs, hypocritically, let their families go on with it.

I was dressed hurriedly and covered from head to toe in blankets and new *leso* wrappers. We headed outside. It was still pitch dark but almost the break of dawn. Shouts and cries of happiness rented the air from women who had been keeping vigil outside as we emerged from the hut. The wind brought news of yet another group of approaching singers. The all-night celebrations to me had seemed as if I was attending my own wake. Cows had been slaughtered for the occasion. I caught flashes and glimpses of torches and lanterns though I was thoroughly covered. We passed a neighbour's *boma*, where smouldering embers of a bonfire, to signify mourning, had been lit. The fire must continue burning for another week and should never be rekindled but be left to burn out naturally. Our papa once long ago told me that the fire burns beside the fresh soil of the grave and that our people, the Abagusii, never leave *ekeroba*, the fresh soil of the grave, before one has received all condolences from well-wishers and relatives. Otherwise, they believe misfortune after misfortune will haunt the bereaved family. The fire should also never be used to cook food or roast any meat. I remembered how paternal Magokoro had to stay put by the dying embers years ago when paternal Sokoro died of tuberculosis. I remember, at the time I was very little, seeing my grandfather using his own special utensils that I was told he could not share with anyone because tuberculosis (TB) was contagious. Magokoro had said that Sokoro had

---

i Kiswahili -- meetings held at village level with local residents and the chief

contracted TB because of the excessive tobacco he used and sometimes sharing of his pipe with other old men of the village. A shiver slithered up and down my spine and I trembled at my morbid reveries.

Now, hordes of women escorted us with traditional songs to the edge of our village. I was then left with about thirty women including my mama, Magokoro, aunts and older female cousins. We began on a trek. A long epic journey was how I was to view it on subsequent occasions of reminiscing. It took us up ridges and we crossed a river and went through several villages. All along we met women in their *shambas* who called out to us wanting to know if I was *omware*, an initiate. Their shrill voices rented the air with *koiririata*[i] upon hearing that I was or was soon going to be. The melodious ululations echoed across the ridges. Arrrrrrrrirrrrrriiiii! Arrrrrrriiiiirrrrrii! Arrrrrriiiiiirrrrrrrriii! Arrrrrriiiiiirrrrrrrriii! Arrrrrriiiiiirrrrrrrriii!

It was very cold because usually during the month of December extreme highland conditions prevail. I was shivering and the dew had made my dress wet. Fireflies twinkled teasingly past my eyes as they flitted into the tea bushes glistening in the dark dawn, the mist tightly wrapping itself onto the evergreen leaves. We went through vast carpet-like tea plantations and I lost track of time. Tears were trickling down my cheeks. No one even noticed that I kept stumbling due to weariness. Later, I could only vaguely recall that a woman had been on each side of me holding my hand to lead me as I could not see because of the smothering blanket.

Finally, we reached our destination. It was somewhere in the forest. We went towards a clump of bushes. I remember wondering if the Government directive had pushed these diehard traditionalists to the forest. By then the blanket had been removed.

---

i Kisii -- ululate (verb): ebiririato -- ululations

An old stooped woman came towards me. She seemed to have been waiting for us. Her face was wrinkled and pinched due to old age and maybe the vagaries of the weather. Her hands were gnarled and reminded me of the bark of the *muarubaini*[i]. She looked grotesque; she seemed to have hit the century mark ages ago. I started shaking and quaking with fear, my knees buckled beneath me, but the two women held me up. My mum looked at me warningly and reminded me not to scream -- why for Heaven's sake was I not allowed to scream? I wanted to wail out loudly, but I could not muster the courage when I glimpsed the outrageous stares of my aunts. It was as if they were wondering why one should cry when she is about to be made a woman? I was feeling so weak. I wanted to shout and scream at them all: "Can't you see I am only ten, and a child? Why can't I scream if you're going to hurt me?"

One of my younger aunts kept whispering to me over and over again "*Rema. Rema*[ii]"

But pray, do tell, how could I be brave? The *leso* was removed from my body and my dress was next. I started shivering again. Little did I know that the *calabashes* and earthen pots some of the women had been carrying contained ice cold water from the river that was going to be used as a local anaesthetic. I could never have imagined that I would experience such a cold drenching in my life.

Suddenly I was thrust down roughly on a large freezing rock, legs held *akimbo*, and flung onto the cold stone. The wet grass, full of dew and lumps of cow dung, covered my ankles. The threatening hysteria bubbled to the surface attempting to break through the throes of fear that had numbed and partially paralyzed my body. My panties were torn off me. I struggled and started

---

i Kiswahili -- Neem tree

ii Kisii -- "Be brave. Be brave."

sobbing, as two women pinned me down, holding my hands. I was conscious of someone else almost straddling my legs and suddenly they were yanked wide apart. I thrashed around wildly as the group urged the old woman to be fast. I saw the old woman get out a pair of scissors and a razor blade from her old decaying banana fibre pouch. I froze with fear. Surely those were not going to be used on me? My eyes must have been glazed with fright because in my subconscious state I heard someone say that my eyes should be covered. A large, dirty palm was eager to oblige and my world was plunged into darkness again. I opened my mouth wide and let out a terrified scream, which sounded like a squeak from one of the moles caught in the wire and steel traps left by young boys in the sprawling tea plantations. Another calloused hand covered my mouth tightly. My mama, sensing my fear, sucked and gritted her teeth, telling me it would only take a minute. One of the women put a piece of stick between my teeth so that I could stop whimpering and, in their misguided notions, not bite my tongue. The elderly granny made a sudden, swift lunge at my vagina, her hands just swiped at me...I felt sharp painful cuts.

That must be the razor blade, my bemused mind registered, a few and more sharper cuts like someone sawing at cloth. It almost gave me a heart attack, and those must be the scissors, my subconscious registered once again...I slipped into a brief fainting spell that I welcomed.

Arrrrririiiiiriiii!   *Arrrrririiiiiriiii!*   *Arrrrririiiiiriiii!*
Arrrririiiiiriiii!   *Arrrrrriiiiiirrrrrrrriiii!*

The ululations renting the air jerked me back to consciousness. I was aware of a sticky wetness pooling at the joint of my legs.

23

The old mama scooped ash from a knot in her dirty *leso* wrapper and rubbed it on my wounded vagina. I was in terrible pain. I gingerly held my feet apart. The women on either side of me sucked their teeth in disapproval and pushed my hips together hissing at me that it was a show of weakness and that I should try and walk properly, like an African woman. Someone lifted me up to my feet. I felt some liquid trickling down the inside of my thighs, and then I realised the sticky wetness was blood -- mine!

The blood continued trickling down to my shoes.

I looked around me and realised that my blood was splattered around us and onto the green grass. The old woman was showing the others something in her aged palm. I guess they needed proof that she had cut me before they paid her. They seemed to be overjoyed at the pieces of flesh they were shown and quickly got money from their bras and paid her. Mama was given my pieces of flesh by the old lady and told to bury them back at our tea plantation in our village.

We started on the same journey back up and down labyrinths and ridges. We crossed streams and rivers at their lowest points using stones to step on, through tea and pyrethrum plantations, this time being greeted with congratulations coupled with even merrier ululations than on our way out.

We met women with tea baskets coming from *etundubari*[i] after delivering tea leaves. To make matters worse, it was Friday; a market day, and we encountered many more people who had gone to sell at the market before dawn with vegetables, lots of fresh farm produce, cattle, sheep and goats, and who were now trekking back from Kebirigo market.

---

i Kisii -- Tea collection centre

The following day being a Saturday, people did not go to the market as most of the community were members of the Seventh Day Adventist (SDA) church. Their faith forbade them from working on the Sabbath.

That was why I was also circumcised today as the old woman would have gone to church the following day. Under the blanket I kept questioning the rationale behind all this. What had it accomplished?

All around us the women continued singing that Kemunto should dance as she had now become a "wife of men and not boys" and could now go to the *shamba* to dig.

> *Ero mbande, tenga ango buya Kemunto ominto kwabeire omokungu bwa abasacha,*
> *Ero mbande.*
> *Ero mbande, tenga ango buya Kemunto ominto kwabeire omokungu bwa abasacha,*
> *Ero mbande.*
> *Kemunto mogondo aree Kemunto.*
> *Kemunto mogondo aree Kemunto.*

Seclusion

Finally, we were back at our *boma* where we were received with more traditional songs and dances. The cows mooed and lowed pitifully as the fattest from papa's *kraal* were chosen and slaughtered for his eldest daughter's initiation. I was taken to join my cousin in the initiate's hut next to Magokoro's to begin a month-long seclusion. I must have passed out at the door of the hut for the next recollection I have of consciousness is lying on my *riyo*, in a corner. I felt hot searing pain around my crotch. The slightest movement aggravated the pain and brought tears to my eyes. I discovered that putting my thighs tightly close together while lying perfectly still lessened the pain.

25

The worst was yet to come. When trying to urinate... the pain was intolerable! I had to do it while sitting down as I could not even squat! My cousin showed me a trick to manage the pain. We had to pour lukewarm water, kept warm on a blackened pot over the fireplace, over our vaginas to lessen the pain.

I withdrew into my innermost self once again. I loved my cousin, but she seemed so excited about all this. While on the other hand, I could not condone the practice. It was barbaric and inhuman. For a whole week I could not walk properly, neither could I pass urine without whimpering and gritting my teeth because of the severe pain. It was torture whenever nature called! Yet people were celebrating. We could not go out in broad daylight, and if we had to, maybe for a visit to the pit latrine outside, we had to cover ourselves in ashes and *lesos*.

While in seclusion we fed on the choicest of foods. My people believe that by the time your month of seclusion is up and you leave the initiate's hut, you should be like the proverbial fattened calf. We always had hot *chinsaga, obokima, ching'ende, amabere amaroranu, amandegera, enyama ye mbori ne ng'ombe*; all Kisii delicacies -- special greens, maize meal cake, beans, sour milk, mutton and beef, you name it.

Our aunts and Magokoro told us stories of how they grew up and were taught that the woman's and children's place was in the kitchen by the fireside. And men's place was in a special hut called *egesa*[i]. Grandma insisted that in those times, there were no shared roles and everything was gender-specific. We also learned that it used to be considered a taboo and a curse for a woman to dress in men's clothes, like trousers. There was only one exception called *ogokobania*. Here, a woman, bereaved of her husband, was allowed to dress in the clothes of the departed spouse.

---

i Kisii -- egesa: singular; ebisa: plural

Being naturally thin, which did not change even after seclusion, my wispy frame was attributed to sulking. I was town-bred. I had not been fed on all the talk about initiation and transition through the cut to womanhood, until just in the recent past, but my cousin had practically been weaned on such tales. So, for her ten years or so in this world, she would have been waiting eagerly for the occasion.

I still remember vividly the day we were released from seclusion, how even some of the old men ogled at her. I think it was sub-conscious. I doubt if they know that one can sense such vibes, no wonder there are so many early and forced marriages in the rural areas.

After a month we were feted, given presents by our family and well-wishers and a party thrown for us. We were taken on an outing and a sort of tour of the rich highlands. But for what purpose?

Regardless, the singing in the *boma* continued as the elderly men and women continued to demand for more traditional brew to celebrate the new initiates.

> *Mbeni chugucha, mbeni gwaya, mbeni chugucha amache kayiare.*
> *Mbeni chugucha, mbeni gwaya, mbeni chugucha amache kayiare.*

Home in Mombasa and back to school.

In later years I came to learn that what I had undergone was called Female Genital Mutilation or FGM as it was referred to in short form and not circumcision as only men and boys are circumcised. Girls and women are either infibulated or go through FGM. Only later would I reflect upon this event and realise the profound effect it was going to have on my life, starting from my schoolwork, which had been affected even before the event by the building crescendo and ultimate climax. I had always wanted to be a writer and had dreamed about it for years.

Though I was only ten, I was already reading the leading three national newspapers and novels by Fredrick Forsyth and Robert Ludlum. This was because, before I was barely seven, I had finished with the Alfred Hitchcock and Enid Blyton. By the time I was ten, I was also through with the Mills and Boons romantic series and had started on the orange African Writers Series and Pace Setters!

To forget about what had happened to me, I developed an even crazier obsession. An insatiable thirst for anything in print -- and I mean anything! Even after what I went through, I still dared to dream that one day I would write my own novel. I started keeping a diary and would journal everything that I went through.

I was going onto eleven years and joined Standard Five for the first term of the new year. I had always been a vivacious, daring and outgoing girl, but something had now happened to me. I was different. Changed. Withdrawn. As usual, my friends Myra, Shilpa and Latifah came to my rescue. On most evenings we walked home together from the Coastal Girls Primary School which we all attended, or we boarded a *matatu*[i] home. We loved the *matatus* which are like discotheques on wheels! Nowadays we have the large forty-two seater ones with large hand air-brushed larger than life paintings of Osama bin Laden and Barack Obama on their sides and backs. It just goes to show the extreme to which teens can take hero worship.

Though I, Myra and Shilpa lived in the same vicinity, our hoods were as different as can be. Myra and I lived at the dilapidated Mbaraki government quarters, 1940s colonial houses adjacent to the magnificent high-rise

---

[i] Kiswahili -The flamboyantly graffiti hand-painted passenger vans expressing street art culture with conscious hip-hop booming from large speakers; also referred to as "*mathree*" in Sheng (Kiswahili slang)

KPA[i] apartments. Shilpa's house was further down the road in Ganjoni, in what was called the Indian quarters. They lived behind a steel gate in a large mansion with their extended family. Latifah lived twenty minutes farther, behind the railway station in a Swahili neighbourhood called Guraya. There you could find fifteenth century houses that were falling apart though they had beautiful trellis and shutters that shouted Arabic influence. As I was saying, my friends came to my rescue when they noticed my withdrawn nature. I told them about the female genital mutilation (FGM) I had undergone. They were shocked as they could not understand any of it. We made elaborate plans to examine our *ka-thingis*[ii] the following day at school. Each of us came to school the next day with a tiny mirror. During the recess break we removed our panties and squatted over the mirrors in the girls' toilets to try and compare our k*a-thingis*. All we could see was one white Arab *ka-thingi* with a red moist slit, one Indian *ka-thingi* with another moist red slit and two dark African *ka-thingis* with red moist slits and not much of a difference – maybe at that age we did not know what we were looking for.

Coming back to my studies, I have never had a head for figures, and more often than not, in that area, I will give you disasters, but give me words anytime, anywhere, and I will give you perfection. That is what I always told my friends in primary school. I was not too modest to acknowledge the fact that my writing was a gift from God. I always came top of my class in English. No one could beat me. I remember always telling my English language teachers that I was one day going to write a novel, and the beauty of it was that they believed in me because they seemed to see it. I remember one day, one

---

i KPA -- Kenya Ports Authority

ii Kiswahili slang (Sheng) -- denoting a small thing, euphemism for vagina, thus "ka-thing": "ka" = small

of my teachers in Standard Four confiscated a Robert Ludlum I was reading during her lesson. I remember it was a second hand book, one of my 'hand me downs' from my older brother. It was titled The Icarus Agenda.

After my teacher confiscated the novel, I went without my lunch for weeks just so that I could get a brand new copy from the bookshop. I had searched round the second hand stalls in town in vain and I just had to know how the whole episode ended. The next time the same teacher found me reading a brand new copy of the same Ludlum paperback during her math class, she punished me with detention after school on a games day. She later asked me about the book to see if I understood the plot. I knew she had been reading my novel, the one she had confiscated, when she kept urging me on at some point. When she finally realised that I understood the plot perfectly well, she just shook her head resignedly.

Through it all, I held on to my burning ambition. I went on daring to dream that one day I would be published. And I thought I would start with my FGM. But I wondered how my best friends Myra, Shilpa and Latifah would take to having part of my history with them documented and put down on paper for the whole world to read.

SERENITY PRAYER

...and wisdom to know the difference ...

...na hekima kujua tofauti ...

Myra

Myra learned fast that in Africa, coming from the wrong side of the tracks meant literally that, because a railway track almost always divides the classes. She would stare across the railway track that divided our dilapidated government flats in our hood in Mbaraki in Mombasa from the high-rise KPA apartments and wonder if it was true that railway crossings in Africa are a preserve of djinns meeting at midnight. Though we also lived in the same government quarters, our flat was better because papa was a district commissioner, and mama a state counsel. The only solace we had in the evenings was hurriedly finishing our homework, going to the Little Theatre Club and begging to be let in towards the end of a play as we never had the money for the entrance fee. The patrons there were always *wazungus* or middle to upper class working Africans.

Myra was an only child. She was thus the typical teenage girl marking time at her parents' house, just waiting to come of age and leave their restrictive boundaries.

Every time Myra did not have bus fare to catch a ride home on a *matatu*, I would pay for her or volunteer to walk home with her. She repeated her vow on all such occasions that she would one day escape from the poverty she lived in. Every time we stared at burgers, hotdogs, sodas and ice cream in the school cafeteria but could not afford them, we were reminded of how much we wanted it all. We started to believe that it was better to be lucky than to be good. When Myra lacked sanitary pads and borrowed from me, her vows were reinforced just like our daily Girl Guide's motto Be Prepared and the promise, "On my honour, I will try to serve God and my country, to help people at all times, and to live by the Girl Scout law." I remember how we would chant the law, 'I will do my best to be honest and fair, friendly and helpful, considerate and caring, respectful, courageous and strong, and responsible for what I say and do, and to respect myself and others, authority, use resources wisely, make the world a better place, and be a sister to every Girl Scout.' I think that in many of our escapades in later life, remembering the motto, promise, the law and the founders' graves of Lord Baden and Lady Olive Powell (which we had once visited in Nyeri on a school trip to commemorate 'Thinking Day') kept us alive!

Myra grew up seeing her Meru father -- who was jobless most of the time -- put down her civil servant mother who toiled hard as a copy typist. Not in so many words but by show of proverbs, especially when he was drunk. Her parents were from different ethnic communities. Her mama was Kikuyu and very hardworking despite her husband's lack of support.

Sometimes I would be present when Myra's drunken papa would tell her mama that, *"guti nkingo yakila mutwe[i]"* or *"aka ni ata[ii]"* despite Myra's mama being the sole bread winner at times. As we grew older, we were to notice how men would use such proverbs in the subjugation of women or to portray women as people with no identity. Myra's mama certainly did not believe her own Kikuyu people when they told her, *"Muka na ng'ombe matiri urata[iii],"* when it came to the issue of land inheritance and property ownership. She worked hard to ensure that Myra completed high school and went on to university.

Just like in my family in my formative years, Myra's parents did not go to church and were always fighting. It

---

i   Meru proverb -- "The neck cannot come above the head."
ii Meru proverb -- "Women are destructive."
iii Kikuyu proverb -- "Women and cattle are not friends."

got worse when her mama discovered that her husband had another wife at his rural home. Myra had step brothers and sisters whom she learned of later in life.

Myra was what at school we referred to as a brainy or a chop. She was extremely bright and worked hard at her grades. Because she loved the sea so much she wanted to be a marine biologist so that she would have all the money in the world. She believed the profession to be one of the best paying and would get her into the world of the elite. Sometimes I would take her to the Kenya Marine and Fisheries headquarters in the north coast. She would spend time pestering the scientists there about sea anemones, coral reef barriers and marine and environmental pollution. This is where we learned to snorkel and scuba dive in the deep seas.

Myra also realised early in her teens that she had a graceful, ageless and charming personality.

As we grew older this trait would make men part with thousands of shillings at the supermarket till and the shopping mall just to make her happy. She decided to put her charm to good use, or so she thought, and got addicted to investing her faith in expensive merchandise. Retail therapy worked wonders for Myra whenever she was feeling low. Men learned fast that if they did not finance her excesses on her feel-good shopping sprees, they risked the boot!

THE SERENITY PRAYER

......living one day at a time...

...nikae siku kwa siku...

Shilpa

Shilpa was our exotic friend and almost oriental being. She always had a colourful and sparkling bindi placed in the centre of her forehead even when coming to school. At home an embroidered veil covering was never absent from her head. I found her family oriental and yet so glamorous at the same time. They were always in Indian fabrics like the beautiful imported Kanchipuram silks sent over by their relatives in India. The ladies were always adorned in jewellery, with diamonds set into filigreed threads of gold and silver twisted together. And always wearing saris aflame with deep colours like the peacocks we had seen at the Bamburi Nature Trail. The saris were embroidered all over with golden sequins shaped like the stars and cusp of the moon with thin silver borders.

Despite the glamorous setting, Shilpa loved coming to our African hoods. We would in turn almost blackmail and bully her into introducing us to their Indian culture despite her parents being very strict. Her papaji and mamadi, as she called her mom and dad, were so conservative that even at primary school during the swimming lessons, Shilpa would never get into the pool without a large oversized T-shirt covering her swimsuit to the knees. By upper primary school, Myra, Latifah and I had broken her. Our legs powdered with the beach sand like grains of gold, Shilpa would run barefoot into the sea impatient for the cool water. Her toes would curl in anticipation and exhilaration, her panting like the lapping of the water. Her rushing making small gusty winds, soon she was an expert in swimming, loving the feel of the water as she swam in several dimensions at once. By the time we were in junior high school, it was a spectacle to behold. At the beach on Saturdays, Shilpa would discard her sari. She would have been holding it up, bunched at her knees for hours watching us, waiting for a bikini and a moment to let go her inhibitions. She would bestride beach, her long ponytail slapping her wet bottom! After clearing senior high school and joining college, dolphins, snorkelling and deep-sea fishing were our pastimes as we tried to help Myra become a marine biologist.

At the same time we learned from Shilpa of the three main Hindu gods; Brahman (the creator), Vishnu (the protector) and Shiva (the destroyer) amongst other deities. Sometimes we accompanied Shilpa and her family to the Shree Cutchi temple for various Diwali celebrations, or to the *melas*, the fun fares organised by their community, to watch the dazzling sparkle of crackers and fireworks displays during Diwali. It was the most awaited festival of charm and joy for the Hindus, which also marks the beginning of the New Year in the Hindu Calendar. In preparation for veneration of the various deities, we would help Shilpa's family light many tiny traditional lamps and lanterns to symbolically illuminate their house and the environment in their garden to welcome Laxmi, the divine goddess of wealth and prosperity. Laxmi was Myra's favourite – I was not surprised, given her obsession with anything monetary. Shilpa taught us that it is believed that the goddess visits mortals during the festivity to bless them. She told us that Diwali is also known as the festival of lights and provides an occasion for people to seek the light of knowledge and dispel the darkness of ignorance. And the light from the lamps rekindles love for humanity and provides impetus for brotherhood. We knew almost everything about Diwali because Shilpa had told us that religious attributes to this enchanting festivity marks the coronation of Lord Rama, who the Hindus hold in high esteem as the King of Ayodhya on his return to the kingdom after fourteen years of exile. It also marks the victory of good and virtue over evil and destruction. We would watch as the Hindus exchanged gifts and gave offerings of *mithai* sweetmeats as a show of friendship and brotherhood.

I remember another time we accompanied Shilpa for a whole week as she rehearsed with others of their faith at their temple for their presentation of Krishna. We learned that it was a ballet based on an innocent, yet at the same time, romantic episode of the Hindu deity Krishna who evoked devotion, love and happiness to his devotees. A special day, Janmashtami, is set aside to celebrate his birthday. Shilpa's group presentation was so musical and enchanting. They magically re-enacted episodes from Krishna's mortal life and his divine boons to mankind. I was mesmerised as I followed the re-enactment. The Lord was born at midnight in a prison cell and his mortal life was full of miracles. Shilpa and her friends brought to life his childhood antics as he was raised up by a foster mother in the Vraj. Shilpa told us that Krishna is adored for imparting spiritual knowledge to the despairing Pandav Arjuna during the battle of Mahabharata. This knowledge is enshrined in a religious doctrine known as Bhagavad Gita. They also believe that Krishna, the dark handsome hero of Mahabharata, spent his childhood in Vrindavan where he was naughty and indulged in pranks with fair, cowherd maidens called Radhika on the banks of river

Yamuna. He subdued the ferocious cobra king Kalia that notoriously poisoned the waters of the sacred river and destroyed the tyrant king of Mathura. Shilpa's presentation glorified the episode of the Lord's childhood days in Gokul.

By the time we graduated from high school, and despite being brought up to respect her faith, Shilpa had forgotten about her sari and was into skinny jeans and halter tops. Soon she also started getting bored of going for her Indian dance lessons, saying that *bhangra* and *tarana* were so yesterday! She totally forgot how to slide her neck from left to right gracefully at the same time lifting the two sticks and hitting them to the drums beats. We also soon forgot the Anghiti and Veraswamy Indian restaurants where she had introduced us to the most delicious Indian curries, chicken tikka and fish tikka. The Tandoori Grill restaurant ceased to be our favourite. We kept on the back burner our frequent visits to Bhagwanji's, the most famous Indian sweet meat and confectionary shop in Mombasa. I could not believe that our obsession with Indian snacks and sweetmeats like *chevdo, penda, laddoo, jelebi, pera* and *kachri* had come to an end.

A time had reached when we thought we had outgrown these festivities. Shilpa wanted to be an architect when 'we grew up,' as we used to say. I hoped her papaji and mamadi would let her follow her dreams.

THE SERENITY PRAYER

...enjoying one moment at a time...

...kufurahia kila wakati...

Latifah

Before she was barely five-years-old, Latifah and her four siblings had to sometimes stay up at night to memorise the more than one-hundred surahs of the Qur'an. She was told the five obligatory prayers were not enough and she had to learn two chapters of the Qur'an by heart every week. She later told us that they were always reminded that it was their sacred duty.

Latifah had only one brother but she and her two sisters were overly protected by their *mahrams*[i]. She had to be escorted by a male relative to the *madrassa* school where she learned the Qur'anic verses. No amount of lamenting and cajoling would get her out of being escorted even to the neighbourhood kiosks for a packet of salt or sugar. Even when she would want to accompany me, Myra and Shilpa to the streets to watch and listen to the brasso band with their Scottish bagpipes (an instrument borrowed from the colonial times via seafarers) or to the playing of traditional Swahili tunes like Kula Menyewe, Twataka Ndogo Ndogo and Unkula Huu, a male relative always tagged along.

We loved her ma's kitchen though, because in there was where we learned to prepare delicious and spicy coastal dishes like mutton biryani and chicken pilau.

Their kitchen was a hotspot for spices and herbs where neighbours would occasionally knock on the door to borrow one or the other. By the time Latifah would sit down to do her homework, her flowing *kaftan* would be veiled in the fragrant aroma of *garam masala*, ground turmeric, ground cumin and mustard seeds, grated ginger and coconut, diced clove garlic, tomato puree and tamarind pickle and sauces.

i Arabic -- Male relatives/male gender in whose presence the hijab must be worn.

45

Every time we were at their place it always seemed like Latifah was being taught to be submissive. Her female relatives, starting with her ma, *shangazis*[i], *nyanya*[ii], down to her female *binamus*[iii], always threatened the girls with brimstone and hell fire at the slightest sign of deviating from the Holy teachings. Her ma and *shangazis* taught her that girls are supposed to get married and have babies. Her ma, older *shangazis* and *binamus* were very vocal and insistent whenever the subject of submission in *ndoa*[iv] came up. Constant admonitions were drummed into her head and rammed down her throat. Her eldest *shangazi* on her ma's side never ceased to tell her that a wife has to be submissive to her husband in all aspects. She constantly told her that brimstone and hell fire will consume her if she did not follow the directives. Nothing more and nothing less. Only hell fire!

Latifah once shared with us that all the women in her life hid their emotions behind the veil. She never knew when they were sad or happy, neither could she tell when they were smiling, laughing or crying. Latifah was always dressed as her ba and ma said, appropriately to social conventions and Muslim doctrine. They insisted that she start wearing the strict Islamic dress and decorum when she was barely ten. She grew up with the concept of duty and how to behave towards her *mahrams*.

She was taught to lead an obscure life[v]. She could not talk. She was only to be seen, not heard. She was taught that the men were supposed to only see the clothes she mended, food she cooked and sons she bore. But never

---

i Kiswahili -- aunts; singular: shangazi

ii Kiswahili -- Grandmother

iii Kiswahili -- Cousins; singular: binamu

iv Kiswahili -- marriage

v This type of behaviour is not an Islamic view, but more of a culture influenced mind-set specific to most Muslim families in Mombasa. In Islamic tradition, the prophet Muhammad married a woman who had a job and is thus seen as a powerful female role model for women in Islam.

her. And never any mention of bearing daughters, as if it was an abomination! The men chose when to notice the women and when not to notice them. When to hear their voices and when not to hear them. She grew up avoiding doing and saying normal things that young girls of other faiths did and said. It was a life of unending servitude. That was why at primary school she got attracted to Myra, me and Shilpa who seemed to have a bit more freedom from our parents.

Despite her parents' attempts at keeping Latifah almost locked up, we still managed to have our escapades and shared so much of our cultures and religions. Sometimes we would follow Latifah to the Baluchi Hall during Ramadan for *iftar*, breaking of the fast in the evening. We celebrated with her family during Maulid, Prophet Muhammad's birthday. On the other hand Shilpa and Latifah learned of Christmas and Easter, the birth of Jesus and Jesus' crucifixion and resurrection from Myra and me, though we hardly went to church. I wondered if Latifah's baba would ever allow her to pursue the dentistry course that she so dreamed of.

We indeed all had different ways of growing up.

THE SERENITY PRAYER

...accepting hardships as the pathway to peace...

...nikubali taabu ilioko nikielekea penye amani...

Different Ways of Growing Up

How time flies! It is unbelievable that we are all grown up. Now, as an adult woman I stare across the open expanse of sea and remember outings with my dad. My papa the district commissioner -- I was so proud of him. I can still remember him in his khaki trousers and matching shirt and colonial style helmet. That was before the fighting started between him and mama.

Pollyanna's kindergarten song reverberates in my mind "If you're happy and you know it clap your hands."

Little did I know at that precocious age that ours would no longer be a happy family. The main problem was that there were a lot of taboo subjects you could hardly talk to anyone about without a miasma of fear gliding up your spinal cord.

* * * * *

I digress, let me go back. I was barely six. Dad quit the government and went into the hardware business. A few years later, he is also running a pub with a couple of his buddies.

Suddenly I was twelve-years-old and I did not know what the fights were about, but I soon learned. My older brother never seemed to notice, my two younger brothers slept through the fights. My younger sisters were too young.

Was it because I was always in the kitchen with mum, helping with the cooking and other household chores? I called myself born 'labelled and limited.'

I soon knew what the quarrels were about. Dad would finish at his hardware yard and go to his bar in the evenings and mum would be home from work.

It became the custom for dad to send us *kuku* or *mbuzi choma* with *kachumbari*. That is roast chicken or goat meat with tomato salad. Every time we had the delicacies, that night my parents would have a mighty fight.

My mind came to the conclusion that Karisa was the culprit. He was the expert meat roaster who would be sent to our house with the meat from the pub. He was carrying tales or so I told myself.

When he and mum were talking, I heard snippets about dad and his mistress.

It is at that time the rumours started doing the rounds in town. It was true. Our father had a mistress. He was supporting her and they even had a child.

Our mama, who had always been docile and submissive to papa, suddenly seemed angry at everything. She said she would not let a tart ruin her marriage. Then she started drinking. Beer became her companion at night. She never missed to have more than four brown bottles of Tusker in the house in the evening. When she was angry she was terrible. She screamed and yelled at us. She told us what ingrates we were for not appreciating her more. Papa joined in her mood swings. If the food put before him was not hot enough, the plates were more often than not likely to come flying past mama's face as she set it down for him. He threw fists and slaps as easily as he did cups and plates.

Overall, I can say that I found mother weak and submissive and I can remember that for many years I vowed I would never get married. I kept asking myself if this was how marriage was supposed to be. It was not a very good example to a young girl growing up and reading happily ever after stories like *Cinderella*, *Sleeping Beauty* and *Beauty and the Beast*. I developed an intense aversion to misery and I kept asking mama why we could not leave. She would say that an African woman does not leave her husband to another woman, and that she fights to save her *boma*! It got worse when mum started leaving the house to go sort out 'the other woman.'

As she left, the food would turn to sandpaper in my mouth. I would hide all knives in gunny bags of cereal in the kitchen because I knew their fights always turned nasty.

My brothers seemed oblivious to all these. Was I so much more aware because several times I was the one who accompanied mama to the hospital and heard her lie about her injuries to the doctor? Or was it because on occasional nights, our youngest brother would have one of his epilepsy fits and I would be the one to take care of him?

My life became hell. Alternating between tending to my epileptic brother to make sure he does not bite his tongue or choke on his saliva, rubbing his hands and soothing his legs which convulsed in spasms at night, and listening for dad's car in the driveway and then waiting for the fighting to start.

To mum, she was fighting to save her family, her marriage. That was the only option for an African woman, she told me time and again. To dad, in the mornings, he would suffer from collective, selective memory lapses. Bouts of self-induced amnesia I called it.

We never discussed such issues. It became ingrained in my head that the scars which I got from trying to stop them from fighting were from falls and swinging from our compound's gate.

Christmas parties would end tragically. Shouts and screams. Broken glass. Blood and gaping wounds. Visits to the ER[i] became commonplace and later indelible scars.

---

i ER -- Emergency Room

Meanwhile, mama was quietly disintegrating. The years began to take their toll on her. She tried all sorts of projects to keep busy but they all floundered as quickly as they started. But at least she had invested wisely earlier and had several rental houses to her name. She was retrenched from her job, but her retirement money was soon gone as she used it to renovate her houses. The monthly pension she got from the government was hardly enough even for her own basic needs.

I, on the other hand, devised forms of escapism like educational school trips. Some fictitious so that I could have sleepovers at friends' homes. Dad never tired of putting his hand in his pocket, maybe out of guilt. We had moved to a neighbourhood near the Mombasa Municipal Stadium and so alternatively, I would spend hours at the local library, or across the road at a forbidden housing estate called 'Buxton' opposite our house and full of dysfunctional families, according to my parents. Was our family any better? I always wondered.

At other times I actually became a liar. I would tell mama that we were having lessons in the afternoon so that I could avoid going home and instead spend the afternoons at either Shilpa or Latifah's place. I could not go to Myra's because it was now a bit far and Shilpa's parents were never home in the afternoon. I liked Latifah's place because her parents were divorced and she lived with her mum, so it was always peaceful with no fights there.

When my mum found out, she gave me a beating with a pair of large scissors. I will never forget that beating. I went to school with a big *nundu*, a bruise, on my forehead for the whole week.

No small wonder I ended up seeing a psychiatrist in class six. Our family doctor gave up when I underwent a series of numerous illnesses; he seemed to find them almost imaginary because he could not seem to find anything wrong with me. So I ended up at the shrink's office!

It was another blow because I knew that some of my friends and schoolmates were wondering if I was insane or something. That was the impression one got in those years, as the doctor was the only prominent psychiatrist in Mombasa town!

I remember refusing to go and see the shrink, but mama insisted as I had already been referred there. Even now, I fail to understand how my parents could have missed to grasp the basics of what was happening to me. They should have known by then that I was a very sensitive child.

It somehow hardened me, but I was dying slowly inside. I remember the first session clearly. I was with my mum and I clammed up totally. At the next appointment when she came in with me the doctor requested her to leave us alone. She looked bewildered, and then it must have slowly sunk in that the doctor wanted to talk to me alone. Without her imposing and intimidating presence. She threw me a warning glance that I did not pretend to understand.

How could I tell the doc of the pain I had undergone with my FGM which had never been explained to me? How could I regale him with all the gory details? Would he understand why I sometimes even now took off my panties, took a mirror and squatted, just to try and see what they had done to me? How could I tell him how I had squatted over mirrors naked with my best friends so that we could compare our *ka-thingis* and try and understand the trauma that I had undergone? How could I tell him about my parents' incessant fights? How could I tell him how their squabbling affected me?

Next, he wanted to get to the root cause of my chronic insomnia.

How could I tell him how I slept in fits of dread and fear waiting to hear the drone of dad's car engine in the driveway and the key to turn in the lock? How could I tell him how I would ask our house-help (whoever it was we were having at that particular time) to assist me in hiding knives, machetes, *simis* and slashers in the gunny bags full of rice and flour in the food store? How could I tell him that was how I averted a dozen fatal tragedies in as many formative years? I looked at the doctor and the tears slowly streamed down my cheeks. I never told him anything, and he eventually gave up when I went on clamming up on subsequent visits for fear of embarrassing mama and my family.

In the meantime, our parents' fights continued. Almost every night their voices would recede towards their bedroom and papa would shut the door. Soon mama would be screaming. Sometimes I would cover my head with my pillow to drown out the shouts. The following morning it was as if none of this had ever happened. I, on the other hand, would insist to papa that he was wasting his money sending me to the shrink as if they did not know what was troubling me.

Yet through it all I still dared to dream that one day I would have one of my novels published. I continued with my journaling and diary-keeping, which I knew would one day come in handy when I wanted to write my novel.

I found refuge in my first love, books, and buried myself in reading. The workers at the local library got to know me quite well. I managed to persuade papa that I did not want to be picked up after school at four and that I had rather stroll to the local library. During that time the education syllabus was not yet very tight. At least one could read a few chapters of a novel before calling it a night!

I loved my parents dearly. I could have given anything to see them happy; I never blamed them for my FGM. I have never been bitter and I never pointed fingers. I did no second-guessing; there were no "what ifs" and no "if onlys." I realised that they were also victims of circumstances and the ills bedeviling and eating into the very fabric of society. Like the way a woman was supposed to hold on to her marriage no matter what.

Papa provided everything materially. I never missed a single school trip, be it to the Maasai Mara or the Tsavo National Parks, but I suffered emotionally.

Sometimes I wondered if papa was trying to assuage his guilty conscience, or did he acknowledge partly and secretly that he was to blame? I always looked forward to school trips, and I joined almost every club from the Wildlife Club, Red Cross, Ranger Guides and the President's Award Scheme so as to get out of the house for a couple of weeks.

I almost got into cigarette smoking once in high school, but I thank God that I managed to avoid the peer pressure because of lessons we had been getting at the Youth Counselling Centre's Mombasa branch, in the mid-1980s. I will eternally be grateful to all our counsellors. They made such a difference in so many young lives in those formative years, though we never realised at the time. There was also the guiding movement of which Shilpa, Myra, Latifah and I had been members. We were Brownies in lower primary school and Girl Guides in upper primary school. In high school we were Ranger Guides.

Though I still found myself getting into escapism, I thank God that I never got into the snares that are entangling so many of our youth these days. All that I can say is that as I grew up, my younger sisters also grew up. I put my foot down amidst all the hype about the banning of FGM. I am glad that they were not made to go through the torture I experienced. Maybe my parents had also grown wiser and realised their folly; the rite was outdated. When I tried to confront my parents years later about the FGM I underwent, they never said they were sorry. I realised then that sorry isn't just a panacea. They never said they wished things had turned out differently. They never acted like their actions were wrong and unfair to me.

I continued reading a lot. My dream was to major in English Literature and write books one day. But then the other blow hit my life. The eight-four-four system of education!

I had grown up adoring my older brother and I would watch him fiercely concentrate on three subjects. I mean just three: Economics, English and Literature. But here, I was supposed to study for more than ten when my love was for only one!!

I was in high school when I came across shocking tableaus. Abortions and children born out of incest. I consoled and convinced myself that my family was better off with the incessant fights.

I sought a better alternative. My writing. It became my own form of self-therapy.

When my older brother cleared high school, a fundraiser was organised and he left for the United Kingdom to study Economics. After high school, I was enrolled in a computer college where I studied and attained my diploma in Computer Systems Designs and Operations. I would have preferred to be enrolled in university to study English Literature, but papa and mama said they could not afford it. I still had five younger siblings and three of them were already in high school. But I wondered why they had organised a fundraiser for my older brother and not me? Why the discrimination? But nobody answered my questions.

In the meantime, while mama was busy fighting her own physical battles, I had my own emotional ones and no one to talk to. Growing up, never knowing what was right and wondering if I had put my foot in my mouth.

I remember papa, a loving, jovial family man, who gradually became a sullen and withdrawn man. My brothers, sisters and I had to learn to be cautious around him. It was as if he was not really there. He became part of the background, blending in with the messy dining table after meals – that is if he had bothered to eat with us. He would silently sink into his favourite leather sofa seat when he wanted to watch the prime time news – that is if he was home on time. He blended in with everything – even our old wooden bookshelf and Christmas tree that we had once decorated and lit on our front porch verandah. Every morning smelling of his Brut cologne, he would dress in one of his designer suits and leave for his office at the hardware yard. He would chat amicably with our numerous neighbours and be swallowed up by them in the driveway as they all drove away. Papa's distant behaviour strengthened my lifelong relationship with all kinds of fiction books, which had developed into an obsession of sorts.

Mama, on the other hand, pretended not to understand this obsession -- the need I had to constantly lock myself in the girl's bedroom. For some reason she felt the need to fake naiveté about this book thing of mine. I always kept a journal and diary. Every evening I would record my day and put down my innermost thoughts before burying my nose in a novel or writing one of my fictitious stories. Mama pretended like she did not understand my preoccupation with journaling and writing. That it was all beyond her understanding. The source of this self-deception was a mysterious and arbitrary decision to place certain arenas outside her realm of understanding. A former senior state counsel, the lady who had become a fire-wall of protection around her marriage and family when its very existence and foundation was threatened by the 'other woman' now felt the need to play dumb. I, on the other hand, learned to concentrate on the minutiae when tragedy struck, an act I was to perfect for the rest of my life.

Things came to a head once. Mama almost burnt down our house one evening in one of her drunken stupors while preparing supper. The incident sobered her up. We sure were glad to have our mama back! Papa sobered up too and somehow got out of the clutches of 'the other woman.' Maybe it had been a mid-life crisis of sorts.

...Nowadays, all grown up, in the evenings when I get home I still get out my diary. Diaries and journaling kept me alive during my parents' fights. To read me is to read the diary of scars on my cheek, my hands, my womanhood, my entire body. My soul: a diary of pain. Oh, this phoenix of my pain. No one can decipher it. Not even Maya Angelou with her healingly therapeutic poetic prose can today be a soothing balm. Every scar on my body is a heliograph of pain, written in bloodied braille so that humanity, blind as they all come, can touch and try to read my pain. Only those who have read me can read my skin, scarred with the braille of brutalization.

That is why I am ever so grateful and careful to be friends with my daughter Nehema now that I am a single mother. I want her to know that she can always come and talk to me openly about any subject under the sun. To always uphold her dignity and know that she can always stand up for herself.

You must be wondering what happened with her dad.

THE SERENITY PRAYER

...taking as He did this sinful world as it is...

...kuona dunia hii ya dhambi vile alivyoiona Mwenyezi Mungu...

Maxi

Everyone called him Maxi. It was because he loved to listen to reggae star Maxi Priest's songs when they were a current hit in the early 1990s, especially his two hit songs *Wild World* and *Close to You*. We met at Myra's birthday party that she held at a night club that he managed. Papa as good as disowned me when he discovered I was dating Maxi, whose ethnic tribe he did not approve of. He even refused to shake his hands. He said that he does not consort with uncircumcised men – his words precisely. He furiously told me that the Gusii who circumcise their men and women do not intermarry with uncircumcised tribes. He was implacable even after I told him that Maxi, who had been born and brought up in Mombasa, was circumcised just like the coastal people. I could not believe that I was being a witness to negative ethnicity of the highest order.

Papa said that he would never allow a circumcised daughter of his to marry an uncircumcised *omoisia!* Mama refused to intervene even after I begged her to, telling her that I loved Maxi. She told me sternly that we have our cultures and that there is nothing like love. She believed that love was a stupid idea brought to us on ships by the white colonialists and currently via Mexican tele-novellas on television. She said love makes one lose reason, and she added a proverb meanly to drive her point home, telling me *"geutere giote gekobamboka gekobambokere!"* Maxi and I had fallen in love and there was nothing papa could do to stop us from moving in together, which we did a year later. Shilpa and Latifah were surprised, but

---

i Kisii proverb -- paraphrased: when you let into your house a freezing camel, it can easily turn against you when refreshed.

not Myra who had seen it coming ever since that party. I knew I had to have my baby soon because I knew that the older I became, the harder it would be to fake orgasms. I had discovered that due to my FGM, I could not feel any sexual stimulation. But I wanted to have my own child and a normal marriage.

I was soon pregnant. My slender figure disappeared, and I ballooned up until I could not see my feet. My toes and fingers tingled. Constant discomfort and frequent visits to the loo were the order of the day. My insides felt as though they were struggling for space. I spent a lot of energy wondering if I would be a good mom. But I already loved the life growing inside of me that I had created with my partner. During the day it was Shilpa, Myra or Latifah who pandered to my cravings for cashew nuts and chocolates. At night it was my partner who got it rough from sleepless nights of my demands for oiling, massaging my feet and endless back rubs at odd hours.

At least I did not hate him the way some pregnant women do with their partners.

We soon had our baby and christened her Nehema which is Kiswahili for Grace. Nehema smelt nice and powdery like all babies as I breast-fed her. Her father took to sitting around idle after losing his job of managing the nightclub. But it soon turned into a typical case of stay put or call it quits for me. To some, it would seem like either way you were doomed. Damned if you do and damned if you don't! Such is the case when desperate situations call for desperate measures.

Maxi became so broke that he even sold his car. I would give him bus fare, but he would use it on beer and cigarettes. Once, I remember when I was still pregnant, I suffered from a bout of malaria and was admitted in hospital for a week. He was unable to clear the hospital bill and he had to borrow the money from his sister. I remember when I went to deliver my baby. I went into prolonged labour and my gynaecologist asked me if I was going to foot the bill alone. The caesarean section operation would cost around fifty-thousand shillings, while a normal delivery would cost between ten to fifteen-thousand shillings depending on the doctor's role in the delivery. I opted to go through the long labour and normal delivery.

Maxi could still not raise the twelve thousand shillings upon our discharge. I was lucky I'd had the foresight to save, though earning a meager pay at the hotel where I was working. Later, on asking him why he was lazing around the house while he was aware we now had a baby to provide for, it would degenerate into a mighty row with him accusing me of violating his space, and that I was overstepping the line and crossing the boundary.

My one-month paid maternity leave was over too soon and I decided to take another month of unpaid leave so that I could train our new house-help cum nanny on how to care for the baby.

After the second month was up, I decided to quit my job at the hotel as I could not survive on the pay and provide for the baby too. After six months, I got a job at another hotel that paid slightly more. I would extract breast milk with the breast pump and leave it with Nehema's nanny. I would settle her in her high chair with her sippy cup of breast milk and a bowl of her favourite Weetabix whole meal cereal. My heart would swell with pride as I prepared to leave. "Bye, bye, bye, bye!" she would chant over and over again, showing off her newest addition to her scant vocabulary.

Things came to a head when Maxi accused me of infidelity – especially when I got a job twice, and yet he hadn't gotten any in a year. It did not matter that one was from an advert in a local newspaper, and another a walk-in interview I chanced upon. Things got worse when he started coming to the reception of the hotel where I was working, especially during my night shift.

I would look up from my cash register or computer rooming list and find him standing there staring enigmatically at me with baleful eyes. He would say that he knew somewhere in the hotel some white man must have fallen in love with my super-model African look of short kinky hair combined with a slim body. Later we would go home and have another fight.

Why did he not trust me? What did he expect when he came to the hotel? Find me holed up in one of the suites with one of the guests in a compromising situation? I thought things could not get worse! I thought in this generation most young men belong to a new liberated generation, but I sadly realised that when it comes to the 'S' word for sex or 'V' word for vagina, they are still dyed in wool male chauvinists.

Another time I suffered from urine incontinence. Maxi thought the world had come to an end and again accused me of infidelity. I was a virgin when we met and I had never been with another man. I swore to him that I was not being unfaithful to him, but he did not believe me. My heart was in so much pain and I could not understand how or why this was happening to me. I saw a doctor who concluded that it was as a result of the FGM I had gone through as a young girl. I then had minor surgery that corrected my incontinence.

In the end, I decided to be totally honest with Maxi and told him that sexually I felt nothing, no stimulation at all because of the FGM I had undergone. He could not understand it and thought I was lying. This was because a lot of myths surround FGM. I remember my aunts and female cousins telling me as we grew up that my *ka-thingi* will grow long, compete with men's *ka-nyamu*[i] and stink if I did not get circumcised.

I was told that I could not get pregnant if I was not

---

i Euphemism for penis

circumcised and that I could not get a man to marry me if I do not undergo the rite, but that if I underwent the cut I would become more beautiful and a proper woman capable of keeping any man. To me, FGM is an injustice society metes out on individuals while presenting the injuries as beneficial to the victim. How have I profited when a pleasure-giving and joy-receiving part of my body was cut from between my legs and buried in a tea plantation? I felt that I had been scarred and not yet healed, but such words belong only to the living, and I felt like I was dead.

After my confession, things were never the same between me and Nehema's dad. Having bad sex is like playing a bad game of basketball or hockey. When your opponent is inferior, your game suffers. And of course I was the inferior partner because I felt no sexual arousal. I discovered soon enough that when it comes to sex, safe sex or sexual manipulation, women always find themselves lame sitting ducks. Every family planning method I used had terrible side effects on me. The pill made me constantly nauseous, the injection gave me terrible pain in my joints and I lost a lot of weight. The coil gave me a bloated tummy. The Norplant gave me terrible backaches. I asked Maxi to start using condoms because I did not want another baby so soon. He flatly refused.

The minute I tried the pill again, I would be sick for days. I patiently asked him to consider the alternatives available to him, short of pulling out before ejaculation like an infatuated teen. All hell broke loose! He accused me of not trusting him. I did not understand where all that was coming from, but the issue caused a rift and a strain between us.

In my heart I started thanking God that we were not legally married, and I could get out if the situation became unbearable. We had lived together for a while.

However, every time his family planned to go the traditional way and settle the bride price, other more important things like Nehema's birth came up. So the wedding was put off time and time again. Like a jinx. So here we were almost three years down the line, nothing settled and we were becoming intolerant of one another.

I remember during my pregnancy I used to suffer from recurrent thrush. When the same condition affected me post-pregnancy months later, Maxi went ballistic again insinuating that I was being unfaithful to him because I worked at beach hotels.

I brought him pharmaceutical pamphlets explaining that Vaginal Candidiasis is the medical term for the condition, and that it is normally triggered by hormonal changes during pregnancy or just before or after one's period. We read that stress factors like poor diet, lack of enough sleep, and emotional stress are also linked to the condition.

I would have a respite from his threats, but as soon as he saw me using the treatment (mostly anti-fungal creams and pessaries) he would become violent again. The way he went on and on, one would think that I was suffering from genital warts or herpes. A month later, I suffered from another urinary tract infection. You guessed right. He blew his top. I was always the delicate and sensitive child in my family and I was not surprised at my allergic reactions to most medications.

It was two years and he still did not have a job. We only survived by God's grace and occasional help from my mama, Myra, Shilpa and Latifah who would chip in. By then, our daughter was two and I enrolled her in baby class, so I had her fees to pay. I also had to take care of other expenses like the house rent, groceries and the food we needed to push us through the month.

Then, one day Maxi woke up and decided he was

going to his family's up-country rural home. He stayed there for almost three months. In those three months he rarely called, not even to ask after the baby, never mind about how I was taking care of all the bills single-handedly. Once during his absence he sent his brother and sister who also lived in Mombasa to check on us. And that was that.

When he came back I refused to have sex with him. I suggested that we go for HIV testing as he did not have any feasible explanation for his lengthy absence. He refused to go for the test. He could not believe it when I told him that having sex with him would be tantamount to handing me a gilt-edged invitation to court HIV and AIDS. He did not have any reason for abandoning us for three months. I asked him to keep to his side of the bed and I kept to mine while waiting for him to reach a decision on whether he would take the test or not.

Two months with no action I decided enough was enough. His disappearing stints may develop into a habit, so I decided to call it quits. I had to get out, because he was not helpful in any way, including even the household budget, and I knew it could only get worse. In the three years, he had never bothered even to find out the price of a pair of bootees or diapers.

I tried to talk to his parents to act as arbitrators but in vain. Everything I tried proved futile.

The proverbial last straw that broke the camel's back was when I found witchcraft paraphernalia and concoctions in our house.

At first he refused to explain their presence but when he saw me packing my bags, he admitted that he had been seeing a witch doctor so that he could get a job. I asked him what his getting a job had to do with me? Why mix smelly concoctions with my body lotion? He knew very well that I did not believe in witch doctors, medicine-men, wizards, *juju* and voodoo, so what were the strange charms doing tied beneath the bed? He seemed lost for words. Maybe he thought that I would never notice the paraphernalia or the black powder he had put in my lotion.

Have you ever tried to find the correct words to convey your feelings but they do not come out sounding right? Words of a popular love ballad kept reverberating in my head, "Love is blind, it does not ask why, it does not think twice, always straight from the heart and not from the head. It just has to be!"

I think also deep down I wanted out. I could not go on pretending in bed. I lay back night after night after night and pretended to be sexually aroused, which I never was and it was taking its toll on me. At one point in time I stopped pretending and just gazed at the ceiling as he pumped away on top of me. As the passions swelled within him I could not help wondering if this was the last time he was making love to me that night. I started dreading the sex. With roughness he would lunge into me. I would feel a lot of pain as I was not ready. His body would quicken and tremble and I would pretend to go along with him, squirming under his jerky up and down movements going on for a while. His body would rotate against me, his penis stoking every inch of me around and around, circling roughly, deeper and fuller. Then he would push his hands beneath my waist so that my lower back was in his palms and my body was raised, freeing my hips to move. I would be in pain, not feeling any sexual stimulation and I would silently pray for him to climax.

I knew that I had to get out of this pretence even if it meant going against my community's cultural practices. Some decisions in life are just instinctive. I remember that last day together and how an eerie silence that neither of us could cross had stretched between us. I had resisted talking because I had felt that sometimes silence is better than many words. If moments define our lives, then I would say that one defining moment of silence was mine. I realised that in our personal journeys such moments have the possibility of great significance, and for me this was it -- I learned how to stand up for myself and what I believe was right. I packed my bags and left with my Nehema.

PART TWO

KEEPING MY HEAD ABOVE WATER

THE SERENITY PRAYER

...not as I would have it...

...badala ya vile nitakavyo...

Going Against the Grain

When people say that women are their very own worst enemies, I understand only too well. Most of my lady acquaintances and colleagues, even family members insisted that I stick it out; some said your husband is your husband no matter what. "Even if it affected my health?" I asked.

I thank God that I got out of that relationship because I do not know where I would be today had I stuck it out. Maybe I would have had four or five children. I cringe inwardly at the thought, especially when I see a long-time schoolmate who has just had a fourth baby in a relationship that is going nowhere.

I remember an aunt of mine who kept telling me over and over again, *"Kemunto, intwe seito, nekeAfrica, omosubati ekero asokire, tarikoirana sobo!"* In simple translation she was informing me that in our African traditions, once a lady is married she does not go back to her parents' home; you stay with your husband no matter what. Whenever she was in Mombasa I would try and avoid her. Whenever I went up-country I would try my utmost best not to spend my time in close proximity with her.

On the other hand, Myra never tired of telling me, *"mtaka cha mvunguni, sharti ainame[i],"* and that she would not rest until she parked her dream car in her driveway – a Lamborghini Marcielago. She did eventually. But at what cost? That is a story to be told later.

I knew it was a jungle out there; everyone for herself and God for us all. I knew that to retain my sanity I would have

---

i Kiswahili proverb -- whoever needs something from under the bed must bend and kneel down to retrieve it.

to go against the grain. Go against society's expectation. After all, communication researcher Herbert Schiller wrote "...when new social forces assume control in society, it is to be expected that the expressions and words of the preceding social order will eventually be eliminated, if for no other reason than that they have diminished applicability."

So, lest I be accused of suffering from literary schizophrenia, I made up my mind to let rip with my pen and not a sword or gun even if it takes dogged determination! Deep down I knew that my sacrifices would one day turn into a success story and not come back to haunt me.

Sometimes I wondered if I was trying to be a Nostradamus in my own life: Predicting my own future. I hoped it did not turn into a tragicomedy of sorts. People say that there's no elixir like love. Knowing that I needed to clear some mental space, I walked out never to look back. And strangely the last song blaring from the hi-fi system as I left Maxi was Miriam Makeba crooning her rendition of our own Kenyan Fadhili William's 'Malaika,' my mama's favourite love song, '*Malaika, nakupenda malaika. Kijana mwenzio, Kijana mwenziooooo, Nashindwa na mali sina weeee, Ningekuoa malaika.*' I still treasure mama's now antique original LP of 1965 on which is printed, 'Fadhili Williams & the Black Shadows – Two Guitars, Bass & Vocal.'

The words of the song reverberated in my mind in the months to come and I sometimes thought my life was a macabre charade turning into a dark comedy with everybody asking me why I had opted out of a five-year relationship with my partner. Why were they asking, I wondered? And yet when I told them it was to maintain my sanity, they could not identify with my train of thought. A dark comedy indeed, with my performance turning into comic relief like I was a clown in a circus!

A vicious cycle was to start, with my baby's father refusing to part with child support even when he got a good job, insisting that I go back to him first – a pipe dream I reiterated! I even stopped trying to ask him to take part in his daughter's life when he started misconstruing my requests to be a case of unresolved feelings.

You are sitting there, reading this and thinking that I am biased. Maybe you want to play the devil's advocate for him? Go ahead, it is your prerogative. I tried the Children's Department. It was a nightmare. They give you summons to deliver to the child's father and if he does not respond, they tell you to get a good lawyer and go to the Children's Court. What if you cannot afford a 'good' lawyer? I realised that our constitution was the culprit. Under the law, the Children's Act says, "Where a child's father and mother were not married to each other at the time of the child's birth and have not subsequently married each other, the mother shall have parental responsibility at the first instance." Maybe that was why Maxi was ignoring any summons he received.

I was soon pushed to a corner by financial constraints; cutting down on portions of vegetables and reducing the amount of fruits I bought!

I thank God that I kept all documentation of deliveries of the summonses, complete with indication of where my daughter's father had signed. When she was ten and asked about him, I told her the truth. I showed her all the papers, some delivered by courier service. It was paper trail of a tale of her father's refusal to provide for her.

She has also, through the years, witnessed how I have had to struggle to provide for her and pay her school fees. Penny-pinching from the kitchen budget became the very bane of our existence. Frequently, I just had to go browsing at a cyber café for ten minutes to quench my thirst for anything from the literary world.

I could not simply wish my obsession with writing away – if truth be told, I thought I was dying.

Isn't that what life is all about? Finding strength through adversity and letting go of the past. My mind had been troubled for a while but I was now at peace with myself. As I went it alone or 'solo' as young people call it nowadays, all the fears that I kept hidden deep inside rose to the surface like smoke from Magokoro's freshly stirred fireside. All I knew was that my baby girl and I, God willing, would beat the odds together. I had to fight to keep my head above the swelling waters or allow myself to hit sea-bed rock-bottom!

On the other hand, when my dear Magokoro heard of my love-hate shenanigans with my ex-partner, she put her hands over her head, lamented, wailed, sucked and clicked her teeth. She tightened the knot on her *leso* wrapper, and stomped around her *boma* hitting with her hands her hips and flabby breasts, of which she never tired of reminding us that they had suckled twelve children. She let flow a string of riddles and proverbs:

"Timogokung'uta ekerandi tigaria enduranerio.[i]*"*

"Banto mbaumerani, mbitunwa bitarikoo'umerana.[ii]*"*

"Engoko enganga tiyana goturagia ebichuchu.[iii]*"*

"Enyoni nigo ekorora omote ekogwera.[iv]*"*

Years later, in hindsight and judging from Magokoro's wise proverbs, maybe she knew how difficult it was going to be for me to raise my daughter alone. I was also not prepared to deal with the fact that I was going to meet a bank manager at a hotel I would work at, who was to almost turn my life upside down.

---

i Kisii proverb -- do not empty the gourd; retain some fermenter.

ii Kisii proverb -- people meet; mountains do not.

iii Kisii proverb -- a hen that never stays on its nest never hatches chicks.

iv Kisii proverb -- a bird knows the tree on which it lands.

THE SERENITY PRAYER

...trusting that...

...kwamini kwamba...

186 Feet Above Sea Level

The present...

The movements of the sailboats dotting the ocean act like a lullaby to me. A sort of hypnosis.

An occasional speedboat flashes past. The songs of the waves almost lull me to sleep.

Local fishermen in their tiny boats go about their business. The passenger ferries go to and fro across the Likoni channel. A cruise ship hoots as it glides into port to drop anchor.

Given the amount of time I spent at this spot when growing up, it is no wonder that the booming, blaring sound of a ship's horn will always remain a part of my childhood.

I have been doing this a lot lately. That is, coming here to spend my lunch hour.

Sometimes even to while away any free time at Mama Ngina drive with the heat of Mombasa, a city that is 186 feet above sea level. Mombasa, with so many different intertwining cultures and an ocean that connects the city with the outside world! My sojourns here to my favourite spot (in town, that is) have been different lately, because I have been in a painful catch-22 situation -- to sell or not to sell my household appliances.

Nevertheless, here I was reminiscing. Swamped by childhood memories – things were much simpler then.

I remember our nursery school chants.

"...Humpty Dumpty sat on a wall. Humpty Dumpty had a great fall... all the king's horses and all the king's men could not put Humpty together again..."

Now I have my own six year old daughter to sing along with. Yes, childhood was simpler then. I remember Madubaa, my childhood's secluded and forbidden beach. Nevertheless, I still ran after my three brothers who disobeyed our parents about going to the dangerous shore. They would try and shake me off, but I would hold on with the tenacious grip of a leech. My younger sisters were still too small to play with. Later, of course, I had my best friends Myra, Shilpa and Latifah, to hang out with.

I remember asking our house-girl on many a day to use a brush to scrub the beach sand off my hair, lest my mum spots the cream tell-tale grains of sand and gives me one hell of a spanking.

Our parents had warned us not to go to Madubaa. They said it was very dangerous, especially when it was high tide. Still, I would follow my brothers across two busy roads. It is a wonder we were never knocked down by speeding vehicles; maybe the fear of a worse spanking than the injuries that could be caused by a car made us be extra careful!

My mind recalls the memory of one of my language teachers. She used to be shocked at my vivid compositions. Sometimes she would get hysterical whenever I told tell her that it was not wild imaginations at play, and that it was what I did over the holidays or on weekends.

She realised fast that I was really getting bored, because while the other children were busy reading 'Hello Children' and 'Read with us' my nose would be constantly buried in a Ludlum or Charles Dickens, Alex La Guma, Ngugi, Okot P' Bitek and even some banned publications.

Anything else, so long as it was not what the class was reading during her lessons. As I mentioned earlier, I owe thanks to my older brother and his hand-me-downs.

I used to feel so irritated with songs like 'Lazy Mary will you wake up' and 'Mary had a little lamb.' I would long for sounds of Manu Dibango and Bruce Springsteen in papa's car.

I realised early that creative expressions cannot be suppressed. My mind glides back to the past again. Crossing the forbidden road to a sprawling estate with Myra. We used to do it anyway despite knowing that our parents would kill us if they found out. Of course, my parents eventually discovered my escapades to the forbidden land. I could not stay away. Girls our age (we were about twelve then) living in these so-called forbidden lands had babies already. We were fascinated by their lifestyles, deprived as they were.

I switch back to when I was barely five, to the Nyali Army Barracks with papa. Being a district commissioner and having many friends in the disciplined forces, he used to take me almost everywhere with him when he was off-duty. He had friends at the barracks and on some weekends mama, my siblings and I would accompany him. I would spend my time at the barracks' sea-front view staring across the sea, while he was at the mess with his friends. If we were not at the army barracks, then we were at the naval base off the waters of Mtongwe. Tranquility that is the sea became a part of me.

One day in the late seventies (I was in kindergarten at the time) papa had picked my older brother and me from school. My brother had diarrhea and so papa decided to drive to the hospital first. Out of nowhere a reckless driver overtaking another car almost had a head on collision with us! Papa jumped out of our car to confront him, shouting 'Bloody fucking!' It was the first time I heard those swear words, but they fascinated me. I wished I could see more of that side of dad. Papa jumped back into our car and we were on our way humming along to strains of Tabu Lay, Marvin Gaye, Jim Reeves and Isaac Hayes. Permanent sounds in papa's car.

My mental camera fast forwards to when we grew older. Papa never put us in public means of transport when travelling up-country for the holidays – mama would not hear of it, so my dad always drove the whole family personally in his car. I had a favourite game – I would read all the road signs from Mombasa to our Kisii highlands, and any that I missed I would read on our way back. My creative juices would flow as we wound through the old road around the Great Rift Valley Escarpment. I would have a new story for my composition class at school.

Sometimes I would break things and hurt myself in the process of trying to re-enact Barbara Kimenye's *Moses* series, *Famous Five*, *Secret Seven*, and Alfred Hitchcock's *The Three Investigators* – I loved Jupiter!

* * * * *

The tangy smell of the sea wafts in the air and teases my nostrils tantalizingly. Bringing me back to earth and the gnawing pain in my tummy. To my peptic stomach ulcers playing up again and the ever tangible presence that is my dilemma.

I caress the two scars on my right arm softly, one a burn mark and the other a reminder left by shards of a broken mug from years back. Both have refused to fade. I remember that silent voice from God last night. Asking me why I have written so much of my past, but jumped this incident.

Collective memory lapses perhaps? Or is it selective amnesia?

He reminds me of what he told me last year when promising me a break in my writing.

A break I would only get if I wrote about some incidents in my life, because that is the problem facing the African woman -- not talking about the socioeconomic crisis affecting us, but bearing the brunt of all the ills afflicting society. He reminds me that my family's reaction notwithstanding, I have to write about it all.

He takes me back to last year. For three straight months I would rise as early as four in the morning to go to church. I remember how I would stay on my knees for hours in church, crying and arguing with God, telling Him that I could not write about some things, and the way He would insist that I do it. Now, I sigh resignedly as I stare in wonder at the two scars. Unwarranted mementos, unwanted souvenirs or an uncalled for talisman of sorts? Or reminders I constantly carry around? Or better still, harbingers of good tidings where my writing is concerned?

I remember that inner voice last night again. "You write about so much," the voice kept nudging at my conscience the whole night, "but why are there pieces of the jigsaw missing? Why the gap? What happened prior to, after and between *To Serenity via Perdition* and *From Shifting Sands* to *Deeper Dimensions?*"

"Don't you want to share with other women?"

"Of course I do! It's my dream!" I cried.

"So write it!" the voice insisted.

So here goes!

You might think that I am digressing. So many paradoxes. I realise I have to take you back a bit.

Flashback to a couple of years ago...

There I was, stuck in the hotel job. A dreary low-paying job, behind the front office desk!

The rent to pay and school fees for my daughter and

the house girl/nanny (I needed one because I worked shifts); the list was endless.

A single parent struggling on a salary of less than ten-thousand shillings with no medical coverage will confess to you that she dreads any medical emergency arising – such emergencies usually turn into horrendous nightmares,

When I broke up with my baby's father and decided to go solo, I said a simple prayer and asked God to guide me so that I would be able to provide for Nehema. And I prayed that He would never let me get into any situations that would make me compromise my integrity or dignity. It was more than enough that I had just opted out of a relationship with someone who suffered from an inferiority complex and seemed intent on dragging me down with him in a demeaning way. I am an introvert, but there comes a time when one needs to say enough is enough!

That is why I know God has always been present for me and my daughter in His own special way. And as coincidence would have it, he was there to hold my hand when the Likoni ethnic clashes broke out. But that is a story for another moment.

So there I was, working there for one year now, stuck behind the reception desk or switchboard, day after day, sometimes night after night. A boring treadmill of sorts. It was thus easy for me to notice a certain man: An African middle-aged guest who would always hang around the reception desk. Because I am trained in customer care it is usually hard to brush someone off, even when they could become too demanding and persistent.

The elderly man always passed by the reception to say hello, and would insist on me solving any problem he had with his room, yet housekeeping was on call for twenty-four hours.

It turned to an obsession of sorts when he would wait for me to come on duty even if the problem was a leaking tap. Yet the maintenance team was on duty twenty-four hours, seven days a week.

I started avoiding him like the plague, in my own way because his behaviour was raising skeptical eyebrows. I would exchange roles with my colleague and ask her to work at the reception and let me work at the switchboard, which was partially obstructed behind the reception area.

One day he found me at the reception and asked me why I was avoiding him. I told him I was not avoiding him, and that I was just trying to show him in a gentle way that we had departments at the hotel for every crisis arising and that he did not have to wait for me every time his room had a slight problem.

I thought we had resolved the issue, only for me to

find out a couple of days later, when I reported on duty in the afternoon, that he had been asking for me!

One day the hotel's front office manager came to me and said "Mr. Kamwanthe says you are indifferent to him nowadays."

I said, "I am not indifferent to him Sir. It's just that he keeps hanging around the reception and I just want to put him in his place."

He continued, "Do you know he's a bank manager?"

I replied, "No Sir. I do not."

He said, "Do not be too hard on him. He just moved here on transfer from their head office in Nairobi and he is still looking for a house. I have never seen him do that before, that is, develop an interest in one of our staff. He might offer you a better paying job, and I know that you need the extra money."

A couple of days later I had cause to think that the hotel manager was a psychic and clairvoyant, to boot!

It was on a Saturday and as usual it was the bank manager's day off.

He dropped by at lunchtime to say hi.

As coincidence would have it, my five-year-old Nehema chose that very opportune moment with swimming floaters and wings to run all the way from the swimming pool dripping wet with my kid sister in hot pursuit.

"Mummy! Mummy! You promised to join us!" she was wailing.

My sister on the other hand said, "I am sorry! I tried to stop her."

She was apologizing because I had asked her not to let Nehema come to the reception area. I knew she would give me a hectic time asking for this and that, especially from the hotel shop cum boutique across the reception.

I picked the wet bundle that was squirming and wailing, ready to take her back to the pool. Then I realised that the bank manager was still standing there, open-mouthed! I was not sure why he seemed shocked, but I decided to come back and find out.

Five minutes later I was back.

"Kemunto, I knew you were single. But I did not know that you have a child."

"Well, I do. Why do you seem so shocked?"

"You do not look like you have a child."

"Why? Do I look too young or what?"

"I do not know what it is, but you just do not look it Kemu. You know. Like you have given birth."

I burst out laughing because he had this funny look on his face, and he kept staring at me.

I do not know if he was mesmerised by my twenty-four inch waist, wondering how I could have had a baby with such a tiny waist or was still shocked by the revelation.

I had to shoo him away because I was not getting any work done.

A few days later he was back again.

"Kemunto, how do you survive with a child? I understand these guys barely pay you ten-thousand shillings."

I looked at him. "I barely make ends meet. I just try my best, because it is all I have. If I dwell on the negative, I will freak out."

He spent a couple of months hovering at the reception. I knew he was just biding his time and something had to give.

Finally he changed his tactics.

One evening before going up to his room, he passed by and kind of blurted out, maybe before he got cold feet, "Kemu, are you interested in a better paying job?"

"Yes, of course I am. My sister has to go to college and I can barely afford her tuition. Have you heard of an opening somewhere? Maybe I can send in my application."

"Umm. Actually, the opening is at our bank. I do not know how you'll take it, but the salary is good. It is better than what you are getting here."

"What is the position?" I asked.

"A tea girl, I know that you might see it as beneath you, but as you say, you have to pay rent, school fees for your daughter and college fees for your sister. It is also essentially an office assistant's position. I have seen your papers in the manager's office and I know you deserve a better job, but at the moment that is the vacancy we have with prospects of a promotion."

"How much is the salary?" He mentioned a figure that was more than thrice my current salary. He then added that once I am confirmed to my position there are other benefits like medical insurance for Nehema and myself, career progression, and later on, educational benefits.

I needed a better salary but I was apprehensive. Tea. Make tea and serve other staff? Me? I had never done that before!

I had an agonizingly nail-biting week of mulling over the whole issue.

I talked to my close friends Myra, Shilpa and Latifah. To make matters worse, they shared my misgivings about making tea for people. The ball was squarely in my court. The onus was upon me to come to a decision. After all, it was I who was suffering and not making ends meet.

I talked to my parents. They were excited and said it was better than being a hotelier as there were prospects of a promotion. But then again, they also said that the call was mine.

Have you ever needed something so much you could not sleep at night? That is how much I needed a laptop, to put down my spontaneous and compulsive thoughts which coalesce into writing. And so I finally agreed to apply for the tea girl's position. I sent in my credentials and testimonials. All formalities were concluded. In a week's time I was officially employed at a certain bank in Mombasa. Little did I know what I was getting myself into.

The first few months

The minute I walked into that bank, I hit it right off with the African receptionist/switchboard operator called Rosemary. The first thing I did when I noticed her having a problem with locating the number of a certain airline that had the knack of changing their contacts every other quarter, was lean over her work station and whisper conspiratorially, "Why don't you dial the airport info desk, the number is 433211 up to 9."

She was so surprised that she dragged me into the bank manager's office and asked him, hands akimbo,

"*Aiiiii. Sir, mbona umetuletea msichana mwerevu na mrembo hivi akuje kutupikia chai?*[i]"

He looked sheepish as he replied, "*Si hiyo ndiyo nafasi iko, ama unataka kumpatia kazi yako?*[ii]"

What an induction!

* * * * *

I soon settled into my routine of making the morning and afternoon tea for the staff and cleaning up afterwards. I do not know what it was, but I soon started rubbing certain people the wrong way. I cannot actually pinpoint it to any one particular incident, but one stands out like a sore thumb.

I was coming out of the kitchen when I came across Salma, the personal assistant to the general manager. She was having a problem with her computer and seemed at her wits end.

I asked her what the problem was and she looked at me askance as if to ask, 'And what will you do about it?' But instead she said, "It was working just fine yesterday. Now it has locked up on me the whole morning. It keeps hanging at intervals."

"Let me see," I lightly pressed the control-alt-delete sequence and rebooted the system.

"No need to call the technicians. This is a sure way to end the lockup when it hangs or freezes. But maybe you can request the techies to install a fire-wall for you just in case?" Salma was really skeptical, wrinkling her pert nose in uncertainty.

"Kemunto, are you sure that you haven't deleted the file I was working on?" she asked.

---

i Kiswahili -- 'How come you have brought such a clever and pretty girl to make us tea?

ii Kiswahili -- 'Isn't that the vacancy we have, or do you want to give her your job?'

"No." I replied calmly. "Here let me show you." I executed the program she'd had open when I rebooted the program. "See. Isn't that your file?" I asked her, pointing to the recovery file on the screen. She looked at me like I was a rocket scientist standing beside her trying to help out.

And there I was, making them tea.

After that incident, life was never the same at the bank. Frustrations became the order of the day from Salma. I could not even read a book during my lunch break. She would summon me imperiously for a cup of tea when the whim struck her. I decided enough was enough. I went to the bank manager and told him that I was having a problem with the PA because I had been instructed that tea was only to be served twice a day.

He called her to his office and talked to her. The problem was resolved. Then she started nitpicking. One day her complaint would be that her tea had very little tea leaves, the next that it had too much milk. I devised another method of going around such a problem. I asked the manager if the bank could buy tea bags, coffee and cocoa so that all I had to do was boil the milk and water, pour it into thermos flasks place everything at a central point and let everybody serve themselves.

Everyone embraced the idea except for Salma, who started making innuendos and insinuations as to my association with the manager. Little did I know how almost right time was going to prove her theories.

A few days later, the problem was that she could not find her special mug among the tea things I had set out. What pissed me off was the way she went about it. She stormed into the kitchen, grabbed the book that I was reading and tossed it on the counterpane, all the while shouting that she wanted her mug!

I stood up and asked her what she had just done with my book. In a very soft voice punctuated with staccato emphasis, I went like, "Listen – my dear. I – am – never – shouted – at -- OK? If you want to shout go and shout at your husband who always looks so henpecked and harassed when he comes to pick you up. Remember that I have a child twice as old as yours, and the next time you shout at me I might just end up at Central Police Station charged with assault."

I picked up my book and calmly resumed my reading.

I only looked up when I realised that the other staff were crowding the kitchen entrance, amusement hovering around their lips – some of them looked like they wanted to clap but could not dare.

You have probably guessed right. She stormed into the general manager's office and I was summoned. I was accused of being insubordinate and I felt that the GM was taking her side because he was Indian like her! I simply told the GM to his face that if his PA did not respect me, I was not going to respect her. After all, it was a two way street. She never allowed me to live that incident down. She started making me pay for it.

She would send me on errands outside (sometimes unofficial ones, even to the spices market in the Old Town) whenever she found me writing or reading a book. She would send me to the post office or say, "By the way would you mind passing by this shop and getting me this and that?"

Obviously a clash of wills was imminent because for one, I was not a messenger. The bank had another male office assistant for such errands and not personal errands at that.

A week later I put my foot down and refused to be sent out.

Things got worse. Frustrations galore! Salma became impossible to work with and she ganged up with the lady assistant manager called Preeti who was also Indian! I did not really mind. The PA had a top job, but I was better at everything. She would even come to me for help with her spelling. I would roll my eyes and say, "don't you have spell check on your computer or a dictionary on your desk?"

Then push came to shove, and finally crunch as a result of many not so obscure incidents. One day, I asked the branch manager why they let a particular family hold accounts at the bank. I thought the reputation of such a family would eventually surly that of the bank. It was an open secret in Mombasa that the family engaged in illegal trade, narcotics and money laundering. It was even known that the patriarch of the family was the leading drug baron in the East African region. They would come to the bank to deposit their millions, accompanied by armed security personnel. They were practically treated like demigods.

Anytime they came to the bank, the other customers in the banking hall would hurriedly move aside and whispers of 'mafia....' 'mafia...' would float in the air.

The bank manager told me not to even dare talk about that family. Years later, that particular family hit the headlines with the patriarch assassinated in a foreign country. That manager must have recalled my words.

Another day one of our account managers, an expatriate Austrian, flung aside a loan application file and it almost landed in the dust bin! I picked it up and glanced at the cover. I looked at him curiously and said "don't you want to be politically correct?" (It was during the KANU regime.)

"Why?" he asked,

"I can see by the name of this firm that you think it is from the Lake region. It isn't. Do you know who the directors are?" I gave him a couple of prominent names from the Rift Valley region, but he brushed everything aside.

Not for long though.

A couple of weeks later, he had a shock.

The directors of the firm whose loan application file had almost landed in the trash, paid the bank a courtesy call.

The 'expat' almost freaked out when he was told that he had visitors waiting at the reception area.

He glanced from his office window and saw some people sitting at the reception. A couple of them had some of their lower middle teeth missing (A cultural rite of passage for some tribes from the Rift Valley.)

The GM called the bank manager and they came to the expatriate account manager's office for a brief meeting before they could talk to the directors of the firm.

The account manager almost fainted!

The whole office was mobilised to look for the missing file – which was not missing, really.

I walked into the account manager's office and asked him, "How badly do you want that file?"

He stared at me and responded, "very badly!"

I looked at him. "I thought so. But didn't you throw it into the dust bin?"

I went to some shelves behind him, retrieved the file and handed it to him. He hugged me, shouting "you're an angel!" The rest of the staff stood amazed. I was so embarrassed but maybe I deserved it for being cheeky with the file.

After that incident, it seemed like my relationship with the bank manager was headed for its nadir of sorts, so to speak.

* * * * *

One day he started the conversation in a very interesting way. "You know Kemunto, everybody here thinks I am protecting you. Maybe I should start doing that."

"You do not have to do anything of the sort. I can fight my own battles," I replied.

"Do you know that they think we're having an affair?"

"No I did not. But I am really not affected by office gossip so long as I know it isn't true," I countered.

The following day after I had set his tray down, he asked me to serve him. He had never done that before. All I ever did was set his tray down and that was it. He normally served himself at his own convenience as the milk was in a thermos flask. I am not sure why, but I hesitated that very first time. My gut instinct is always razor sharp and that day it was telling me not to serve him. I had a feeling it would become routine. A bad precedent, my intuition whispered. Because I have always considered knowing how many sugars or how much coffee a man takes rather intimate.

I served him and thought that it was only for that day. He was at it again the next day. And the next. And the next.

One day he said to me "Kemunto, you seem very uncomfortable serving me. I like it when you serve me. It is the African thing for a lady to do."

I just stared at him, and asked albeit a little sarcastically, "African?"

He replied, "that is the problem we are having with you young ladies of this generation, Kemu."

Why did I have a nagging feeling about this?

I was soon to find out.

A month later...

"So Kemunto, don't you want your promotion?"

"Of course I do, sir."

"I told you to join banking classes. Why haven't you signed up?"

"It is too expensive; I cannot afford to pay my sister's college tuition and mine at the same time. Not forgetting my baby's kindergarten fees."

"Kemu, do whatever it takes and go to college, bring back some tangible results and then we can see about your promotion."

I thought about it and finally signed up. It was very difficult because it was extremely expensive.

However, I talked with my sister and asked her to put on hold a couple of her semesters while I started with my bridging courses.

A few months and some exams later, I finally brought in my results for Business English and Commerce. Then I commenced studying for my diploma in Banking.

He said that, at least now, he could start working on my promotion.

Two months later he had not done anything about it yet.

All I could do was feel him staring at me whenever I was in his office. One day, after I had finished serving him, as courteous as ever, I asked him, "do you need anything more, sir?"

"Just you, Kemu."

I froze.

"I beg your pardon?"

"I want you Kemunto, are you shocked? Haven't you realised that by now? I fell in love with your short kinky African hair and slim body the minute I saw you!"

I stared at him in shock and said "Aren't you ashamed of yourself? You are my father's age. I thought you recently went up country to attend your daughter's wedding, a daughter as old as I am?"

"What has that got to do with me wanting you?"

This was hopeless. I simply walked out. It became a refrain, like a scratched CD! Every time I would ask him if he needed anything more in reference to his tea or office duties, he would stare at me and say 'do you really mean that?' or 'only you.' Or 'just you.' I stopped asking him the question. I even dreaded going to his office. But I had to enter his office at least twice a day. When taking him his tea tray and when going to remove the used cups in the evening.

I could not avoid or escape that.

One day in the evening I asked the other male assistant to do me a favour and clear up for me because I was running late for classes.

The following day I found the manager anxiously waiting for me. He called me to his office. "Kemunto, yesterday evening you did not ask me if I needed anything before you left?" Was that a question or a statement of fact?

"I am sorry Mr. Kamwanthe, but I asked Barasa to clear up for me because I was late for class. What did you need?"

"Just you. I wanted us to have dinner together, Kemu. I have wanted you ever since I laid my eyes on you at that hotel reception, and I think I am going crazy."

I looked at him for quite a while. Finally, I spoke.

"You do not know me. Aren't you scared of AIDS?"

"I know enough, Kemu. I have my own ways of finding out, and I know that currently you are not attached. As for AIDS, remember you were asked to go for a series of tests before your medical coverage was approved?"

No! I said to myself, what he wants to say cannot be true!

"Do you remember?" he insisted.

"Yes." It was barely a croak. I remembered that day because my baby had been sick and I had just picked her up from school and passed by the bank's doctor for the bank's mandatory pre-employment medical check-ups before proceeding with Nehema to the hospital.

"Well, I know you are ok Kemunto, because your HIV test came back negative and that is why your medical coverage was approved."

I was so shocked!

"That is a low-heeled thing to do! How dare you subject your staff to the HIV test and lie to them? If I remember well, when I asked you what the blood test was for you vaguely talked about meningitis and hepatitis! God! You people are insufferable!"

I was so angry and pissed off I could barely talk to him civilly over the next few days!

A week later...

"Are you still mad at me, Kemunto?"

I had to laugh at that. He looked like a small boy, asking for forgiveness!

The following day at least I started answering his good morning wishes.

In a couple of days' time, he resumed his pestering and cajoling for me to have dinner with him.

I flatly refused. He soon changed tact and he decided to play dirty.

"*Unajua,* my friend Kemunto, *ni uwache kuringa ringa. Hiyo kitu uko nayo hapo katikati ya miguu yako si dhahabu, ni sawa tu kama zengine.*" (You know my friend Kemunto, stop with the pride. What you have between your legs is not gold. It is the same as other ladies.)

The man was really something else!

"So what if what I have between my legs is not gold and is just the same as what all the other women have? Why do you want it? And by the way, I thought you had a wife and girlfriend?"

"There you go again. Almighty and proud. Can't you even talk in Kiswahili? Every time I hear you talk, it

101

is in English. I know! I know it is because of your so-called constant writing! And yes, I have a wife and the occasional girlfriend, but it is just something with us men – we never seem to get enough!"

God No!

"I know that young ladies always have an older man on the side, Kemunto. I understand you call us ATMs. I do not care if you have your young boyfriend. *Unaona huyu* PA *wetu? Ako na* Zed Form Four."

"What?" I was shocked – getting a Zed grade in Form Four in the old system meant that you'd flunked in all your subjects! Was that why she looked at me with venom in her eyes whenever I filled the daily newspaper's crossword puzzles, Sudoku or the Code

Word in ten minutes or less, while she would be stuck in the first few words for the whole day?

"*Na huyo* copy typist *ako na* D minus *kwa hiyo* eight-four-four *yenu.*"

What! The Indian copy typist Rupti had a D minus aggregate in the current eight-four-four system! It meant that she had practically gotten E's in all subjects undertaken and had maybe been a point away from an aggregate grade of E! I was way above her as I had scored a mean aggregate of C plus and had only missed a point to have a B minus!

Still, I liked the copy typist. She was down to earth and appreciated that we could help one another out in the office.

"*Unajua, alikuwa anafanya kwa benki ingine hapa karibu tu. Siku moja weekendi, alipatikana juu ya meza wakifanya hiyo mambo ya mapenzi na* boss wake. I mean directors from Nairobi just walked into the boss' office, and there they were on top of the table! Obviously she was sacked! But you know Indians and their banking fraternity – her former boss was owed a favour by the GM of this bank, and so naturally here she is!"

Oh my goodness! I could not believe I was privy to this. Why was he telling me this? I wanted the ground to split in two and swallow me up!

"I know you're going to college, Kemunto, and you have brought some results, but whether you bring a diploma or degree, I am the one who conducts staff appraisals and forwards names for promotions to the head office; I can pass you up if I want. So go think about it, or you'll go on serving them tea and yet you have better grades than they do!"

"What?! Did I hear you right? What have you just said?"

I could not conceal my shock at his words. He did not bother to reply.

"Is that why you offered me this job and made me quit at the hotel? To come and frustrate me? I only took this job because you said that there are prospects of a promotion. I can walk out anytime I want, so do not hold your breath because I won't sleep with you!"

He looked at me, "Maybe you think I am joking, Kemu." He walked to his rows of shelves holding various files. He came back with two staff files and flipped through.

I did not want to look, but my curiosity got the better of me – there it was in black and white!

One school leaving results slip with a Zed and another with a D minus!

I knew the other staff had good qualifications because I talked with them a lot, but I had begun to have misgivings and reservations about the two particular cases Mr. Kamwanthe was referring to.

By the time I reached the kitchen I was in tears. I was in so much pain, I was shaking. I held onto the sink for support. Salifu, the motherly lady officer, opened the door. She had grown close to me once we realised that she lived in an estate across from where I lived.

103

"You're crying. I saw you leave his office. Is he frustrating you? You know you can talk to me."

I just nodded but told her I was fine. Two days later, she would find out that I was not fine at all.

The following Saturday...

It was around eight in the evening and my daughter had gone to her grandparents for the weekend.

As usual I was deeply engrossed in my writing. It is usually the only time I have to myself and for my writing.

There was a knock at my door. I went to open without asking who it was, because I lived in a block of flats in a safe neighbourhood.

I froze. My blood went cold. I have only heard of people talking about their blood turning cold, but that evening I experienced it. My knees went cold and I felt a chill climb from the soles of my feet to the crown of my head.

Mr. Kamwanthe was framed in my doorway!

I did not let him in. Instead I asked him, "how did you find out where I live?"

"Aren't you going to ask me in, Kemunto?"

"No. How did you find out where I live?" I repeated my question.

"Have you forgotten the private eye files in the office? You know we use them for background checks on prospective clients."

The cold rush went through my body again as I mentally pictured the logo of a human eye I had seen on some files in the office. Was someone paid to poke their dirty nose into my private life?

I thought that surely this man was becoming irrational and obsessed!

"Why don't you dress up and let me take you out to dinner, Kemunto? Where is your daughter?"

"She's not here. She went to my parents with my sister." I mentally kicked myself. Why was I offering him any explanations? "And no, I do not want to go out to dinner with you. I am very busy."

"Doing what, Kemu?"

"Writing."

He stared at the pen in my hand. "So you're really serious about your writing?"

"Yes." I wanted to reduce my conversation to monosyllabic responses so that he would just go away.

"You seem like a good and bright girl. I can do so much for you, Kemu. I can pay your rent for you, your sister's fees, your daughter's, yours and even buy you a laptop for your writing and college assignments. What do you say?"

"Please, just leave me alone!" I shouted.

My opposite door neighbour opened his door. Most of my neighbours on my floor were bachelors and were very protective of me, my daughter and my sister.

"Are you ok, Kemu?" my neighbour asked hesitantly.

"Yes, I'm fine." But I looked at my 'visitor' pointedly and in a soft voice meant for his ears alone I said "Please, leave before I cause a scene."

My neighbour closed his door.

"Well, I will leave for now, Kemunto, but I brought you some shopping to help you out."

That is when I noticed the large Nakumatt shopping bag at his feet! Was the man out of his mind?

He actually had the audacity to walk away and leave the full supermarket bag at my door?

What to do? The bag was heavy. By the time I run down the stairs after him, he will have driven away! And obviously I could not carry it to work with me and dump it in his office!

I had no alternative but to take the shopping inside. It pained me to do so.

Once inside, I was shocked to find that the shopping was worth more than five-thousand shillings.

Almost the equivalent of my rent, and it was going to last for ages. What was he trying to do? Wear down the last vestiges of my resistance? The bastard!

Everything was in the largest of quantities, not the five-hundred gram quantities I was used to buying due to budgetary constraints. He had bought everything in excess from the large portion of five litres of expensive olive cooking oil to ten kilogrammes of the finest Mwea Pishori rice! I stared forlornly in my kitchen at the *uto* and *samli* (unrefined cooking oil and fat) I had bought from the slums behind our flats to cut down on cost. I then understood how a girl starts yearning for pampering and lets someone do it – and of course pays the price.

I started thinking. I had been doing some research, and from legal notes I understood that sexual harassment has been defined as: "Unwelcome sexual advances, requests for sexual favours, and other verbal or physical conduct of a sexual nature. When submission to or rejection of such conduct is used as the basis for employment decisions or such conduct has the purpose or effect of creating an intimidating, hostile or offensive working environment."

I had tried talking to ladies who had gone through such experiences. I found out that most succumbed to the pressure or quit their jobs when the emotional abuse went overboard. They were too scared of talking about it as they seemed to get no support from any quarters!

That definition seemed telling, because even most social workers say that such cases are hard to take up. The courts need tangible proof before they can even think of prosecution. Neither a helping hand nor support structure is available. One is left feeling as if she is grasping at air.

My take on the whole issue is that in Kenya, sexual harassment is not recognised explicitly. Period.

I went to bed, saying a prayer to God and asking Him to help me hold on to my dignity because I was faced with a prospect of what us girls call 'horizontal interviews' -- that is, you decide if you will sleep with your boss to get your promotion or refuse and face the prospects of no promotion.

The following day...

Being a Sunday, after church I came back to my place to get some more writing done before I could go get my daughter from her grandparents.

Salifu (the lady officer from the bank) came to see me. She stayed just near my place. She had this look in her eyes.

"Last night I saw his car parked here, Kemu. I thought it too much of a coincidence that his car should be parked where you stay. I really feared for you. Please tell me he was not here. Tell me it was not him!"

I looked at her and simply said "It was." And I promptly burst into tears.

Maybe it was the result of all the pent-up frustrations I had been bottling up.

"You do not say."

I just nodded. I could not talk. I was barely coherent. I cried my heart out, the heaving sobs tearing me apart.

She just held me in her arms, till my sniffling abated.

When had calmed down, I told her exactly what had happened the previous evening.

"Good for you, Kemu" she told me, "but what are you going to do about him?"

"I don't know."

"I think I will have a talk with him, Kemunto."

"No Salifu. Please don't, he might get worse and start victimizing me instead."

Salifu left soon after without agreeing with me.

Later that evening...

In the evening I went to pick up my daughter.

I had a conversation with my papa and was profoundly disturbed. "You know my daughter, your boss has really helped you by giving you this better paying job."

"Yes, but..."

"I think we should give him a present, Kemunto. Something small to show our appreciation."

"Papa, there is no need to do that." (In my heart I was thinking 'Dad if only you knew...').

"It is just being courteous. Maybe a meru oak coffee table and stools."

(He was now also a timber dealer, though not doing very well at the time due to the runaway bank interest rates.)

"I said no! Didn't you hear me?"

Mama was shocked. "Hey, Kemu! No need to shout."

Papa dropped the subject, but mama continued with the same thread in the kitchen.

She was wondering why I was so defensive.

I just told her the truth, that the bank manager had changed and that he was sexually harassing me.

She was very concerned about my job, because if I quit, they would be unable to help me as they had been victims of the Likoni ethnic and land clashes and were still trying to pick up the pieces. Rent for some of their properties had to be reduced by half (nobody was willing to pay more in an area prone to clashes), plus they had to pay fees for my two sisters who were still in high school.

I told mama I was contemplating quitting. That it had crossed my mind. She just told me to be strong and not to quit. In my heart I agreed with her because I could not depend on borrowing from my friends Myra, Shilpa and Latifah should I be jobless again.

* * * * *

On Monday...

The kitchen door was pushed open.

"Kemunto did you have to go and tell Mrs. Salifu that I was at your place last night? You have really disappointed me. She's just given me a lecture like I am a small boy, and yet you're talking of a promotion!"

I did not answer him. He'd closed the door behind him.

"I am talking to you, Kemu. Do you know, if you joke with me you're going to continue making tea here forever, your intelligence notwithstanding?"

I still did not answer him and I guess he was really irked!

The next minute I felt his fumbling hands as he grabbed me by the waist and turned me around. (I had been facing the electric hotplate which I had switched on but was yet to put the milk on to boil.)

I struggled but still managed to burn my hand on the red hot coils as he tried to kiss me forcefully!

"You bastard! Leave me alone!"

He pressed me against the counterpane and held my hands back. In the process, we knocked over one of the China cups from the mug tree, and it crashed on to the work space in smithereens!

Oh no! What a bad omen! Of all the cups it had to be

the PA's mug! A jagged piece of enamel from the broken cup cut into my arm and the blood gushed out!

The other employees were bound to hear the commotion.

He still went on trying to kiss me. I kicked at his shins and kneed him in the groin. He stifled a scream but he let go and in the process crashed headlong onto the door, which swung open.

"You bastard!" I repeated, "Can't you see I am hurt? And I have also burnt myself."

He appeared dazed, but he noticed the blood.

"God! I am sorry, Kemunto, I did not mean to...." He was interrupted when Patrick, the junior officer whose work station was adjacent the kitchen, came to check, concerned when the door crashed open at the sound of the breaking mugs. Strangely, when he found Mr. Kamwanthe picking himself up from the pieces of China on the floor, Patrick pretended like he needed a glass of water.

I switched off the hotplate, walked past both of them, picked up my handbag and told Rupti that I had hurt myself and was going to the hospital.

I did not come back for two days. Eventually when I did, I was not talking to him. Even when he would say 'Good morning,' I would walk right past him. I did not think he deserved to be wished a good morning! What sticks in my mind from that incident to date is my daughter's reaction to the scar on my arm, where the piece of jagged ceramic had torn into my flesh.

She asked me how I hurt my arm and I told her that I had slipped at work and cut myself with a knife. I asked her to always be careful when handling knives.

She still says the same thing today when using the knife, or she'll tell her friends, 'Be careful with the knife; you might cut yourself the way my mum did.' And she brings them over to show them my scar.

The short and long of it is that from that day Mr. Kamwanthe grew very cold with me. Who would not when I could barely even spare him a glance?

I was already desperately looking for another job! I did not think that trying to seek legal redress for sexual harassment would help much, when all the court would do was demand evidence.

A month later...

Trust financial problems to force me to be the first one to break the ice.

I had to because I needed money to offset a hospital bill for our youngest brother who was still epileptic.

I was in Mr. Kamwanthe's office.

"Kemu, why do you blow hot and cold with me?"

"I am not blowing hot and cold with you Mr. Kamwanthe. I just need a small advance to tide me over because the college fees are overwhelming, and my brother has been sick. I'm not asking for your money, so please do not make this personal. I just need the money and then it can be deducted from my salary at the end of the month."

"We do not do that here, Kemunto. It is month-end to month-end here. I told you I understand the responsibilities you have, and I am willing to help you out, but you're so stubborn."

I walked out of his office. I was not going to beg.

I talked to Salifu and she introduced me to a shylock that some of the staff normally used. He helped me out though his interest rate was very high. He spread the payment in installments over two months, which was not very bad.

I bet that Mr. Kamwanthe was holding his breath, waiting for me to go back to him and grovel!

* * * * *

Meanwhile, the frustrations with Salma went on unabated. She particularly cherished one hour of the day. She had succeeded in managing to tie me down with the onerous task of taking the bank's closing statement to the CBK[i], as is usual with all commercial banks before they start with clearing house. Commercial banks have to do that everyday. It is the procedure to ensure they finalise their obligations to each other. Salma knew the deadline was mid-day, but she would take her sweet time typing the figures once the officers gave them to her. All she wanted to do everyday was hand me the statement at exactly five minutes to the hour and expect me to rush to the CBK on the pretext that it was only down the road. I would be late and the officer in charge at CBK would really scold me even after explaining that it was not my fault. He would point out that ours was the only bank handing in late almost everyday. I wisened up and refused to be rushed by Salma. People say that women are their own worst enemies and I was experiencing from her the worst case of what my friends Myra, Shilpa, Latifah and I call PhD[ii]. But I knew how to hit back. Whenever she would hand me the statement late, I would take my time and reach the CBK fifteen minutes late! I would be sent back promptly by the CBK officers.

Once I was back at our bank, Mr. Kamwanthe would be forced to call the CBK and apologise, saying that there had been a slight hitch thus the delay. I would be asked to go back. I would refuse, and someone else would be sent.

The management realised we had a big problem. When asked, I explained how the PA was frustrating me

---

i CBK -- Central Bank of Kenya
ii Pull Her Down!

and I would rather it was Rupti the copy-typist who would be in charge of the closing statement preparation.

Salma was instructed to at least try and give me the statement ten minutes to time.

She complied but I knew she was going to make me pay for that in other ways!

Two weeks later...

There was a banker's strike going on and all union members were taking part. They were clamouring for promised increments.

Naturally, like all other banks we were also involved (apart from management) and would stage sit-ins and would walk to the union office everyday.

By the fourth day, letters had been issued threatening to sack us. The staff at our bank were torn in the middle of whether to go on or cave in.

There was something nagging at my conscience and I could not resist being naughty about it!

I got along fine with Rupti and we talked about everything under the sky. I think it is because she's not from a rich family and is really down to earth. So there we were just laughing about a lot of silly things when I suddenly blurted out, "Tell me something Rupti, I have been dying to ask you, where you used to work before, were you actually caught making love with your MD on his desk?"

I watched the shock fleet across her face. She flustered and indignantly said a big no. Finally after a reflective two minutes or so, she looked at me and asked, "By the way, where did you hear that from, Kemu?"

I looked at her and said, "Rumours go around, and Mombasa is our own global village!"

"Ok. Yes I did it. We used to do it often. I had to though, I know it was wrong, but I am from a poor family. My dad passed away and being the oldest I have to help my mother pay fees for my younger brothers."

Why was I experiencing a sense of *deja vu?*

She continued saying, "I was going through what you're going through right now with our bank manager, and don't think I haven't noticed."

"Oh God!" I said, "don't tell me it's so obvious?"

We were soon called into the bank and handed letters. I put a rain check on our conversation, to be pursued some other time! We were all there including the general manager. We had a day earlier been given letters terming the strike 'illegal' and were threatened with dire consequences.

So what was in this latest letter?

All staff were huddled reading and signing their letters. Strangely I hadn't signed mine.

Salma, as imperious as ever, pointed at me and called out in front of everyone, "Hey you! I need a copy of your signed letter." She actually shouted it.

I did not want to be sarcastic, but I told her, "These letters have a wrong spelling and I think you should change it first before people sign them and they are filed."

She went up in arms and was very defensive. Her voice went a notch higher. Sharp as it already was. She grabbed my letter from me and went through it. "Where? Which wrong spelling?" her shrill voice rising an octave higher.

We had come into the bank in a jovial mood chatting amicably. Now there was pin drop silence and everybody was staring at us. Watching the unfolding scenario with bated breath, listening to our exchange.

People say that the Queen's language is tough. I realised how tough because it seems to give some people nightmares! As for me, I usually cross all my Ts and dot all my Is; check all grammar and spellings until I am satisfied.

The letter had passed through the assistant bank manager and most of the staff had signed it.

Now they were all staring at me.

"Why do you always refuse to accept help? Here, let me show you," I told her. I stretched my hand and took the letter.

The letter in part read, 'Due to your willingness to return to duty, the management has decided to invoke the earlier warning letters issued to you.'

I pointed to my bone of contention, every one crowded over my shoulder to see.

"You have used the word *invoke* and it is wrong. I think you intended to use *revoke*."

If she were a clever lady, she would have sensed that I was giving her an easy way out and admitted it was a typing error. Which I knew it was not, because she had glanced through it just now and not seen her mistake. Instead, she started arguing. Saying I did not know anything.

She was almost hysterical!

I gave her a curious look and started explaining in a patient voice saying "Invoke means like to call on God with prayer, and I think it will be blasphemous to use it in that context. Revoke means to annul, and I think that is the word you meant to use."

She was staring at me as if I was explaining to her the second theory of thermodynamics!

She was still reluctant to admit her mistake even after some cajoling from the other staff who realised I was right.

Why couldn't she gracefully accept the olive branch I was extending?

Rosemary, our receptionist, cheeky as she was, went for her dictionary (in my heart of hearts I honestly felt like she was going for Salma's jugular).

There it was in black and white! I was right. In front of everybody. I really felt sorry for Salma!

To placate her, I said, "why don't we settle on *rescind*, it means the same as revoke, you seem to have a certain phobia towards revoke!"

Everybody assembled in the banking hall burst into laughter.

It seemed that unintentionally, I had put my foot right into my mouth, because for the rest of the week the other staff kept laughing at her and calling out 'Invoke!' every time she passed their desks. In the coming weeks, I constantly felt like I had jumped from the proverbial frying pan into the fire to battle with Salma's encounters with venomous eyes, and invisible daggers into my back.

After the 'Invoke' incident, Mr Kamwanthe had looked at me saying "Kemu! You're something else altogether!"

"I know!" I had answered back cockily with my tea tray. One could almost certainly see my tongue in my cheek!

Staff annual party...

It was a month later and I knew I looked stunning and dignified in my black evening number.

The other staff kept staring at me in wonder (especially the ladies).

They were used to seeing me in my green (awful!) and white tea girl's uniform. Didn't it occur to them that I had been a hotelier and that I had another life? I kept smiling to myself the whole evening. I had been with them for one year. Didn't they realise that I was a proud lady and liked to look good? My hair itself should be a testimony in that office daily, with never a strand out of place. Bad Hair Day was never in my vocabulary no matter how broke I was. So why were they surprised to see me in this evening dress?

The bank manager sidled up to me and whispered saying, "Now, I really wish you were my PA, Kemu. Have you seen those envious stares?"

He then stuck by my side! I looked for another seat, and he found a way to tell one of our clerks sitting by my side to excuse him! "I thought you were concerned about the rumours flying around the office sir? So why on earth do you want to sit beside the tea girl?" I asked him snidely. He still stuck there as if telling other people 'hands off.' He could not believe that I didn't drink alcohol.

"Stop calling me sir, at least for tonight. I thought tonight of all nights I will see you loosen up a bit, Kemu. What will it take to make you lose your composure and control?"

"Nothing, Mr. Kamwanthe," I replied ignoring his invitation to drop the formalities. I continued gazing at the antics of some already drunk colleagues. "I can't afford to lose my cool. I have to remain in control. I have a child to take care of and provide for, so the short of it is that I do not want to die of AIDS, especially seeing that I am not privy to staff medical records like you." He just stared at me stunned by my forthrightness. After the usual speeches were over, feasting started on *mbuzi choma*[i] sizzling and turning on a spit. It was a buffet dinner of sumptuous traditional delicacies of *mukimo, chapati*, pot roast, *ugali*, beef stew, fried tilapia, *kachumbari* and mutton biryani.

Finally, the hired transport was ready to start dropping the staff at their homes. Some of us decided to stay behind to dance. The bank manager came to me and asked me to accompany him to town for a drink.

"I told you I do not drink. Anyway, I have decided to

---

i i Kiswahili -- roast goat.

stay for the beach party with the others. Maybe that will show you how old you are!"

He was furious and remained so for the whole of the following week!

Another month later...

A day before, when I realised that our salaries were late, I had gone to Mr. Kamwanthe and told him that I had issued two cheques to outside parties and they were going to bounce because our accounts had not been debited with our salaries. He said it was ok because I had explained it to him. I was surely surprised to be summoned to the general manager's office and told to explain in writing why cheques drawn in my account were bouncing.

Now here I was today, addressing the GM.

When the GM looked at Mr. Kamwanthe who was also present for an explanation, to my amazement the bank manager told the GM that he was not aware of my situation.

"You told me to write a letter explaining why two cheques have bounced in my account. I have done that, and explained that I needed the money for tuition arrears and my brother's hospital bill. You asked for copies of the hospital bill, and I have brought them from a reputable hospital, and you have even called the hospital and confirmed the outstanding amount. Now you're telling me that you are not satisfied with my explanation and to explain in another letter all over again? How come when cheques of other staff members bounce you do not subject them to this sort of humiliation? And why are you asking me to hand in my cheque book?"

The GM was known to suffer from hypertension, and I thought he was going to suffer from a cardiac arrest right there. Maybe he was not used to someone questioning him on his decisions.

The branch manager on the other hand kept opening and shutting his mouth like a fish out of the Indian Ocean. He finally managed to find his tongue saying, "you're placing your job in jeopardy, Ms. Kemunto."

I gave him a withering look. "How can I place my job in jeopardy, Mr. Kamwanthe, when I am just about to quit? That is a ludicrous claim."

I wrote my resignation throwing into the bargain what I thought of their management!

When saying my goodbyes to the other staff they begged me to stay, but I was in so much pain.

I could not take it anymore. I walked out never to look back again. The only regret I had was that I was going to miss out on all the procedures that were going to make the bank Y2K compliant as we bid 1999 goodbye and ushered in the new century. I had been told that I could take part because my staff appraisal was good and I handled the switchboard and reception sometimes. I also regretted that I would now be unable to complete my banking course due to lack of tuition.

Later in the evening, Salifu came to my place and begged me to reconsider, telling me not to make rash decisions, but I told her that she of all people knew how frustrated and hemmed in I was feeling.

Mr. Kamwanthe sent emissaries with messages, asking me to go back, that things could be resolved. I refused. Mama also came to my place several times and we talked about everything, but she was still of the opinion that I should have stuck it out. She was rightfully concerned, knowing that I needed the money for heaven's sake!

Myra, Shilpa and Latifah said I was a prig and that I was pretentiously being sanctimonious and puritanical. They said this rightfully because they knew very well that I was going to start struggling again to pay the rent and school fees for my Nehema.

Was I supposed to just sleep with him? Do what the American marines on call at our port say – 'Bang! Bang! Thank you ma'am?'

Well that was not for me. I could not stand the humiliation. I swore to myself that I would never make tea for people in an office again, not even if the pay was good! I promised myself never to accept a job offer from anyone, not unless it was an advert placed in the local dailies. And that is how I have gotten most of my jobs to date.

Back to the present...

I come back to earth and continue gazing across the picturesque expanse of deep blue sea. From my vantage point 186 feet above sea level. I caress the two scars on my arm. Now you know how I got them! I have been jobless for months now. Last week my landlord locked my house. My neighbours broke the lock saying that he was being inhumane as he knew very well that I did not have a job.

He let me stay but threatened to send over court brokers and auctioneers to carry my household appliances for auction if I did not settle my arrears within the week. Forgetting rather conveniently that he still had my two month's deposit! I am back to my catch-22 situation. Should I sell or should I not sell all my electronic household goods? I just could not fight it anymore.

Next time you hear someone say, '*nimesota, nimekula ngumu. Hujui pale Mungu amenitoa,*' (Swahili slang – 'I have suffered and come from far. You do not know where God has brought me from.) it is best to shut up, unless what you have gone through will make their experience pale in comparison!

I go back to caressing the two scars on my right arm thinking. I might be depressed and dejected, feeling like

I am three-hundred feet below sea level, you know, the lowest point in the hemisphere. In the murky depths, but I hear that inner voice cajoling, reminding me that this is lovely, sunny Mombasa, 186 feet above sea level. Hoping that climate change and global warming does not alter the statistics. A city holding so many hurting hearts needing healing. I believe that despite the many paradoxes, God will see me through. I am not a quitter but a fighter.

I was ill-prepared for the further trials I was to encounter at a casino job I got that I thought would be exciting. My resilience and world renown Kenyan optimism were about to be tested again.

Little did I know that I was about to end up in more hot water. If paternal Magokoro who had passed on a year earlier were alive to witness my next misadventure, she would surely insist that I had been staring at myself vainly in the mirror for too long at night. And as a result ended up a thief, like the colonial *wazungus* who came to us with gifts of mirrors and such stuff including the Holy Bible, and yet ended up stealing our land from us!

THE SERENITY PRAYER

...He will make all things right...

...yote Yeye atayawezesha kuwa mema...

Kernels of Hope on Backstreets of Despair

I could not believe it. I did not dare to. How had I ended up in a police holding cell?

My mind was in a whirl. I had never for the life of me thought that I would ever be associated with terms like 'theft by servant' and 'docket number.'

Oh my God! Why did the cop on duty want my belt? I was lucky I was in jeans. Did he think that I would try and commit suicide using it?

They even wanted my spectacles!

Next, one of them ordered me to remove my sneakers. Was I going to be barefoot in the cold police cell?

He shouted at me saying I was too slow. I almost jumped out of my skin.

He was pointing at my tiny silver dolphin ear studs. What did he think I would do with the earrings? Swallow them?

Then my matching thin silver chain with a dolphin pendant and my money. Next they gave me an inventory to fill out.

I persuaded them to give me back my spectacles, which I'd recently started wearing; otherwise, I was going to get a terrible migraine exploring my new surroundings without them.

One of the cops gave them back to me and pushed me roughly into the cell.

I heard the clang of metal as the doors were banged shut behind me.

The steel doors only had narrow slits with grills – just enough for peeping in or out.

Shivers feathered up and down my skin. God no! How had I ended up in here?

Just because of the loss of a few thousand shillings at my work place? I did not want to kid myself – I knew that it was that, coupled with personal vendetta.

As I lived alone, I knew that my house girl must be worried sick by now. I did not even want to think of little Nehema. I stood still staring absentmindedly ahead. I felt someone shift near my feet.

I looked down. I saw this dirty, filthy woman, with her whole right leg in a plaster cast.

She had urinated on herself and human waste was littered around her.

I understood immediately. My take on it was that she must be unable to move to the toilet and no one was willing to help her.

I looked for some space and shifted to my left. Actually, a shuffling of my feet.

The cells were overcrowded and that is an understatement.

The place was crawling with people packed together like cockroaches! A twelve-by-twenty-four foot police holding cell was packed with more than a hundred people!

Someone (I could not tell who it was) shouted that if I was here indefinitely like the rest of them, then I had better look for a place to sit.

It seemed like an induction of sorts. I went and huddled in a corner.

Not long after, one of the cops came in, saying the inmates were too noisy and rowdy.

He was brandishing a *nyahunyu* in his hand. The rubber whip kept landing on our backs, indiscriminately it seemed.

After a while I focused my eyes and realised it seemed to avoid other backs discreetly.

I wondered why. Only later did I come to learn about protection fee and money changing hands while you await your court appearance.

It was early morning. I thought I was only going to be a guest of the state for one night, but I was dead wrong. I was to stay incommunicado for almost two days before my family knew where I was. By mid-day I was hungry and the food was really a mockery of the term. I could not bring myself to touch it. It would just upset my metabolism, and instead of helping to eliminate toxins from my system, they would increase tenfold! Worse, I may die by contracting cholera, typhoid or bilharzia. As it were, I looked into what was ladled into the plate of the inmate nearest me, strange particles of some flotsam they called 'cabbage' stayed atop the watery liquid they called 'soup.'

The toilet cum bathroom was overflowing with raw sewage, which spilled into the corridor in between the women's and men's cells, and yet at night some inmates slept on this space because the cells were overcrowded. The congestion was terrible and indescribable!

At first, I was so scared that I recoiled and withdrew. I huddled even further into a corner of the women's cells. The tears slipping down my face silently.

I stared at the dirty walls covered in graffiti. Most in broken English slang.

Some had engraved obscene statements. Some had engraved their names for posterity: so-and-so was here. 'Nasty dread *mnoma alikuwa hapa.*' Some in Kiswahili *sheng*.

Women always came across as tougher, because after a while I noticed that the women, though mostly in the same state as the men, were more vibrant, more outgoing and more vocal of the need for our country to have a change in governance.

I got myself into the thick of it. It was a refreshing change to have such views expressed openly and not to be on our guards looking over our shoulders.

I noticed one man who kept on staring at me. Was it because I had warmed up to the other women and was back to my outspoken self?

I was not surprised, most people usually wonder at my size eight, five-foot-two stature.

Some do not even believe it when I tell them what I have gone through unless a third party confirms it! One person I met, two years down the line, refused to believe it until he went to the police station to check out the records.

Talk of women having to fight twice as hard as men to prove our worth!

Coming back to the man who had been staring at me. I remembered that during the earlier roll call his name had rung a bell. As he kept staring at me, one of the ladies nudged me and whispered something in my ear about the Kwale mosque shooting to death of a Muslim youth by a cop. So he was the one. No wonder his name was familiar – it had been all over the news. What on earth was he doing here? It had been almost a month ago, I whispered back.

Someone answered that the cop had been taken around several cop stations, with no charge being preferred against him.

The whole saga was most likely to die a typical Kenyan death and fade into oblivion.

I guess that is what happened in the end. We never got to hear of the case again.

Then there were these emaciated looking Arab youth who called out to the cops on duty and then used them as errand boys to go and buy them illicit drugs from the tiny alleys of the nearby Old Town.

None of the inmates knew what the teenagers were in for, but the boys were specific in their demands and I gathered the cops knew the source of the supply well.

'*Nunua kwa yule mama mweupe, unga wake ndio msafi,*[i]' one said.

They sent out for an assortment of drugs and one syringe.

I could not understand why they were sending for only one syringe, yet they had thousands of shillings falling out of their pockets. Why had they been allowed into the cells with their money, while most of us had to ask for some of ours every-time we needed to send out for something?

I remember my high school days and what we had been taught at the Youth Counselling Centre, and I could not take that lying down.

I approached them and talked to them about the dangers of these drugs.

"*Mimi siwezi kuishi bila ndong'a*[ii]," the youngest one replied.

I told them that they could contract HIV by sharing syringes, but even talking to them was difficult. They seemed disoriented, but at least they sent out for more syringes.

My other fight was with the cops. How dare they? These were only children I fumed indignantly.

The cops looked at me saying, "you do not know what we go through."

It seemed the boys in blue had decided to join the goody bandwagon. From their talk I gathered that whenever they arrested the drug peddlers and took them to court, the peddlers usually got off scot-free due to what they termed as corruption of the highest order in our court corridors. I had another bone of contention, and I wanted to pick it thoroughly with the cops! I wondered aloud why they were confiscating our belts, chains, etc. and yet they were bringing in syringes and bottles?

---

i Kiswahili -- 'Buy from the brown lady, her cocaine is the purest.'

ii Kiswahili -- 'I cannot live without heroin.'

Somehow, from that moment for the few days I was there, the whip stopped landing on my back. I sensed a begrudging respect in the cops' eyes, and some of the other inmates even asked me if I was a Criminal Investigations Department (CID) officer; they thought I was a special branch officer sent undercover to investigate the goings on at the police post. For one, I had refused to clean the police offices and sweep the yard that morning. Secondly I had asked the cops if I had been sentenced. They had not even charged me yet so I was innocent until proven guilty.

I also refused to shout out *'Afande!'* or 'Yes, Sir!' when I heard my name during roll call, and only said 'Yes?' Under my breath silently I muttered 'assholes.'

One cop had looked as if I had spat in his face and had told his colleagues, "*Wachana na huyu msichana, ni mwendazimu tu! Anaweza kutuletea shida na hawa wengine!*[i]"

"Now I am mad because I know my rights?" I had asked him. By the second day my family had finally managed to track me down. At least I was now getting real food prepared real well. Right away they tried to sort out the mess, but I felt embarrassed every time they were asked to taste the food before I could have it.

I remember when my mama and papa came to the station; I started crying and had to talk to them through metal grills, asking about my daughter in our mother tongue.

The cop on duty shouted at us to speak in English or Kiswahili, saying it is the law that they must hear what we are talking about!

Papa explained that it was just by chance that my brother had gone to my place and missed me.

When the house-girl told him that I had not come

---

i Kiswahili -- 'Leave this girl alone, she is mad! She might incite the others to rioting!'

home the previous night he had become worried and decided to go to my place of work where he had heard the whole story. Mama told me that Nehema was alright and that I should not cry, but I could not help myself. That is when one of the senior officers chanced upon the scene, and was slightly taken aback saying, "why didn't this girl tell us that she's your daughter? No wonder she's such a tough one."

Papa's reputation as a former DC always preceded him. Even though it was so long ago.

I answered the cop, "And then what could you have done? When I can't even place the single call allowed per person because your telephone is constantly out of order."

And I went further and told him how one of his junior members had cheated me out of five-hundred shillings yesterday claiming that he was going to look for a functional telephone booth outside to make the call for me. He had come back late in the day saying that he had changed the money into coins and gone around to many booths. According to him, all the telephone booths had been malfunctioning and coins had all been swallowed!

Swallowed? My foot! Coins worth five-hundred shillings? Who was he kidding?

Anyway, to cut a long story short, I languished in the cells for two more days, but at least Shilpa, Myra and Latifah came to visit while my parents tried to sort out the whole mess.

I call it a mess because most of the cases in police cells do not deserve to be there, most suspects are arrested on mere basis of suspicion, take the case of this sixteen-year-old girl I found there. She told me she had been there for three weeks and was into her fourth...

It was unbelievable. You may be asking -- her crime?

"Found loitering with intent to prostitute". So what was the most logical step for the boys in blue? Bundle her into their Black Maria and bring her to the police station. The Black Maria is the name given to the notorious black police vans that do the rounds in the town estates. And the van never returns to the station empty-handed. Many are the unfortunate young men and girls who reluctantly get the Black Maria lift as they saunter nonchalantly back from escorting their girlfriends or boyfriends to the *matatu* stage.

Maybe you think you have heard the worst from this girl. Brace yourself.

It was not the first time the young girl had been arrested -- she had even lost track. She narrated to us her first arrest and lift aboard the Black Maria like it was an initiation into womanhood!

She confided that she had not been having any intentions to prostitute; she had actually been doing it! She was an orphan and it was her source of livelihood.

She was then taken to an approved school which in essence is a correctional centre from which she ran way. Are you wondering how that is possible?

This is Kenya. Remember corruption and graft are officially a lifestyle and movement here.

She had even been in *rumande*, the corrupted word for remand. As she talked to me, I could see the pain in her street-wise eyes mingled with the world-weary look of a jaded cynic. She narrated to me what she had undergone at *rumande*. The beatings, orders from sadistic women prison warders to squat in her birthday suit, lesbianism, seeing fellow inmates die of communicable diseases like TB and waterborne ones like typhoid and bilharzia because government hospitals where inmates are treated provide only rudimentary medical care, and seeing some of them released to go and die at home of HIV and AIDS.

As the girl went on talking, I looked at her properly.

She looked about thirteen and I guess she was lying about being sixteen. I shuddered at the unimaginable thought that my daughter was going to be the same age in eight years. I came to the sad conclusion that in Kenya, poverty has been criminalised.

She continued that she had been brought here three weeks ago from Shimo La Tewa to make a court appearance, which she never made because her case had allegedly not been listed for mention. And another time, her file had disappeared as Kenyan files are wont to do. But that time she had been charged with the murder of her five-month-old baby girl. The assessors had said that she was guilty of murder. The High Court had then convicted her of the murder, but given that she was only sixteen -- she did not know her age and it had been determined by assessors from the Children's Department -- when she committed the offence, the court had ordered that in accordance with the law she be detained at the President's Pleasure. The court of appeal had viewed it differently. Given that her baby was under twelve years old when she had allegedly killed her, the judges thought she may have suffered postpartum depression as a result of giving birth and therefore she should not have been convicted of murder. A few months ago, the judges substituted the conviction with infanticide, and considering the time she had spent in prison, they set her free.

When I asked her if she had killed her baby intentionally, she stared at me with her enigmatic street-wise eyes and asked if I were in her shoes, would I bring a baby into the sort of life she was leading?

Now she was back behind bars again.

She surprised me as she seemed well versed and conversant with all the jargon on legal technicalities. She said that even if she did make the appearance before the magistrate or judge, the ruling would be that she be taken to back to Kirigiti, the Girls' Approved School in Kiambu, and anyway she'll never make it there. I asked her why. Brace yourself again.

She looks at me with her worldly eyes and tells me that they are normally given a police officer to escort them (you guessed right – by public means) to ensure they reach the Approved School safely.

Most never make it, she informed us casually, because they give the cops money or sexual favours in exchange for their freedom. They then let them off on the way and later the cops report to their superiors that the girl gave them the slip.

Where is our country heading, I wondered? All we could do was pray that during the coming general elections, *wananchi* will vote wisely, especially for a change in government.

I tried to talk to her about going back to school or a vocational training centre if she could get a sponsor, but she kept interrupting to ask me if she will be given money, and if not I could just as well as forget it.

I am happy though, that nowadays these Approved Schools are called Rehabilitation Centres. Aside from being centres for delinquents as perceived by the public, they are also for kids that are victims of circumstances like this young girl; victims that are making the best of what they have.

On the second afternoon I was summoned and escorted upstairs to the office of the Officer Commanding Station (OCS's). I had quite a number of questions for him, amongst them why the inmates were being made to sweep and wash the whole police station, and also why the cops insisted on tearing apart loaves of bread as a security check for smuggling drugs into the cells by the inmates' families while the cops themselves were being used by some inmates to buy them drugs. I did not even get the chance to voice my thoughts. He started shouting at me, telling me to pay up the money I had allegedly stolen at work while on duty or else the New Year's millennium celebrations would find me still behind bars. That was on my third day of incarceration. I could not bear the thought of spending more days there. Then I remembered how one of the cops, who was a Christian (at least there are still some) and not the nefarious chaps some of us have had the misfortune of encountering, had come to the cells and told me that the OCS had been given fifty-thousand shillings to ensure that I spent the New Year celebrations behind bars. It confirmed my suspicions that my incarceration was a personal vendetta by the security officer with whom I worked. After all, the money lost was half what they had given the OCS. I was brought back to earth by the OCS's barking voice.

I had told my parents not to pay the lost money, because I knew that come the New Year, my younger sister will be needing tuition for college, and that I had rather see the whole mess go to court.

Little did I know how gruelling and stressful it was going to be locked up in there.

The crackling static of a radio call interrupted my reverie.

The OCS picked up the vibrating hand set. I could not hear the person at the other end clearly due to the static, but from our side I gathered a few facts.

Earlier that morning there had been an attempted armed robbery at one of the south coast five-star beach hotels. The gangsters had been intercepted by Flying Squad (the special crime prevention police unit) officers as they crossed the ferry at the Likoni channel in a car they had apparently car-jacked. They had been arrested and the officers had recovered firearms used in the foiled robbery. They were now on their way to the island, and would be at the station anytime from the radio call.

A chill feathered down my spine. I felt sorry for the suspects. It was an open secret that it was woe unto anyone arrested by the dreaded officers, as you would live to rue the day you made a slip-up and were arrested by them. I really started to pray for them when the OCS started shouting into the radio and asking the officers why they hadn't shot them! I was bewildered. Why kill them?

I guess mine is what people call a baptism of fire, seeing live and first-hand what you only get to hear at maskans[i] and neighbourhood pubs as rumours.

The sound of my name brought me down to earth with a thud.

"*Msichana, mbona unashangaa? Mambo ni hivyo bwana. Kama ni mimi na ua hawa majambazi, maana tunapeleka kortini, kesho naona hawa nje.*[ii]" He trailed off suggestively making a shooting sign with his hands. His eyes had such a spine-chilling emptiness.

"*Tena hapana angalia mimi hivyo*[iii]," my eyes were very expressive and I guess the contempt was evident. His tone scared me.

I dropped my eyes. I did not want to be hit. These cops beat you, maybe kill you accidentally, and then tell your next of kin that you'd been trying to escape, their standard response to deaths in their cells.

Next, he asked me if I was going to pay up. I told him I was not and that I had rather go to court. He was simply amazed and ordered that I be taken back to the cells. Back in the cells I was withdrawn and the other inmates crowded around me. It was almost mythical to get summoned upstairs. A real event. Naturally, they wanted to know what gives. I explained to them what

---

i Kiswahili -- Open Public Spaces

ii Kiswahili -- "Girl, why are you shocked? This is how things are. If it were me, I would kill these gangsters because you take them to court and tomorrow they are released ..."

iii Kiswahili -- "Do not look at me like that!"

had happened upstairs and also told them about the robbery suspects.

The hard-core criminals (mind you, we were sharing cells with people on capital offence charges, ranging from murders to armed robbery with violence) just shook their heads sadly, saying, *"Hawo watapelekwa Urban mwanzo wakafinywe, wakifika hapa, ole wao! Watakuwa kama maiti[i]."*

Little did I know what it meant, till sometime after nine that night, when the two suspects were brought in by plain clothes officers. I guess that is how Flying Squad officers look like. Just like ordinary you and me, and not gun-toting with dark glasses like in the movies; that only happens in Hollywood. You could not even begin to imagine that they could do that much harm to someone. I mean, to make you look like you'd been involved in an automobile accident. I have never seen such a bloody sight, it was gruesome.

The two men were bloodied all over. One had his eye almost gouged out. The other had some of his toe and finger nails missing and his arm seemed broken. I did not want to move near because I already had tears in my eyes. I guessed I would make the painful scene worse by looking so soppy and sissy, but I really felt sorry for them. We did not even have painkillers, but the toe and fingernail issue was too much to resist. I had to see for myself; I moved nearer. God! It was true -- some nails were plucked out! It was a phenomenon some of us only get to hear of in the streets from hard-core criminals. How the cops use pliers to pluck out finger and toe nails and also almost crush men's balls!

It was sickening to say the least, and yet the two suspects had the guts to tell the other inmates about it. I moved back into the corner of one of the women's cells. I did not want to hear such gory details.

---

i Kiswahili -- "They will be taken to Urban station, their private parts tortured, by the time they are back here, they will be as good as dead!"

Amongst the women sharing the cell with me was a mother and her grown-up daughter. They had been brought in earlier in the morning from Shimo La Tewa prison for a court mention of their case the following day. The woman's son, also charged alongside them for the murder of their father and husband, was in a different cell. Their case had dragged on for four years with no end in sight. The old woman could not even talk. To look into her eyes was like looking into mirrors of despondency and hopelessness. Her daughter told me that their mother had been traumatised and shattered when their kinsmen had accused them of being *wachawi*[i].

I was not really surprised because their home district of Kwale in the South Coast of Mombasa has the notoriety of getting tongues wagging when someone dies unless it is from a car accident. And fingers point in the direction of dark elements to do with witchcraft.

All in all, it was sad and disillusioning for a case to drag on for years, while one left her or his property at the mercy of relatives, not knowing how your young children are doing, only to come back sometimes and be unable to claim back what is rightfully yours.

Hormonal imbalance came calling that night! I guess I was worried sick about my little girl. I could not believe I was having my period – let's call a spade a spade and not a big spoon. If I use words like menses, I may confuse some of my enthralled readers! What a terrible time. I consoled myself that my sister was going to pass by in the morning and I would send her for some tampons.

Girl! Was I glad to see her in the morning. But first I slept, only to wake up in the morning to the most amazing tableau. We woke up to curses of one man that one of the women had infected him with rashes and that he was itching all over. I wondered what he

---

i Kiswahili -- Witches/wizards.

meant, only to hear some of his pals castigating him, "*Si tulikukataza kuchimba maiti?*[i]"

I was shocked. The lady they were referring to seemed to be of an unstable mind. She was constantly stoned out of her head. She was high on the cocaine and heroin that was making the rounds in the cells for anyone who was willing to pay up. Maybe that was her way of paying for the drug?

I had even questioned the cops about her; she was a common face on the streets of Mombasa.

The cops were non-committal, saying she had been caught stealing and had to face the consequences. They claimed that the money she had stolen had been found hidden deep inside her vagina. I believe that we should try to help these street families because most of them are drug addicts and have no source of income. They become thieves by default to finance the habit.

As always, I could not keep quiet and started talking to her. I wanted to know if what the men were saying was true. She confirmed that it was true.

I was curious. How on earth had they managed to have sex in such a crowded place?

Even breathing was difficult. I had almost suffocated the previous night. Some of the women in my cell, most who were hard-core criminals, had almost fought over space.

When the woman told me that they had sex in the toilet, I was shocked!

The toilet! With all the overflowing waste, sewage and human faeces?

Maybe by then I should have become shell-shocked.

I doubt if she heard a word of what I said. She was floating in the clouds. At least when she confessed that

---

i Kiswahili -- "Did we not warn you against having sex with a corpse?"

they did not use a condom, she gave me cause to talk to her about HIV – but pray what was the man thinking? After all, he was in his proper mind. I was furious that cops could supply drugs in the cells but could not supply condoms! As I was on my period and feeling dirty, I forced myself to have a bath in the over-flowing toilet using water provided by one cop – I lived to regret it. I developed a skin disease and sensed the untreated water must have been drawn from a bore-hole.

On a lighter tone, a pastor was thrown into the cells and he spiced up our prayer lives considerably!

Apparently, he had been car-jacked and had come to the station to report on the incident, record a statement and have the crime put down in the OB (Occurrence Book). Wonders never cease – only to find that someone else had been there before him to report that the pastor had allegedly conned him of a car! It was just his bad luck that the car was newly bought, and the log book and all documentation were in the dash board! Your guess is as good as mine as to what the car snatchers did with the documents.

The cops just looked at him disdainfully saying, 'Most pastors nowadays are flamboyant con-artists masquerading as clergymen,' and promptly locked him up!

Please do not ask me how it came about, or how it ended because I left him in the cell.

The list was endless. A lady was locked up because she had a fight with her man friend – not boyfriend! He had her promptly arrested claiming that she had stolen from him.

Another, working with a local tour operating firm, was arrested because she could not account for a substantial amount of money, including some foreign currency, allocated to her department. Though her family paid up, her employers still insisted on charging her with negligence.

Another lady was also going through a nightmare, accused of 'handling stolen goods.'

Goods she did not know had been stolen but had been brought to her house by her boyfriend.

I was disturbed by one couple's case. The husband had allegedly been embezzling funds at his work place. He had been charged with fraud and using his position as the accountant to do so.

The sad part is that his wife was also arrested because she was proprietor of several prominent businesses. Even after protesting that she was innocent and her husband confirming the same and that they had young children at home, she was still locked up.

When I left the cells before them, they sent me to check on their children who were with the house girl. We had realised that we lived in the same estate. Uncanny, how you get to meet your unknown 'neighbours' in 'strange' places.

My family finally came to an agreement that my employers work out my dues and deduct the lost money. Little did I know that in a couple of months to come I would find myself in a worse situation, believe you me.

My short stint in the police holding cell was a scary experience inscribed in my person, etched on my body and embedded in my subconscious, profoundly shaping my view on life. The fact that I could have died in there does not escape me.

Lastly, I remember this ten-year-old Muslim boy. He told me they lived in the Old Town, and that he had been arrested that morning because he had snatched a lady's purse.

When I was leaving to go home on thirty-first of December at seven in the evening, he grabbed my arm and pressed a piece of paper into my hand. It had a telephone number written on it. He asked me to call his mother and ask her to come pick him up from the station.

I looked down at him, he was only a baby. I saw my five-year-old daughter in his eyes.

Out on the street I took a deep breath. I could not believe I was free.

The first thing I did was look for a public telephone booth to call the boy's mother.

The mother hung up on me when I tried to pass on the message from her son.

She actually banged the phone down, hanging up on me after hurling unprintable Swahili *matusi* (abuse) and screaming that the boy was a little thief and she was tired of him! And that was that! In weeks to come I would sadly think of the little boy and wish that there was nothing like petty crime or minor infractions, only the law which could also take care of such children.

To cut a long story short I was re-united with my baby who was none the wiser. She thought I had gone on one of my sojourns and jaunts of escapade from stress to Malindi! I would have died had I missed the fireworks display she had requested we buy for the New Year's millennium celebrations!

You have not heard the last of this. I had to undergo a gruelling year long court case and discovered how corruption stalks and rules our court corridors. I encountered hopelessness, despair, despondency and disillusionment especially with an 'officially' corrupt Judiciary, and how the phrase 'Why hire a lawyer when you can buy a judge?' was coined.

How I constantly thought that the very next minute I would discover my personal Pinocchio!

Worst of all, how court sessions seem to bring out the verbosity in everyone, including your former colleagues who had been threatened with the sack if they did not testify against you!

Two months later...

I am seated at home with knees pressed together and my arms tucked tight at my side the way ex-convicts sit when freshly released from jail. That is what the few days at the police cell did to me.

I am watching the KTN *Prime Time News* in disbelief. The same OCS of a few months ago who had ordered his officers in my presence, via radio call, to shoot dead the two robbery suspects, is now on transfer somewhere in Nairobi and is defending some of his officers who have apparently shot dead a couple of suspected gangsters. Spewing forth the force's standard phrase he was saying, "the gangsters shot at the police officers first, and in self-defence my boys returned the fire, and a shoot-out ensued."

I detect double-talk in his statement as I remember his cold eyes and voice when he'd told me boldly that he shoots to kill and that there is no need of taking gangsters to court.

I met him again a year or so later (after my short incarceration at his police post) at my local church. He was investigating (apparently he was back in Mombasa on transfer again) an alleged attempt at arson in our church. The arson attempt was a form of retaliation and revenge by some disgruntled Muslim youth over some skirmishes after a mosque in Nairobi was burnt down.

He had stared at me asking me what I was doing at the church. I looked at him and said, "I work here in the church. Aren't suspects supposed to work? I am the one who called the police." He had looked very uneasy, but that is a story for another day.

Fast-forward to March 21st, 2004

I was reading today's *Sunday Nation*. In particular, an article by Patrick Mayoyo titled:

'Wrangle ends as Moi gives up land'

Snippets of the article read as follows:

> *'Former President Moi has surrendered 16 acres of land on which stands the 16th century Kongo mosque in Kwale District. This has brought to an end the 10-year-old dispute between the government and the Muslim community. The row over the Kongo mosque started in the early 1990s when Muslim leaders discovered that the mosque's title deed had been altered and part of the sixteen-acre plot sub-divided and given to powerful people in the former regime...Although President Moi's name had not featured among those who had benefited from the controversial allocations, Lands and Settlement Minister Amos Kimunya recently announced that the former head of state had surrendered the land.'*

Umm. I reminisced. I remembered that day four years back when I was held at the same police post where the police officer who shot one Muslim youth dead was in hiding. The young man, with other faithful, had declared jihad (holy war) and had armed themselves with bows, arrows and machetes and guarded the mosque day and night.

I wonder...whatever became of that case? Did the family of the dead boy ever get the justice they demanded?

* * * * * *

Wondering about that case was not going to be of help to me as I had to prepare for my own court case.

THE SERENITY PRAYER

....when I...

...mimi nitakapo...

To Serenity via Perdition

As I lifted my leg to haul myself over the side of the Mahindra police jeep, I met my mama's eyes and mine filled with tears as time stood still. I will never forget that moment in my life. I could not believe I was getting into a police vehicle to be driven to court.

Mama insisted the cops give her a few minutes with me.

"Kemu my dear," she said my name gently, "we do not have to do this. You do not have to go to court. Your papa and I have just come from seeing the security officer to pay off the money, but he refused." She was referring to the security officer at the casino where I had been working. "Kemunto, I do not understand," she continued. "Why is he refusing the money, yet the OCS told us to settle this out of court?"

"Mama," I replied, "It is personal, as I told you. Frankly speaking, right now I do not care, I would rather meet them in court."

And with that I heaved myself into the back of the Mahindra.

I started musing and mulling over in my mind the events of the last couple of months. This was the second time I was being arrested over the same unresolved issue.

My thoughts switched to the altercation of the previous evening between myself and the OCS.

"You see, my problem is that I do not kiss ass and I do not lick boots. I know my fundamental rights and you are violating them because you have held me here for three days without any charges being laid against me. You either take me to court this morning, or I am going to sue you and the state for unlawful detention and infringing on my human rights."

The OCS had stared at me shocked. Seems like he was used to trampling on people's rights, but I was not one to take any nonsense lying down. Especially not after what I had seen one of the inmates, who was being held for alleged murder, subject him to the previous evening.

"Matako! Mavi wewe! Mimi nikifungwa ole wako![i]*"*

This morning the inmate had been released unconditionally. I started thinking about my re-arrest three days ago; that three police officers could be sent to arrest a harmless lady was beyond comprehension.

There was so much crime being committed out there and the police force is always complaining of shortage of manpower.

Yet they had come to arrest me because I had not paid a few thousand shillings that I had lost while on duty at my now former work place.

I had promised to pay back the money after spending a few days in the cooler a couple of months ago, but had been unable to because I had not secured another job yet.

Nehema had been in the house with me when the boys in blue came calling this second time. I thank God they had not been in uniform. They were in plainclothes like ordinary civilians.

When I had realised who they were, I had silently prayed for them not to use handcuffs on me.

Such a scene would have traumatised my little baby.

I had pretended to Nehema that there was an emergency at work, and that the men were my colleagues who'd come to pick me up.

My daughter was used to such emergencies due to the nature of work shifts at the casino where I used to work.

---

i Kiswahili -- Abusive -"Asshole! You are shit! Woe unto you if I am jailed!"

My house girl was on her off day so I asked the cops to drive over to my parents so that I could drop Nehema there.

Her grandparents were not in so I left her with their neighbours after alerting them of the situation. You never know with Kenyan cops and extra-judicial executions. You may go with them and never be seen again.

* * * * * *

...I was jolted slightly when the Mahindra came to an abrupt halt and I stopped reminiscing. We had arrived at the Mombasa law courts. I was stunned when we were bundled into some sort of underground cells where we were supposed to cool our heels while awaiting the magistrate to make his or her majestic entrance.

This was the second time in many months to see walls with graffiti. Reminders of who had been here at what time and on what date. Girl! Was I glad to be in court to be formally charged, finally!

As we waited in the underground cells I looked around me. I was saddened all over again because I was faced once more with desperation and hopelessness in the eyes of most of the inmates from police posts.

The convicts from the remand prisons were worse. I have always thought the whole point of imprisonment and incarceration is to rehabilitate offenders and re-integrate them into a decent crime-free life once their term ends, but the eyes of these jaded cynics did not spell hope but a hollowed disillusionment; eyes with no hope. Lifelessness stares as if someone had snatched the life out of them.

It pained me to realise just how deeply ingrained into the very fabric of our society injustices were being perpetrated. I stared around the cell. Mothers with babies strapped on their backs; arrested for some slight misdemeanour, maybe a fight with a neighbour. Young girls, some as young as twelve, on charges of alleged prostitution, some real, others trumped up charges.

Some held on personal vendettas being waged against them. Yet we were mixed up with diehard hordes of jail birds and bunches of hard-core criminals, some on capital charges. Having previously spent three days and nights in police custody in the filthy cop station with some of these people, I felt like I knew them. Yet, some had come from Shimo la Tewa for the mention or hearing of their cases. It was scary to listen to them talk; even more scary to listen to their harrowing tales. Some of the women on capital charges had gone through years of domestic violence and abuse and were here because they had finally succumbed to their anger. Literally snapped and committed heinous crimes substituting their personal prisons of abuse for maximum security prisons of brick, steel and electric fences.

Some were even welcoming me to the fold beforehand, saying I may not be released on bond.

What an induction. I cringed inwardly at such a possibility. I could not imagine such an outcome -- that of going to a place they described with such terror. They talked of the dehumanizing congestion at Shimo. Cells meant for five were accommodating fifty, while those meant for seventy were holding up to two-hundred!

The women and girls talked of women wardresses with sadistic streaks, and how they would yell at you to '*kaba!*' that is squat in your birthday suit, while they checked your private parts for contraband, especially after visiting days.

The men talked of bullying and forced acts of transactional sodomy, especially from the older and stronger inmates who preyed on the weaker ones.

Women talked of being asked to grant sexual favours to cooks and warders in exchange for better food than what was on offer from the kitchen. They talked of food being diverted to staff quarters as the inmates faced near starvation, while being fed on half cooked meals.

They talked of the tattered prison uniforms.

Talk of justice being for sale was rife as I was going to find out. It seems like the authorities do not identify with the saying that goes 'justice delayed is justice denied!'

It was painful, and especially so for the ones who claimed they were convicted for crimes they had not committed. They said that our judiciary has now become a rotten institution that took auctioning the rights of the poor and weak in our society as standard practice! They act with breathtaking impunity and total disregard for the rule of law.

They desperately talked of brutality and corruption due to the fact that some inmates had been in remand prison for so long they now called the shots.

Some stayed put until they were released to go and die at home of AIDS, tuberculosis and other chronic infections too far advanced as medical facilities were almost nonexistent in the prisons. The sick would be taken to the provincial hospital only to be given Paracetamol for all ailments. It was a miserable no-go zone and I was so terrified of ending up there. Some crossed their fingers praying that they'll be put on community service or non-custodial sentences, the government's way of dealing with petty first time offenders and reducing the congestion in jails. Later, I found out that even being put on community service was up for sale.

I guess the only thing being poor does to you is grind down your nerve endings to a point that you work harder, and yet stoop lower than most people are willing to. Poverty chips away at your dreams to the point where the hopelessness shows through; to that lowest point when you cannot afford to buy food and your five-year-old child can differentiate between a need and a want; to the point where your child knows the wisdom of not having that extra slice of bread and saves it for tomorrow. Where you swallow your pride one more time and give her what you know will be a broken promise for a better tomorrow. That is where the devil wants you -- in a hopeless corner. If poverty is not a crime then the jiggers that infest our countryside are not a disgrace either...

...I was startled out of my reverie when we were called to go upstairs to the court house. We all trudged through alleys of the underground cells and found ourselves in a court room. Now I understood where inmates used to pop from when I was sitting in a court room, and they would seem to appear out of the blue.

I was later to learn this was court number five, and in the coming months I was to become synonymous with it. When we emerged from the staircase leading up from the dungeons called cells, we found ourselves in the dock!

I glanced around the packed courtroom and saw mama, Latifah, Myra and Shilpa. I heaved a sigh of relief at the familiar faces. Another hour-long wait and His Majesty came in. I expected him to wave a wand or something to that effect, like a magician, but he only had his gavel.

Charge after charge was read out and pleas entered. Finally, my turn came.

The lawyer my parents had retained for me entered a plea of not guilty on my behalf.

As the magistrate talked, I just managed to get wisps of some words, so bemused I was.

"...bond...surety...mention date...hearing..."

And then I found myself out in the beloved sunshine once more, after more than three days in the dark cells of the police station where I had been held.

I could not wait to get home to Nehema. I had not seen my baby for three days.

FIRST MENTION

Little did I know that I was going to spend almost the whole year in court. Mention after mention. Hearing after hearing. Every other week. All because I was accused of 'theft by servant.'

The term never ceased to shock me. I had never imagined in my life, especially after working in a bank -- even if I had been making tea and had dreams for a brighter future -- that I would be associated with such a term, leave alone having my own 'docket number.'

It is an open secret that emissaries reign in Kenyan court corridors. Middlemen of all sorts for hire and brokers par excellence make sure that the suspect with the highest bid gets off scot-free; it does not matter what you're accused of.

The *wananchi*, especially the hapless poor ones mostly victims of circumstances, watch these brokers hanging around the court corridors – and of course the *wananchi* know right down to the minutiae of which broker hangs around the chambers and court corridors on behalf of whom and for what favour!

These broker's faces are familiar in the court corridors such that even the policemen greet them and cleaners salute them! Rumours are that they have been known to confidently stroll into the registry and get all the help they need because the registry clerks know them.

No wonder disillusioned *wananchi* coined the phrase 'Why hire a Lawyer when you can buy a judge?'

At the end of day one I could not believe that I had spent the whole morning and afternoon in court, only for the magistrate to declare an adjournment later, and

_____
i Kiswahili – Citizens

fix another date for my case. I went home dejected. I needed a job desperately. But how was I going to get one if I had to come for mentions in court every other day?

And if I got a job, how was I going to manage to hold it down, with a possible conviction hanging over my head like the sword of Damocles?

Several times while awaiting my case to commence I would wander into other courtrooms and listen to ongoing proceedings. The one-billion hashish case was most intriguing. It was a case study on how scapegoats ended up in jail only for the real culprits, the drug barons, to get off scot-free. The other was a case involving the disappearance of containers at the main port and tyres worth millions of shillings. Yet again scapegoats on parade. What of the tonnes of cocaine worth millions seized in Malindi – we've never heard what happened to the cocaine or the suspects.

Some of the scapegoats are our neighbours and we know they are innocent. But what to do?

As my papa says everybody has her or his own cross to carry. Fat cats involved in corporate fraud, money laundering, fishy offshore investments and drug dealing would stride nonchalantly in court corridors with big grins knowing they would soon be set free.

Coming back to my own problems -- my court appearances always used to coincide with those of a sick man with whom I would share the dock. He was a pitiful sight. He would spend the whole session racked by coughs. He was in remand at Shimo la Tewa and he seemed to be suffering from tuberculosis. I kept thinking that he should just be acquitted and allowed to go home.

One day he pressed a piece of paper into my hand. I knew he did that because he had noticed that I usually came from home for my mentions.

Later, I opened the crumpled note. He had written

in a shaky hand, "I am a dying man. I see you have a lawyer. Please ask him to come see me though I have no money and no family here. God will bless him."

I was so saddened. Later, I handed the piece of paper to my lawyer and asked him if he could take it up on what I understand the legal fraternity called "Pro Bono." He was stunned and said, "Kemu, your case is proceeding very badly as it is, and I do not have time for such. But I will see what I can do."

I do not know what he did and I have never asked him. All I know is that at the next mention the magistrate acquitted the man. The man thanked me when we were leaving. I was really happy for him.

Something else bothered me. Why was it that the court sessions seemed to bring out the verbosity in everyone? Some people were even falling over each other just to perjure themselves. I looked at my workmate in the witness stand. The conniving bitch! How dare she be in cahoots with the security officer?

She knew there was no way one of us could leave the cashiers terminal with the money the way they were suggesting, unless one was an acrobat. We were always checked thoroughly and we left our handbags with the bouncers after recording the amount of personal cash we had in our bags and on our persons, like in our jeans. And when one's shift ended the same procedure was carried out. They were suggesting that I had snuck out with the money or handed it to an accomplice. But how and at what time? The only place you could go to was the loo and not the exit door!

The way the proceedings were progressing, I knew that miraculous manna was surely confined to Canaan and the children of Israel. I thought that the only thing that could save me now was not my innocence but for someone on the prosecution team of witnesses to walk or drive home via Damascus and see the light, the way

Saul of Tarsus, a persecutor of Christians, had and be transformed instantly into Paul the Apostle. All of a sudden all these thoughts came to mind when I recalled what I had learned of the Bible from my high school CRE[i] teacher.

Later, I thought that perhaps I should have coughed up the lost money as I sank wearily onto a filthy broken cement bench at the Makadara Grounds.

The noise of lunch hour preachers intruded on my thoughts as I fed on air burgers -- that is stayed hungry -- and re-read Paulo Coelho's *The Alchemist*. I wonder what Paulo Coelho went through as a child. His descriptions are too vivid to be fiction.

I identified with the characters as Coelho talked about the searing pain of a father's dream that had been long buried by bread and butter concerns. I felt that the little boy, just like my daughter Nehema, could see in his father's gaze a desire to be himself. To travel the world. A desire that was still alive despite his father having to bury it over dozens of years under the burden of struggling for water to drink, food to eat and a safe place to sleep every night of his life.

I did not even seem to notice that the bench was covered with *kunguru* (black crow) droppings.

The public toilet nearby was stinking. I thought it strange that the land hadn't been grabbed yet.

* * * * *

Several times in the coming months my case would be put off because my file could not be traced. I was saddened to realise that it was true that corruption and graft ruled our court corridors.

How could files just get lost? My file had started the famous antics that Kenyan files in court are known for. I was proved right when during one of these "file

i CRE -- Christian Religious Education

disappearing and re-appearing" acts, I was approached by one court clerk who told me that a beautiful lady like myself should not waste time in court corridors, and that *'niongee na wazee vizuri*[i]*'* for my file to disappear permanently and then I would not have any case to answer. I finally realised why some of these clerks are always hanging around the court corridors with bundles of the purported 'missing' files – they know their way around the registry and they make court files disappear as if the files have legs and 'walk' off the shelves by themselves. They can make your file disappear if you 'don't talk nicely' to them until the court goes on recess! This can even result in minor infraction cases pending for years waiting for a 'walking' court file to 'walk' back to the shelves – and you are lucky if you are still alive and the file has all your documents and evidence intact.

DAY OF JUDGEMENT

Mama had come to my place early in the morning to give me even more depressing and disturbing news. How could someone call papa at four in the morning to suggest that he sees the magistrate privately at his residence before the ruling? That my parents should not let me go to jail when there was a way out. And that papa should carry something small 'for elders' because the ruling was going against me?

I always go against the grain and maybe that is my Achilles heel. I had looked at my mum aghast. How could they even think of such a thing?

I told her to go and tell my dad that if he bribed anyone (it did not matter who) I would never speak to him again, and if I am sent to jail they should take care of Nehema for me.

---

i Kiswahili -- "Talk nicely to elders."- Euphemism for bribe.

Already the hit American TV series 'Prison Break' series one and two were going through my head.

I told mama that I was leaving everything in God's hands, and she told me they would respect my wishes. I was so scared because suddenly everything I had heard in the holding cells was happening to me; the judiciary does sell justice to the highest bidder using the litigant's bank account statements and business balance sheets as the scale. Otherwise, why should such an emissary be sent to papa? It was being proved to me that indeed the judiciary is an institution where judges and magistrates take judicial notice that in Kenya big bucks are mightier than the law – from paralegals who take bribes to court clerks who make files disappear, to compromised magistrates and judges who delay cases for years and make the defendants seem to have more rights and liberties than the complainants or aggrieved parties. So many Kenyans learn the hard way that the problem with justice in our country is that it is no longer admissible in our court of law. Period.

Later in the day, my faith did serve me in good stead though. I think because my papa never obliged their request!

The magistrate had looked at me and said,

"Kemunto, I understand you have a little girl. Don't you have anything to say?"

What did he want to hear?

Should I tell him about the time I lost my job because my boss had sent me on an errand to bribe a customs official? He had wanted the official to falsify documents to indicate that upon inspection, his imported containers at the port carried relief maize and not energy drinks so that he could be exempted from import duty, but I had refused. Or the way he had freaked out when I went on to explain to him calmly that it was a principle of mine not to bribe anyone and that I was not going to start then? And that after my refusal the same boss had a talk with Human Resources and when the annual appraisal was conducted and the yearly list of non-essential employees came out I was on it. Did the magistrate want to hear how one expatriate boss had drawn a gun on staff at the casino where I worked? And had only gotten deported after the media highlighted the incident?

Should I tell him how we had gotten a worse 'expat' security manager who would not increase my salary because I had refused to go out with him? How one morning he called me to his office to collect the day's float money only to find him in his boxers, watching pornography on his computer, pretending at the same time to be working out on his dumb bells and then tried to force himself on me sexually?

Should I tell him how I had to put my foot out, jamming the door and screaming for the security personnel? How he then started to hate me and refused to give me my increment. Yet some of my colleagues, the selfsame ones who are now witnesses in this case, had gotten theirs.

I only got to understand this when I accidentally bumped into him with one of my workmates on his arm, when I was having dinner at the Tamarind with some friends from Nairobi.

Or how he kept on deducting money from my salary every month, claiming my computer entries had reflected a shortage in money? The same trick he had used to land me in police custody.

What did the magistrate want to hear of my eventful and colourful short life? Perhaps I should tell him of the bank manager Mr. Kamwanthe and the sexual harassment I had undergone at his hands?

Or how I had walked out of a new job during my first two months because the married boss kept touching my hand and pretending that he was guiding me on the know-how of the office PC and files? How he then started talking of fictitious business trips and that I was supposed to accompany him?

Did the magistrate want to hear how I would feel ashamed, when in between jobs, of going back home in the evening with no food and no money. How I kept breaking into tears at every slight provocation especially towards the end of a temporary job with no other in sight. How sometimes, my frustration would bubble to the surface and I had fight to contain it, praying hysterically for it not to spill over, and for me not to lash out in anger at my daughter when she would ask for something that we did not have. Praying for her not to notice the extent of my pain at being unable to provide the basics, sometimes asking her to save an extra slice of bread for later!

Did this learned man want to hear how I had my back against the wall and sometimes felt that the only way out was to slide down to my haunches and crawl away. I was so dejected I could not even dig in my heels to try and help myself. At best it was a cry for help and at worst a suicide attempt!

I looked at the magistrate. I was so tired. What did he want to hear? I could not bring myself to speak. My chest hurt with suppressed tears. I thought I was going to choke. I shook my head and signalled to my lawyer to talk on my behalf. He went through all the injustices I had suffered at the casino and rested his case.

The magistrate was ready to deliver his ruling.

Time stood still as I reminisced on past milestones...

The labour ward at the Aga Khan hospital. The delivery room as I had gotten ready to have my baby. How the nurse had found me sitting on the floor, stark naked, and had scolded me saying that I would get an infection. How I had told her I liked the cool surface as it dimmed the labour pains.

How an entire Indian family had come to watch one of their own bring a baby into the world, and how they had to be shooed out by the nurses.

One clear memory that I hold dear is the blue primary school prefect's pinafore uniform hovering before my dazed eyes. My baby sister. Maybe that is why she is so close to Nehema. And that cherished moment when I held my baby for the first time, even though I was broke and in the midst of shattered dreams.

The magistrate was waiting for an answer from me. Did he want to hear of how most recently I had been forced to feed my daughter sugarless porridge because I had no money to buy the sweetener?

I remembered how I would walk to Mama Ngina drive and stare so hard at the passing ships and then start meditating. I have always loved the sea and the beach. Such tranquility. I would get on my knees and cry to God for a job which seemed hard to come by. All I encountered everyday was a disillusioned people with a free falling currency, a flagging economy, and an impoverished population growing into its millions. Yet, the gap between the rich and the poor kept widening into a huge chasm. I remembered how a neighbour friend had lost her receptionist job. My friend and I would go our separate ways in the mornings then meet in the evenings to compare notes or console one another. One evening she came to my place and told me that she had gotten a job offer as a telephonist but she was not very comfortable with it and the salary was twenty-thousand shillings.

I had lived in Mombasa my whole life and I knew the salary scales like the back of my hand. There was no way someone was going to offer you that kind of money in 1998 as a telephonist. It was almost double the regular rate! So she told me to go check out the prospective employer and ask for a job and then we link up later and I give her the feedback.

The following morning I went to the bureau. On one wall was a sticker that proclaimed 'No Job Without Sex,' I did not give it a second glance. I thought it was a sick joke. I find this Indian gentleman. He looks sick. He has sores all over his face. I also do not give this a second thought. I enquired about the telephonist vacancy. He interviewed me and then offered me the job. He looked at my Curriculum Vitae and asked where my daughter lived and with whom. I always indicate on my CV that I am a single parent with one child. I answered that she lived with me. Then he said that I would have to work odd hours. I did not understand him because I had passed by that bureau on several occasions and they operated normal working hours from eight in the morning to five in the evening. His next comment started the warning bells ringing in my head.

"*Mimi pana taka sikia mambo ya matoto,*[i] in heavily accented and broken Kiswahili. "*Wewe nasema nakaa pekee yako lakini na matoto, mimi tapata hiyo maneno ingine namna gani?*[ii]" he asked looking pointedly at the location of a particular anatomy below my waistline.

To say I was shocked is the understatement of the century! I did not even answer him. I picked up my papers hurriedly and tumbled out of the bureau, literally running. I paused long enough to enquire at a boutique shop next door on the nature of the bureau. The lady owner told me that the bureau rarely operated and the ladies employed there barely worked for two months.

As I was going home, I kept thinking of the sticker in that office and the sores all over the man's face and hands.

Later, I linked up with my friend. She shocked me saying, "So he tried that on you too? I just wanted a confirmation."

---

i Kiswahili (broken) -- "I do not want to hear about children."

ii Kiswahili (broken) -- "You say you stay alone but with your child, how then will I get the other favours?"

I told her we should hold on to our dignity and integrity and God will open ways for us.

She wondered how I survived with a child and no job. I told her it was due to a lot of prayers and the fact that I was a Virgo and we were known to be resilient and persistent!

Sometimes it was hard putting on a brave face when encouraging a friend and this verse from the Bible slipped into my mind, Romans 5:3-5 which says "Suffering produces perseverance, perseverance character, character produces hope and hope does not disappoint." Only later at night to be so confused when reading a quote by Francis Bacon which says 'Hope is a good breakfast, but a bad supper.'

After a month my neighbour moved out and we lost contact, meeting two years later on the streets of Mombasa. At first I passed her and she had to run after me. I could barely recognise her because she had lost so much weight. I was in a hurry and I just told her to pop in at a shop I worked. She did not have a job again. Soon, she became a regular visitor at the mobile phone shop where I worked. She was always coughing terribly, but would insist that she was not sick.

She told me she had a one-year-old daughter and her baby was very sick.

She occasionally came to ask for bus fare and money to buy medicine for her baby, and I would always give her whatever tips I had managed to gather that day.

One day she had to pass by the shop with her ailing child. I was shocked. Not by how sickly the baby looked, but by the fact that she had Indian-like features. For all I knew she had never had an Indian boyfriend before.

All I said was "Oh, my God! After we parted ways did you go and work at that Indian's telephone bureau?" She looked at me with tears in her eyes and nodded barely noticeably. That was the last time I saw her. She did not have a phone and never told me where exactly she lived. Only that it was in Likoni in the South Coast of Mombasa.

I would give anything to know where she is today and if she and her baby are ok.

...The magistrate's droning voice brought me back to reality; he was finishing his ruling. "One year's probation." and he rapped his gavel and stood up bowing. The security officer from the casino walked out in protest at the ruling. After all he had been doing the rounds in town saying that he would not rest until he made sure that I ended up doing time at Shimo la Tewa.

My siblings were at school as it was a weekday, but mama and papa were in the packed courtroom. I looked at them with relief in my eyes as mama gave me a thumbs-up signal. I had been so scared of going to jail. I remembered a colleague who had worked at the bank where I had quit a few years ago. She had done time for fraud. To date she swears her innocence saying her signature had been forged. She had only served two years of her three-year jail term before she was released through a presidential pardon or clemency, an amnesty that she said was also up for sale to families with the highest bid to have their loved ones released. It was a chilling indictment of the justice system in our country and a horror tale for the poverty-stricken majority.

We walked over to my lawyer and he gave us a very simple explanation as to what probation meant. That I was going to be under surveillance for the duration I had been placed on probation and that a probation officer would be assigned to me. I would have to report to the probation office once a month and stay out of similar trouble for that duration.

Little did I know that the term 'probation' in modern day corrupt Kenya had a completely different definition from the standard one you and I know. It was like another mini-trial at the hands of an uncooperative probation officer. A horrendous nightmare. Of all the escapades I have ever been involved in, some cases at extremely risky rendezvous, my probation ordeal takes the cake!

PROBATION

My experience at the hands of Kenyan probation officers was a once-in-a-lifetime experience!

I had to report at their offices with my probation card once a month as the lawyer had told me.

Here I was without a job, and when on some days I missed to report at the probation office, the officer would not understand that I did not have bus fare.

I saw people being subjected to punishment because of missing to report on their scheduled dates. When you missed an appointment, the next time you reported you would be asked to sweep the compound, slash the overgrown grass, clean the offices or even wash the curtains.

One day I met one lady who had come to report on her weekly basis and she told me that I did not have to go through such manual labour, that all I had to do was be friendly to the probation officer and meet his demands. I was soon to find out how!

First, he asked for a coffee date. For the life of me I did not get it. What on earth did my probation have to do with coffee dates? I refused.

Initially, I reported once a month and then without any reason he changed it to twice a month.

I wondered. Did he have carte blanche to do as he pleased?

He knew it was hard for me financially. I knew there had to be a catch somewhere, and I waited anxiously for his move.

It came eventually. He dangled a very tantalizing carrot.

One day I went to his office to 'report.' I found him with some forms. He showed me some of them and said that the government was able to help deserving cases on probation, like myself, so that they do not regress into their 'bad habits' by paying school fees for their children until they get jobs.

He showed me the forms of some needy cases whose fees had been paid.

Then he asked me out to dinner. I refused again. He put the blank forms I was supposed to fill back into his desk drawer.

He told me that if I continued being stubborn, I would not get any help from him, unless I came back to my senses.

I stared at the pictures of his wife and children proudly displayed on his desk and told him that I would never ever go out with him no matter what.

He stared at me enigmatically and told me not to use such strong words like "never" with him. He said that he'd heard it all before. I left his office with suppressed tears.

Another day, he told me that the government could help me start a small business, as I was one of the more disciplined cases, but first he wanted to come to my place.

Didn't the man have ears? I told him I did not want him coming to my place. He said that as my probation officer he had the right to. So I told him that if it was official, he should tell me the day and the time, and I will make sure that my sister or one of my family members or friends was present.

To cut a long story short, you have probably guessed right, he never did make that visit, and I never got any school fees for my daughter, nor any grant or capital to start a business.

But I did get a hundred shillings one day from him for my bus fare!

To date, I still wonder what criteria the government uses to vet the deserving cases.

Eventually, I got a job even though I was still on probation.

When I informed the probation officer, he told me that if I got a job I had to inform him. I thought he would be happy for me, but instead he looked miffed, like I had slapped him on the face!

He had been gloating at my inability to find a job, and now here I was telling him I had gotten one. Because this job was in town, I had no difficulty making my twice monthly reporting visits to the probation office.

Then I landed a better paying one at a garment factory. He set out on another route of frustration. My new second job was in Mombasa West, a long way from the city centre. Instead of reducing the number of times I should report to him, he increased them to reporting twice a week!

Every time I would come to report, I would not find him and I would spend hours hanging around waiting for him.

Sometimes I understood he was in court. But once court was over I would call him on his cell phone and ask him to come to his office, and he would say that he was first going for lunch. Or he would tell me to go to the court house and he could sign my card for me there. I would rush there only to be told he'd just left yet he knew I was on my way there.

I almost lost my job, but luckily enough my one-year probation was drawing to an end.

Once or twice I would find the other probation officers, one of whom was a lady, and they would sign for me after I explained to them the situation at my work place.

On subsequent occasions they refused to sign saying

that my assigned officer had refused their interference, but why couldn't they meet my eyes?

On the last day, I could see it in my probation officer's eyes that he could not believe that I had finished my one year. Neither could I, but I could hear my mother's words ringing in my ears, that I am a strong lady. That, coming from an African woman who has brought up seven children and buried another who was stillborn, is more than a compliment.

The probation officer had looked at me and I have never forgotten his words. He had the audacity to tell me that he had a feeling a miscarriage of justice had occurred somewhere along the way. But that as I was not showing any remorse either, he was going to write a bad final report unless I talked to him nicely. Remorse? I doubted if the man could recognise the emotion if it walked right up to his front door, rang the bell and punched him right in the face! Anyway, doesn't one need to be guilty in order to be remorseful? I looked at him disdainfully as he continued talking. He said that with a little fee, all traces of my 'criminal record' could disappear. He said that I would never get a job with multi-nationals, blue-chip firms and important organizations like the UN who request applicants to produce the Certificate of Good Conduct provided by the police, if my criminal record continued 'existing'.

I was stunned. He had the nerve! I simply told him that he can go to hell as I did not care what he wrote.

And that was that. I wish you could have seen the look on his face.

My probation was over and it was a relief. I have never even wanted to know what he wrote in my file. But what I do know is that he did not measure up to the definition I had looked up for probation officer which said, "A social worker attached to the prisons department and who provides information to the court on the life and attitude of a person awaiting sentencing or a person already committed to community service but reports to an officer weekly – that is on a probation period of maybe one year."

A man I later met, who was interested in dating me, expressed shock when I openly talked of this experience. He challenged me to show him proof and I simply told him to check police records. It was certainly within his means to do so. He had the cheek and he said he will call my bluff and went to check. It profoundly confounded him to find my confessions true! He disappeared from my life after barely a week. Maybe he was scared of what society would think if he got involved with a near convict. I will repeat myself, I do not care what people say or think so long as I know I was innocent. I was set up. Whoever is interested can go dig the archives!

During the entire probation period I was so frustrated. I thought the pain would kill me. All through the gruelling ordeal, I thought I had died and gone to a sort of perdition. My own private hell but then I would sense God's presence. That maybe it was His own highway to my serene heaven. I would rely heavily on His Grace and my fortitude and serenity to see me through.

I would walk long distances looking for a job. I simply refused to compromise my dignity. People said there were no jobs, but the jobs were there, because at numerous interviews somebody with no papers or any sort of qualifications would land the job.

I needed some slack and I knew something had to give. Either I would lose it and go insane, or I would get a job. One day it leant towards the former and almost proved fatal.

I had walked into every office on all the eleven floors of a high-rise office block looking for a job. Any job. I was tired of the indignity of borrowing money all the time. Shilpa, Myra and Latifah said it was pride. But it was not. I could no longer keep accepting money from them yet have no idea when and how I was going to pay it back. I started being reactive with the little finances I had instead of being proactive. I used quick-fix solutions to my problems with no long term plans in my head.

That day I was so exhausted, the fatigue heavy like a cloak around my body. I had wiped my brow and moved away from the elevators towards the windows that overlooked the city and the strip of ocean in the distance. I had rested my feverish forehead on the cool panes. Shock rippled through me when I realised that in between the large panes of glass there was enough space for someone to slip through.

I wondered. Was that why there had been several suicides committed from this eleven storey building? Shuddering, I had moved away from the windows.

Why had my thoughts wandered so? Wondering, I had wandered back again and stared down. Eleven stories below the hustle and bustle of Digo road, the main avenue snaking through Mombasa's Central Business District (CBD). A peculiar sense of floating outside myself engulfed me. A curious foreboding had settled over me. I had felt a detachment from my being, my very soul. My breath had slowed, filming the glass. My bitter self-recriminations had faded. There had been only the distant pavement glinting and beckoning seductively at me. Until that afternoon, my infrequent considerations of suicide had always been along succinct and logical lines. I had never been one to entertain suicidal intentions, and always thought it a cowardly act. But that afternoon, gazing down from eleven stories at the shimmering square cuts of pavement, my normally acute mental processes and faculties had been distorted. Thoughts had floated like insubstantial wisps of clouds that could not be grasped. There are no grills; it is so very easy to jump out and end all this suffering...

But then the elevator's ringing sound had intruded, breaking the spell of the betraying thoughts. The lift had ground to a halt and the impatient people, in a typical Kenyan way, had pushed and shoved to get in and out, the ensuing melee bringing me down to earth. I had been shocked. What was I thinking?

I had gone and sat on the stairs, hugged my knees to my chest and cried my eyes out thinking of my Nehema and asking God for a job.

People going up and down the stairs had stared at me with questioning glances.

I walked home later. When I looked deep into my daughter's eyes I knew then how innocent she was. I vowed then to soldier on and see the end of the sordid mess, but the experience of that moment remains with me to this date, reminding me how transient life can be. It was only a year down the line that I shared the horror of that day with Latifah, Myra and Shilpa. We had cried together and became even closer. Talking about it served to exorcise the demon that had been tormenting me. The demon of an untold near tragedy.

* * * * *

God says that we should not seek revenge and that vengeance and retribution is for Him alone.

How so very true. Barely two years down the line, the casino was closed due to financial problems. The perjurers got no benefits. All their dues were still outstanding. The expatriate security officer was involved in a terrible car accident and both his legs were broken. Do I hear someone out there whisper 'poetic justice'? But doesn't God possess a sense of irony or what? Karma sure is nature's way of punishing someone who has wronged us without us having to lift a finger.

I did not have the last laugh for long though, courtesy of a near fatal illness.

THE SERENITY PRAYER

...surrender to His Will...

...kubali Nia Yake Mwenyezi Mungu...

A Sabbatical Sojourn

Medicus Curat, Natura Sanat.

The age-old Latin aphorism had been resounding in my head these past couple of days. I remembered the refrain from a medical journal I had once read.

Medicus Curat, Natura Sanat, the doctor treats, nature heals, *Medicus Curat, Natura Sanat*, the Doctor treats, Nature heals...

The refrain had been going on and on...

I remember when it had all started. I had said "no! It could not be! Not when I do not have a job! Oh dear God!"

I should have seen it coming – yet I did not want to believe it.

I had been experiencing some pain when I slept on my chest, my favourite position.

I went and stood before the mirror, I lifted my hands above my head and stared critically at my breasts. Nothing out of the ordinary.

I wondered. What did I expect? Some protruding lumps? Yet I had felt them.

With a wry smile (I could still afford one), I lowered my right hand and lifted my left even higher.

I used my right palm to tenderly feel my left breast. I went over the whole breast.

I felt it again, the slippery lump that I could not grasp properly.

I felt it slip towards my armpit. I lowered my left hand and repeated the process again with my right breast. Another slippery lump. God no! I went and laid down on my bed. I knew I was lucky. Very lucky because it was routine for me to examine my breasts and if it was breast cancer then the earlier detected the better. Still, I hit my pillows over and over again, screaming 'God no! No! No! No! No! No! No!'

The tears streamed down my cheeks. I did not need this. I asked God not to let me be sick. I did not have a job. Sometimes I could not even afford to put food on the table, let alone buy a snack for my baby to carry to school for her recess break.

I did not go to the hospital for months, how could I? I did not even have the bus fare to go to town and look for a job! The job I had gotten towards the latter part of my probation had also ended when the garment factory was shut down.

Meanwhile, the pain in my chest and back got worse. I started experiencing intense pain in my legs. At night I would be gripped by panic attacks, I would feel as if I was suffocating. I would be dizzy and feel as if the ceiling was pressing down on my body. I would break out in sweat and get down on my knees to pray.

I felt frustrated. I sacrificed a lot and at least went for a full medical check-up and pap smears religiously every year. Weren't these tests supposed to detect such developments? This time, I was truly on my own; Myra was busy trying to get her Lamborghini and Shilpa was busy in college. On the other hand, Latifah was married and also had a one-year-old son. I could not even ask for help from my parents who, as you remember, had been adversely affected by the Likoni ethnic clashes and were yet to recover financially. Their income had been halved because the rental houses my parents owned in the South Coast of Mombasa were now deserted -- devoid of tenants who had fled to their up-country origins. Now, a room that would normally be rented for two-thousand shillings was going for around five-hundred shillings – and the story doing the rounds was that the landlords/

ladies had to take it or leave it. It was now the year 2000 and my family had still not recovered – economically that is.

It reached a point that I could not take it anymore. I had to go to the hospital.

I scrimped and saved and managed to get the required consultation fees. The doctor first did the usual examinations. My weight was down to forty-nine kilogrammes from my usual fifty-eight kilogrammes.

My haemoglobin count was six point five – the doctor said it was cause to panic as a normal person's count should at least be eleven. He said that he was surprised I was not dead which was not very comforting!

He said that it appeared I was not eating well. I did not argue with that, I could barely put one meal on the table.

He also felt the lumps, but he said that because I was having some other symptoms he preferred that I have some chest X-rays before coming to any conclusions.

He saw my hesitation and asked me if there was any problem.

I told him that I did not have any money, and I asked him if it was a must for me to undergo the scan and if was possible for him to just prescribe some painkillers for me?

He told me that I had to undergo the X-ray, as it was the only way to determine what I was suffering from.

I asked him how much it would cost. He gave me a rough estimate of around one-thousand eight-hundred shillings.

I was shocked – even getting the five hundred shillings for his consultation had been a big hassle.

"Does it mean that if you do not have any money in this country one dies?"

"I am afraid so, yes" he replied, "that is why we have such a high rate of maternal deaths and infant mortality."

The doctor prescribed some painkillers to keep me going until I was able to afford the scans.

I could not even afford the painkillers – they were costing around eight-hundred shillings.

I asked the doctor to write me the prescription and I would go and buy the drugs from a pharmacy in town. The hospital pharmacy was too expensive.

I went home and I did some thinking. I was in so much pain. I had to get those drugs, yet I did not have any money. Back home in deep thought I considered my options. I hated borrowing money, especially when I did not have a job. And my family – well, that was out of the question. I felt as if breath was being squeezed out of me!

Talk about being stuck between a rock and a hard place! This was a typical catch-22 situation.

Finally, I settled on selling my DVD machine. It was all I could think of, and at least the money, though half of the machines value, paid some bills and I managed to have my X-rays taken.

A couple of days later I found myself in the doctor's consultation rooms. He looked like a worried man. I was soon to find out why. He took my hand and led me to where he had hung up my X-rays so that we could view them using the fluorescent tube light. He started talking slowly.

"Kemunto, you are a very sick young lady. Do you see this black mass here?" he asked, pointing to the overhead X-rays. "You have pneumonia and it has spread all over your chest, your back and probably into your bone marrow too. Come here." He led me to someone else's X-rays.

"Do you see how clear this X-ray is? You can see the rib cage clearly defined and even the shape of the lungs. But when you come back to yours all one sees are these fuzzy black patches in spots."

We went back to our seats. "In my opinion," he continued, "you are a very strong person. Someone else could have died of this kind of spread six months ago. I need to know something. How did you contract pneumonia? Have you been to any cold places lately? Or are you a fan of cold drinks?"

"No. I haven't been to any cold places and I do not take cold drinks."

The Doctor stared at me, forming a steeple with his fingers while resting his elbows on the table. "It is very strange. I need to understand the genesis of all this.

Have you had pneumonia before?" he asked.

"Well," I started, "my mum tells me that when I was three I had a severe attack of pneumonia and had to be in the ICU for close to a month. The Doctor told my parents that I was highly susceptible to chest infections." I came to a stop.

"Alright. What about your family? Do they have any chest problems?" he asked.

"Well, my middle brother used to have asthma when he was young, but he later overcame it. And one of my younger sisters is prone to attacks of bronchitis. Our youngest brother suffers from epilepsy. I also have vague images of my grandfather using his own special cutlery. I was later told that he died of TB. "

The doctor looked thoughtful "No. That is not it. What about more recently? You must have done something to bring this on. Normally such pneumonia is brought on by exposure to extremely cold conditions. And sometimes cold surfaces."

Recognition dawned in my eyes.

"Wait a minute! I think I know when it happened." I said excitedly.

"You do?"

"Yes. In December I was in police custody for three days. I promised myself I would not sleep on the cold

179

cell floor, but I always inevitably found myself waking up from that very same floor. And then again in February I was back in custody for three more days. We are now in October. I guess that explains the pneumonia." I finished calmly.

You would have given anything to see the doctor's face. He was incredulous.

"Kemunto, you're talking about this so calmly as if it was nothing. It must have been terrible. You do not look the type to end up in police cells. What happened?"

"You really do not want to know. In fact, I just completed a year's probation. Can you believe it? I do not like talking about it. I always end up crying. So what are we going to do about my sickness? More drugs?"

"Actually, I am placing you on a tough regime of drugs. Your pneumonia is really extensive. I do not know how you have managed to stay with it this long. The lumps are still there but let us first treat the pneumonia. Go buy these original drugs and no generics please. And then come and see me after two months when you are through with the dosage."

I was in for a big shock. The original Augmentin tablets the doctor had prescribed cost around four-thousand shillings. I thought to myself, "Surely, I am going to die!"

I went around most chemists comparing the prices. They were more or less the same.

The pharmacists said that they were the original ones from Germany, but if I had rather buy the generics which were costing around two-thousand it was up to me. They would trail off suggestively insinuating that the generics were not as good as the original tablets.

At first, I survived on applying Deep Heat and Vicks or any ointment with ethanol on my chest and back to relieve the pain.

In the end I had to do something I dreaded. I borrowed money to buy the drugs.

I was in so much pain, especially at night. I could not stand it.

Two months later...

The lumps were still there, but the pneumonia had healed after the regimen of drugs.

I had taken some X-rays which showed that my chest was now clear.

I was in my doctor's office, and what he was telling me about the lumps was not good news.

"Well, there are women with a number of abnormal cells. The risk of developing breast cancer goes up fourfold. Hopefully the abnormal cells can be targeted before they become malignant, that is, when they are still benign." He droned on and on. I was scared stiff and barely paying attention to his words. "In some women it is hereditary. They have a family history or genetic disposition for breast cancer. There is chemotherapy, and also sometimes in the more developed countries especially in the west, oncologists give some women a preventive agent to see if they can eradicate the abnormal cells and thus prevent the cancer from developing further."

I learned a lot of technical terms. He talked of a mammogram that I could not have because I was still under the age of thirty-five and that it was not advisable. Noticing my bemused look, he explained that it was a scan of the breasts. He talked of Alopecia and further explained that it was loss of hair, a condition occasioned by the effects of chemotherapy. He then said that what I would have to do was have an ultra sound scan of my breasts.

All I could ask tremulously was "will I have to lose my breasts, doctor?" The doctor just looked at me gently saying, "no Kemunto, I have not said that. Go for the ultra sound first and then we'll move from there."

"I do not have any money doc. It must be very expensive."

I had already explained to him that I was a single parent and currently jobless.

"I won't lie to you. It will seem that way especially as you do not have a job, but it is something that you have to do. Why don't you go to Coast General Hospital. It would be cheaper there with the cost sharing introduced by the government."

Everybody knew it was a nightmare paying a visit to the government provincial hospital.

It was always packed with masses of sick people who could not afford the private hospitals.

Stenches of uncollected used hospital dressings overflowed from the dumpsters. Winding, unending queues of patients sometimes miles long into the sunshine characterized the corridors.

There was always no stationery. You even had to buy an exercise book from vendors or kiosks outside the hospital to be used by the doctors as your appointment card!

A day later, I found myself buying the famed exercise book and joining the unending queue. I was shocked. I thought because of the government cost-sharing scheme it would be much cheaper, maybe two hundred shillings. I was surprised to be told that it would cost around eight-hundred.

I did not have that kind of money. I thought to myself saying, "is this why so many people are dying at home and on hospital steps? Because they cannot afford medication and treatment?"

I should not be surprised. After all, we've heard of expectant mothers in labour dying and losing their babies at provincial hospitals because they could not afford a pair of surgical gloves and the doctors and nurses refused to attend to them. I went home dejected. I had to get that money.

I managed to get one of our church members to buy my music system.

At least I paid my daughter's school fees, part of the rent and managed to go for the ultra sound.

The nurses were so demoralised, maybe due to being underpaid and overworked. The one attending to me twisted me this way and that way. She hurt my breasts squeezing them roughly as she positioned them between the two plates for the scan. Even when I tried to voice my protests she said something rudely to the effect that it is what Kenyans get for wanting cheap services! I thanked God it was over quickly.

One day after Bible study at a church member's home, Nehema seemed unusually quiet.

Later, when we went home she asked me suddenly, "mummy, was that our music system at Ian and Carl's place?"

I reflected for a minute.

Should I lie? Should I tell her that it was not? That they had just bought a similar one to ours? That I had taken ours for repairs?

Isn't that what authors of most positive and self-help literature talk about? That we should not burden our young ones with our worries?

At least John Gray stresses in his book *Children are from Heaven* saying, 'There is a big difference between being manipulated by a whiny child and being motivated by a brilliant negotiator.'

Upon reading his book a year before, I had started learning fast how to self-correct in the way I was bringing up my daughter! I thought of John Gray's words now as I prepared myself mentally to answer Nehema.

She was only six, but I decided to be honest.

"Sweetie, come sit on my lap." I held her saying "yes Nehema, it was our music system."

"Why did you give it to them mum?"

"Baby, I did not give it to them. I sold it to their dad. You know I have not gotten a job yet and we needed the money to pay your fees and for me to go to the hospital."

She knew I was having chest and back pains at night because I would ask her to sit on my back while I lay down. Her weight would relieve the pain especially in the chilly weather when my Deep Heat was finished and I did not have any painkillers. Now she surprised me by taking my hand and practically saying, "It is ok mummy. Do not worry. Let us get down on our knees and I will pray like we've been taught at Sunday school. God will provide us with another one."

We got down on our knees. She said a simple prayer that was music to my ears and brought tears to my eyes. "Our dear Heavenly father, I am praying that you give my mummy a job so that we do not sell anymore of our stuff. Please, also heal my mum and do not make her sick. Help her to pay for my fees and also our rent because that is what you tell us in Philippians 4:19. In Jesus' name we pray and believe. Amen."

I was not brought up by faithfully church-going parents, though they went on Christmas and Easter but I thank God for his saving Grace that I am now going to church and teaching my daughter to pray and to appreciate God.

Later that night, after Nehema's prayer, I remembered how when I had broken up with Maxi I had asked God to help me not to subject my daughter to a succession of "so-called uncles" and a string of "wannabe dads."

I asked God to sort me out and protect me from the sin that is covetousness against all odds, to help me not to compromise my dignity, because He tells us in Psalms 118:8 that it is better to trust in Him than to put confidence in man. In the Good Book, He tells us over and over again that He provides for us and that His timing is always best and perfect, never too early and never too late. Always just on time.

That night I repeated my prayer. I added that I needed help seriously to maintain my self-preservation and not to self-destruct or to crave for too much too soon.

Strangely, God had a sort of inspirational message for me in a moment with Him a day later. He told me that He would heal me but I will not get a job for a year; until I write about my experiences with my three friends Shilpa, Myra and Latifah and the trials and triumphs as a single mother who has had to struggle every inch of the way. I was shocked.

It was a surreal experience. I had gone to church very early in the morning, around five, to pray before the Morning Glory Service began. For several weeks I had been coming to church and I would just kneel at the altar and tell God that I just could not go on with my situation of being jobless and penniless. I had literally heard this booming voice tell me to write of my experiences in book form. I had looked around me scared and stupefied and the voice had repeated itself. I was alone as other worshippers had not started arriving. The voice had repeated itself. I had cried silently, the tears trickling down my cheeks. Was this God's voice? How could he expect me to write about my tribulations?

A day later I asked God if I had heard Him right. He repeated Himself: I had to put all my experiences in print. That it was when He would give me my break. I had to write about everything, even my stint in police custody.

I was reluctant at first, but I realised how serious God was after missing job after job.

I also remembered that in Isaiah 55:8-10 God tells us that just as the Heavens are higher than the earth, so are His thoughts and ways different from ours.

I got down to it. I wrote about everything. Then I decided to look for a publisher.

More horrendous nightmares. I could not get a publisher to touch my work. Perhaps because my genre stepped on sensitive toes?

God gave me some slack anyway and I got a job after exactly one year. Perhaps because He saw that I was obeying His instructions and really trying to get published. A job that did not last long but that is a story for another day in another volume.

* * * * *

I started doing a lot of reading then on breast cancer, particularly on the experiences of one brave Kenyan lady, Ms. Julia Mulaha (God rest her soul in peace). She had been a victim of breast cancer. She started an organization whose main aim was to help women affected by the disease and to sensitize them on the same. Thankfully, in my case it never came to a requirement of a biopsy (taking of sample tissue from my breasts!)

A week later I went to see the doctor and he got out my scan. He had this strange look on his face.

He told me to get on the examining table. He did the usual preliminary checks and then examined my breasts. Finally he looked at the X-ray once more and asked me

"Kemunto, do you believe in miracles?"

"Very much so, *daktari*. I know God has healed me. There are no lumps because recently I cannot feel them," I replied.

He looked confused and said "I do not know about God healing you, but your ultra sound is clear. No signs of any abnormal growth or cells and I have examined you and I cannot feel any lumps."

I think that was the last time I visited his office.

After that I was without a job for close to one year.

I remember I sold almost everything in the house including our beds. The only remaining things we had was the foam mattress we would sleep on, pots, pans, crockery, cutlery and other basic utensils. I would walk for long distances looking for a job.

At times in the sweltering heat after the bottle of water I always carried from home was finished, I would crave for a cold can or bottle of Coca Cola and would think that the craving was going to kill me. I remember one day I was so thirsty I stared so hard at a Coca-Cola vendor till my eyes hurt!

I thought I would end up begging for a sip from the ten-shilling containers. I was that broke and that thirsty! The moment passed though.

There were times I would feel so dejected because even the emerging micro-finance institutes seemed to set some unrealistic goals or targets to be achieved by someone before she or he became a beneficiary. Like getting involved in women's self-help support groups, where individuals have small businesses and then get small loans with group mates as collateral and also items in your business premises. But more often than not, these groups are normally riddled with nepotism, cronyism and tribalism.

I befriended one newspaper vendor who always gave me the newspapers to read when I could not afford one. I especially felt bad if I missed the Sunday ones which contained literary discourses. Sometimes I would read the financial papers. I would go through articles by Victor Mandi, Manyara Kirago, Robert Shaw, Abel Kabiru, Dennis Kabaara, and I would be thinking, 'these guys do not know what they are talking about. Have they ever been jobless with no income and a child to bring up alone?' Where do they want us to go? No wonder talk is rife that most of the young call girls plying the street with their trade and sometimes even getting arrested are graduates who cannot secure jobs.

Needless to say, I would read through the articles diligently. Maybe one day, who knows, I might be able to practice what the financial gurus were preaching. Things became even more difficult that year. At times I would share a hundred shillings with another jobless neighbour who had a more pressing need. Later, I would wonder if I had epitomised philanthropy only for me and my daughter to do without a meal in the evening.

Still, I refused to let pessimism replace optimism. I tried to strategize on a shoestring budget with whatever few coins I could gather.

The phrase from donor agencies and countries on poverty stricken people in the developing countries living on less than a dollar a day took on a whole new dimension and meaning for me!

Sometimes my daughter would be sick and I would not have money to take her to a private clinic in the estate where we stayed.

The owner of the clinic was very surprised at my total honesty. I would simply tell him that my baby was sick and I did not have a job and that once I got one I would pay the money I owed.

I do not know what it was, but I think he was used to people lying about the reasons for their inability to pay up. One day, he surprised me by saying to his staff, "if this lady comes in with her daughter and they have no money, just treat them. She'll settle the bills when she's able."

I never forgot that kind doctor because several times it did happen that I needed to take my baby to the hospital when I still hadn't gotten a job. Nehema was treated, once for malaria and twice in the course of the year for other minor ailments. I always made sure I settled my bills whenever I was able to.

Over the weekends, sometimes I left my baby with neighbours because I could not afford a house girl. I knew of rich people who were employing under-age girls as housemaids and paying them one-thousand or one-thousand five-hundred shillings a month. I always wondered how such employers expected the girls to survive on such a salary? Actually, such a stipend? I promised myself never to underpay a house-help. I would rather struggle without one until the time I would be able to pay her the salary stipulated by the law or more. Because even what it stipulates as minimum wages is beyond belief! People do say the law is an ass!

During the weekdays, whenever I got a temp job like relieving a secretary going on her annual leave, I would be at work but I had a feeling I was developing into a clock-watcher.

Constantly, I would be racked by separation anxiety or was it mother's intuition? I would be worried sick because Nehema had to stay an extra hour after school with the teachers waiting for me to pick her up.

I remember one day I was so late it was almost six in the evening when I went to pick Nehema up. I found her sitting alone at the school gate. She had such a forlorn look of reproach on her face, one that is forever etched on my memory as she rushed to hug me saying "Mummy, I thought you were never ever coming for me again!"

I looked deep into her eyes asking "baby, what made you think that?"

She said "because my papa left you and me and now here at school I have been left all alone. All the other children have been picked up." I do not know why she thought of her dad then, maybe it was because of joining school and seeing two parent families and also dads picking up their children, but I told her "honey you know I love you. I would never leave you alone and even if I am late, just stay put. Do not talk or go with strangers. Wait for me to come pick you up, Nehema."

Though such moments are like fleeting images captured on celluloid, I cherished such incidents with Nehema. I felt like we bonded more and I was able to show her how much she meant to me.

* * * * *

In the coming months I was to thank God over and over again. I counted my blessings because by His strength, He was able to keep me at my writing, never letting up. Not even after several incidents of losing my work, like the time one vindictive managing director deleted all my manuscripts. He did not want to see me typing my personal work on office computers even after hours or during my lunch break!

Sometimes, I would feel like giving up. One day, my cowardly actions suddenly seemed duplicitous and I knew it was retrogressive and damaging to my self-therapy of putting down my thoughts on paper.

When I read what Anthony Robins says in *Notes from a Friend*, I knew I had to have a positive outlook with no metaphors!

…Suddenly I was jerked back to the present by Craig David's crooning 'I am walking away from the troubles in my life. I am walking away to find a better life.'

How appropriate! That is what I intend to do, walk away and work very hard!

Lastly, I told God that He was our (mine and my Nehema's) medical coverage and education policy, and that I intend to hold Him to his promises. He had come through in His own special way. Nehema had never been expelled from school, nor do I remember taking her to the hospital in years. I was thankful, even though sometimes we used rough caustic soda soap to bath and even put the empty container of cocoa butter body lotion upside down overnight to use whatever drips down for the next day. Other times, we cut the empty toothpaste tube in half to make sure it was really empty or used salt. The fact was that we were still alive, and I learned to thank God for the gift of life and good health!

Such resilience, faith and trust was what a moment with God was like, if you learned to listen carefully to what His voice could produce. That still inner voice. Perseverance. Our God is a God of miracles if only we worked hard, had faith in Him and partnered with Him. My initial substantial sabbatical sojourn commissioned by the Almighty God Himself had almost turned sour! Strange bedfellows these were. I mean sabbatical and sojourn.

I had scares and then some! But I never bargained on the fact that soon my three best friends and I would be separated forever.

PART THREE

STRIKING FOR SHORE

THE SERENITY PRAYER

...that I may be....

...kwamba nitakuwa na...

Monsoon in Mumbai

It had reached a point that Shilpa did not find it odd to join us at night clubs like Club Rio in the CBD or the underground one, Tiffany's. Florida overlooking the Indian Ocean at Mama Ngina drive had also become one of our haunts. Just Drinks and Bob's in the north coast were our most favourite hangout joints. If not at any of these clubs, then we were definitely at the Reef Hotel's Yamas Beach Pub.

That is why I never gave it a second thought one day at Just Drinks when I introduced Victor to Shilpa. I was so used to Victor. I took his presence for granted. He was like a brother to me. We called him Vic for short. Vic had been in school with my older brother. Even when my brother left for the United Kingdom, Vic, who had joined the Kenya Navy, continued to visit our family.

When I introduced the two, I never expected what would transpire a couple of months later. It was an event we were later in life to refer to jokingly as Monsoon in Mumbai! As usual, Myra, Latifah Shilpa and I would go almost everywhere together. So when Shilpa started preferring to frequent the Officer's Mess at the Naval Base at Mtongwe at invitations from Victor, I did not give it a second thought as we constantly crossed the Mtongwe Ferry or used the Navy's tug or K-Boats to go visit Victor. Our seven foot, dark and handsome African naval officer had captivated our Indian girlfriend!

I should have noticed their shared intimate glances at Just Drinks. Shilpa had kept blushing. One day, dropping her eyes, she asked me why Victor was so bold as to ask her to dance, when for weeks he would have noticed that she did not like dancing to Hip Hop music.

Later, when she had given in and as I watched them dance sometimes to R & B or Rhythm & Blues if you rather, I would let the music wash over me and seep into me like the confidence of falling in love. I would pretend that I was the one who was smitten.

Victor was too handsome to ignore. Shilpa's chin hardly reached his chest and she tried to ignore him for several weekends but in the end she fell for his charm like a ton of bricks.

When they started going out as a couple, peoples' stares changed from ones of indulgence to shock. An African man and an Indian girl flirting so openly? Such things were best done in secret, the indignant looks said. It was only in retrospect that I did remember that Shilpa had always liked African men and boys! I recall one time during our secondary school days, she had a crush on our new biology and chemistry teacher whom students had nick-named Speedo[i] because of his tall and slim physique. Suddenly, bio as we referred to biology and chem which of course is chemistry became Shilpa's favourite subjects. Out of the blue she started dragging me, Latifah and Myra to all MSC (Mombasa Sports Club) hockey games to watch Speedo, who turned out for the side. But just as suddenly, her infatuation died.

Now she had a new love. Every time Vic entered Just Drinks his eyes only scanned the pub for her. Shilpa, who never drank alcohol before, now took the occasional tot of Tequila and Amarula. Her dressing had changed. Skinny jeans and balloon tops which were so in became her new wardrobe and her modest skirts became so yesterday! The girl who hated dancing would now spend a whole evening on the dance floor gyrating to the latest hits.

She savoured *chapati* and liver stew. *Ugali* and fried chicken became her favourite too because Victor loved

---

i Brand of slim ballpoint pens.

these African dishes. She, in turn, introduced him to chewing *paan*. He was so modern and exciting that once at the naval base he even had invitation cards courtesy of the American Embassy for all of us to attend a cocktail party aboard an American submarine to welcome US marines who were on training on the Kenyan coast with their Kenyan counterparts! Eventually, the two love birds decided they wanted to get married.

* * * * *

After dating secretly for three months, Vic and Shilpa decided to come clean with their respective families. Victor's family accepted Shilpa without any reservations. Surprisingly, when she told her mother that she was in love with an African man and they wanted to get married, her mamadi was baffled and shocked that she could not find a nice Indian boy whose roots and generation they could trace back and investigate! Shilpa did not know what her papaji would say. She soon found out. He was so shocked he forbade her to see Victor. He told Shilpa that she, being their only child, had disappointed him and had dishonoured her family by dating Victor. Shilpa, in turn, told her papaji that his attitude towards Vic was a kind of xenophobia dishonouring mankind! She asked him why he was applying double standards in judging Vic yet they had taught her that a passage in the Bhagavad Gita instructs them to know the people around them? Why couldn't they accept Vic? Shilpa was baffled that now black seemed like a metaphor to her parents, yet the majority of customers to her papaji and mamadi's spices and fabric shop in the Old Town were black Africans. She could not understand their hypocrisy.

Nevertheless, Shilpa and Victor continued going out. Her papaji was infuriated that she had become so confident to the extent of defying him. Her other Indian friends gave her mother the 'we told you' so look, which said albeit silently, 'we told you so. Look what her two African and Arab girlfriends have gotten her into!'

One day we went to pick her up at her home. Victor decided to accompany us in order to try and break the ice with her parents. Her mamadi had come rushing into the living room in her usual clouds of chiffon. She had screamed at Victor to get out and not to shame her daughter. In the mayhem she had slipped when her sari pallu caught on an armrest and she stumbled and fell to the floor. Luckily, she had not hurt herself. Shilpa's papaji dressed in his usual Dhakai cottons in monsoon colours sent from their relatives in Mumbai and a white dhoti had come into the living room screaming "*kemcho? Kemcho?*[i] at Shilpa as if Victor had done something terrible to her. He had shouted that his daughter will marry an African man over his dead body. He had screamed that he did not want *chotara*[ii] grandchildren. Shilpa had become hysterical and her aunts and uncles had intervened siding with her papaji and mamadi, and calling her *neemakaram*[iii]. We had to leave as Victor was not apologetic. Shilpa's papaji had shouted at Victor that he only wanted to see auspicious things in his house, and asked him not to ever come back to their house again, because his presence was certainly not welcome. He instructed the watchman never to open the gate for him.

I could not help but think of the time my papa had refused to bless my intended marriage to Maxi saying that he would not sit down with uncircumcised men! That was negative ethnicity at its highest, and was this now ethnic bigotry or buffoonery? I think it was the first time Shilpa had encountered racial perceptions and racial prejudice as reality and not a myth!

---

i Gujarati -- "How are you? How are you?"

ii Hindu -- "half-cast" or "half-breed"

iii Hindu -- Ingrate

From then on Latifah, Myra and I had to sneak to their house when her parents were out. And all we ever found her listening to were Hindi classics like '*Pyar Divana Hota Hai*' (Love is Crazy) and '*Gata Rahe Mera Dil*' (My Heart is Singing). She was so depressed and told us that she was being banished to India to live with her grandmother. I remember her saying, "I am never coming back." Shocked, I had countered saying, "Shilpa, bite your tongue and take those words back!"

We noticed her parents had replaced all her English CDs with Hindi favourites like Chupke Se, Jao Na, Jiya Maine Jiya, Hum Dono Hain Khoye, Yes Raste Ye Masti, Dil Mera Dil Gaya and Mera Kajal.

On our last day with Shilpa we found her preparing to cook *Aloo Gobi*, their favourite Indian curry, for dinner. She had become like a robot and mechanically prepared the mustard seeds, red, yellow and green peppers. It was as if we were not there. She had reached automatically for the onions, potatoes, turmeric, cumin, coriander and *garam masala*. It was as if she had no control over her fingers as she dropped the cauliflower to the floor. I picked it up, washed it and cut it into florets for her. Myra got the mushrooms and ginger.

I had wondered how Shilpa managed to maintain her sanity. Her eyes glazed over as she took the sugar, water, salt and pepper for the taste. I knew that cooking kept her mind busy. She chopped the onions and peppers without talking. She started grinding the turmeric, cumin and coriander.

Silently, Latifah, Myra and I got to work. Familiar with their spotless kitchen shelves, we started preparing the *naan* bread to serve with the curry. The *moong daal bhajias* would be a side dish.

Shilpa's mama had taught us that *naan* needs perfect measurements and no shortcuts the way samosas are made nowadays full of bubbles because of lack of patience to produce the smooth bubble-free hard patty covering. Myra helped me set out the ingredients. We needed a spoon of yeast, a quarter teaspoon of warm water, 500 grams of self-rising wheat flour, a teaspoon of light vegetable cooking oil. A quarter teacup of milk, one-hundred-fifty millilitres of natural yoghurt at room temperature and a half teaspoon of sugar. For the garnish we set out three tablespoons of melted butter and a tablespoon of sesame seeds.

I put the yeast into a small bowl with the sugar and water. I mixed well until the yeast had dissolved and left the mixture in a warm corner of one of the kitchen cabinets for fifteen minutes until the mixture became frothy. I sifted the flour and salt into a large bowl. I made a well in the centre and poured in the yeast, milk, yoghurt and oil. I mixed it well for ten minutes until the dough was smooth and elastic. I placed the mixture in a bowl and covered it with cling film and left it to rise in the warm cabinet for an hour and a half as we cooked the *bhajias* and *aloo gobi*.

After the hour and half, I took the dough and turned it onto a kneading board and kneaded for a few minutes. I then divided the dough into eight pieces; patted and rolled each piece into a round shape. I placed them on a warmed baking sheet and baked them in the oven we had preheated to two-hundred-forty degrees Celsius for ten minutes, though sometimes one can preheat to four-hundred seventy-five degrees Fahrenheit.

I then removed the bread from the oven and brushed it with butter and sprinkled it with sesame seeds.

Having spent years with Shilpa as childhood friends, we were no strangers to preparing sizzling hot Indian curries like *Aloo Gobi*. We heated the oil in the heavy-based non-stick saucepan. We added mustard seeds, covered the pan and waited for the seeds to pop.

Shilpa still did not utter a word. We added the onions and peppers, sautéed until the onions became translucent. We added the potatoes and fried them until golden brown. The silence was unnerving. We added turmeric, cumin, coriander and *garam masala* to the pan and fried it for a few minutes until the spices were well mixed.

It was as if Shilpa had taken a vow of silence. We added the cauliflower and mushrooms and fried them until brown. Stirred in the ginger, sugar and water and seasoned with salt and pepper to taste. We let it boil, reduced the heat and covered the curry, letting it simmer for twenty minutes, until the vegetables were tender.

As I switched off the electric cooker the dam broke. It was as if Shilpa had been waiting for us to finish part of the cooking. She burst into tears saying that it was the last time she was seeing us! We just shared cup after cup of masala tea and hugged and consoled her. What else could we do? Weren't we the ones who had gotten her into this mess in the first place by introducing her to our carefree lifestyles and thrown handsome Victor into the bargain? Helplessly, we prepared the *papadums* and rice alongside which the curry would be served. Finally, we helped her prepare *daal bhajias* as a side dish for the family. We got the onions, gram flour, rice flour, wheat flour, the *chana* chickpea flour, *garam* masala, green chillies, cumin seeds, coriander leaves, yellow mung daal and black jeera. Next was the chilli powder and the *amja carom* seeds. We cut the onions into rings, chopped the green chillies and coriander leaves and ground the *daal*. We mixed the dry ingredients with just enough cold water to make the batter-like paste smooth enough to drop into a pan. We added salt, olive oil, pepper and a little turmeric. We mixed all the dry ingredients with our hands in a bowl making sure all the lumps were broken down. We left the flavours to soak and then deep fried them in tiny portions. We heated the light vegetable oil on a deep frying pan on medium.

The silence was as still as night. It was actually almost deathly because we had no words of consolation to befit the occasion. Nevertheless, we continued to do what we knew best – cooking! We dropped in the onion rings, and as they browned nicely we dropped in the *bhajias* mixture, a few balls at a time using a wooden spoon and mixing them up with the onion rings without crowding the pan too much. As one side of the *bhajias* became lightly browned we flipped them over to cook and brown the other side. We drained off the oil by holding them with a slotted spider spoon and set them on a plate lined with a few paper towels to soak up excess oil. We sprinkled them with *chaat chilli masala* and they were ready to be served with the *Aloo Gobi* and *naan* bread.

Later as we sat in her room, we realised that Shilpa's parents had confiscated all English and American DVDs too. They had replaced them with Hindi movies. Today she had *Khushi* featuring Kareena Kapoor and Fardeen Khan. We sat down to watch with her as it at least had English sub-titles. The story was about a young man, Karan, and a young lady, Khushi. Karan intended to go to Canada for further studies, but due to an accident was forced to enrol at Mumbai University. On the other hand Khushi's father decided that she had studied enough and she should get married, but she insisted on pursuing her education. She also enrolled at Mumbai. The two met and sparks began to fly immediately and the chemistry sizzled between them.

Their respective friends also fell in love and it was up to Karan and Khushi to play matchmaker and bring them together. They managed to bring their friends together, but the time also came for the two to decide whether they wanted to be together. Next we watched Made in India for the hundredth time!

The bottom line was that Shilpa's parents were trying to tell her that in India she could find a nice Indian boy to marry!

Shilpa was right though. It was the last day we saw her. Her architecture course was cut short, and just like that Shilpa was gone from us. I felt so sorry for her and Victor, who had thought that he would beat the dynamics of the odds stacked against an inter-racial marriage and emerge with Shilpa victorious like his name. A couple of months later I received a letter from her. The only one we would ever get from her.

* * * * *

Dear Kemu, Latifah and Myra,

Hi gals! I miss you all so desperately, especially Victor. I miss our hanging out at the Cinemax and mall and our raves at Just Drinks and the Naval Base. From the minute I landed at the airport in New Delhi, the Indian capital, I felt disoriented. Even though our plane touched down at 3am, you'd expect the roads to be clear of traffic, but no! Delhi never sleeps. It is like the new Nairobi with the twenty-four hour economy. I have even seen a couple of tame elephants and camels ferrying passengers on the streets – I am so surprised because even in Kenya we only see the camels at the beach where they ferry children for fun for a little fee!

But as with most cities in developing countries, the poverty is in contrast with the opulence. Like the five-star Trident Hilton, latest models of cars which are all over versus the dogs, cows, shacks and lopsided buildings. And girls -- the culture! Here it is so entrenched that my grandma has even given me this Indian-style calendar printed on thin white rice paper. It has no pictures. She says that pictures are frivolous and we should focus more on our future which is a serious affair. The Indian days and months are printed in red Bengali lettering. The English translations printed beneath in small innocuous blue. The calendar indicates all our Indian festivals like Jamai Shashhi, when son-in-laws are invited and served their favourite meals. The calendar tells us which days are auspicious and which are harbingers of bad luck. Small diagrams mark full moons and no moons, as well as the thin sliver of the eleventh night which is a time for women without husbands to fast and pray for purification. Handwritten notes on the bottom of each page warn us of the dangerous hours rahukal, which shifts each day with the movement of the planets. Grandma said she paid an astrologer from Calcutta a lot of money for him to calculate these days for me, her granddaughter, who has come to India to begin a new chapter in her life, and would soon pay dowry to get married to a nice young Indian man!

She accompanied me to make sure I hung the calendar above the dressing table in my room when I moved to my aunt's place, so that every morning I would take note of all festivals and keep track of holy days. She insisted that I should never forget to look at the cautionary hand-written notes on the margin of each page. I was amazed at some of the notes. People who begin a journey in the month of Bhadra never come back! A wedding conducted in Aashwin ends in calamity. Grandma has underlined this for me to bear in mind when setting a wedding date.

Books should not be read but worshipped on Saraswati Puja, the day dedicated to the goddess of learning. I was amazed, because all this juxtaposed against the pasteurised modern day Mombasa and western-type Indian families I had been brought up with. These traditions seemed suspect, yet here in India they are still followed to the letter!

Aunt has taken over the chaperoning from grandma and she always insists on a colourful silvery bindi adorning my forehead -- which you know I had stopped putting on -- and almost weekly pilgrimages to Varanasi and the Ganges Keshav temple where food and flowers are offered to the spirits of ancestors who hover near the banks of the holy and mighty river Ganges until sent on with prayers.

Ever since I was banished to India, my life has been as devastated as any terrain that has been hit by a monsoon. Mostly because I miss you: Latifah and Myra, and more importantly Victor, the love of my life. As you both know, he was my first love but rarely do first loves turn out the way we want them to. But I am not surprised at our separation as nothing in life is permanent as grandma now cautions me.

Aunt lives in Mumbai, and everyone here seems to be waiting for the south-west monsoon rains to hit India. From the geography lessons we had in school I never thought that I would ever witness the sub-continent's annual deluge that brings both sustenance and death to my people.

The heat has become unbearable and everyone's eyes have been glued to the heavens for evidence of rain clouds that would alleviate the high temperatures. Mombasa's humidity cannot even begin to compare with this heat. The temperatures have hit the fifty degree Celsius mark, and people have died from the heat wave and crops have failed. The monsoon is no modern phenomenon. The annual transformation from the searing heat to the chaos of the monsoon has taken place for millennia, and I am a little bit glad to be here in Mumbai to experience this love affair between this natural complexity and my Indian people.

The monsoon first hits from India's southern tip to Mumbai. I had first gone to stay with grandma in Kerala, which is located between the Arabian sea and the Western Ghats, southern India's mountainous spine and a tropical paradise. Trivandrum, the laid-back capital, is only minutes from sandy beaches and palm-fringed paddy fields. When I was offered the choice of living with my elderly aunt in Mumbai, India's financial hub, or India's capital city, New Delhi, with another aunt, I grabbed the chance for Mumbai as I would once again rub shoulders with a pulsating modernity and at least communicate with you guys!

Now in Mumbai we too have been waiting for the monsoon's opening salvo. I watched the clouds, felt the growing humidity and waited for the rain. And girls did it rain! The massive thunderclouds built up each afternoon and sneaked away under the cover of darkness. I kept comparing the monsoon to what has happened to my life. In abridged form; it seems the monsoon is sometimes a fickle mistress. One moment its front is dark, the sheet-like falling wall of water imposing yet vulnerable at the same time. Some days it appears like a powerful beast from one of Vic's favourite Sci-Fi movies, combating every distraction with its natural desire to reform and plough relentlessly north.

Huge waves breached the sea wall and flooded shops and houses at the water's edge. When we are in the bus it looks like we are driving through a car wash. The downpour takes its toll. The street drainages are full and cockroaches and rats scamper around looking for alternative abodes. In an hour's time the streets are waist-deep in raw sewage. Getting off the bus I have to lift my kanchupuram *silk sari up to my thighs. Yes girlfriends, I am back to the basics of wearing saris!*

The hundreds of manual and auto-rickshaws here remind me of the tuk-tuks *in Mombasa and how everyone seems to be looking for one to hire in the rain! Street hawkers sell hot oven-baked* rotis, bondas *and* pakodas, *the chickpea flour patties being fried in the open, which do very well because everyone wants a bite of something hot in the rain. I have never seen so many* Mullahs *in my life. They seem to be everywhere with their long flowing beards and dressed in* kurtas and shalwars, *the long shirts and loose trousers.*

My elderly uncle, aunt's husband, dressed always in traditional Rajasthan *outfits,* dhotis *and* mughal gharb, *goes to perform* Kalaripayattu *every day in the course of the monsoon and I asked him to take me with him. One day he took me with him to a dark cellar lit by candles in the farthest part of the city. I was not allowed to go inside with him but I got to peep through a window. I caught glimpses of grown men in underpants beating each other with rods.*

Kalaripayattu *is said to be the world's oldest martial art form. Much like most of Indian life, the age-old traditions of* Kalaripayattu *owe much to the monsoon. The martial arts master in India says that during the monsoon the body is at its most receptive. Thus boys begin their training on the eighth day* of their eighth monsoon. I am sharing all this with you because I know how much Indian cultures and traditions mesmerise you girls.

Today, I have come to Juhu beach, one of the best in Mumbai to write this letter. As you both very well know, it is hard to be sad by the beach. Even though the sea here always seems to be gray with age and weight, not sunny, captivating and alluring like back home in Mombasa where the gigantic blue and white waves are never still but seem to be inviting you to be on a mysterious cruise voyage with them, the white stretch of Indian sand is still illuminated with turbulent memories of you guys! It is not all gloom though. You girls know that despite my architecture course being cut short, it is still my dream to pursue it to the end. I am unable to talk to my aunt and uncle about there being a possibility of me enrolling for the course at the Mahatma Gandhi University after my wedding.

On the other hand, despite some of the areas being steeped in poverty, I love the Mid-Eastern and Oriental architecture I have encountered here. I have been to the Qutab Minar, an architectural masterpiece in the form of the largest sandstone tower in the world, a great example of Indo-Islamic architecture built in 1193. I have also been to the Red Fort, one of Delhi's most famous tourist attractions. The entire building was built from red stone between 638 and 1648. It was here that the British deposed the great Mughal ruler Bhadur Shah Zafarin in 1857, ending three centuries of Mughal rule.

By the way, my substitute here for the best of Mombasa's Swahili dishes and Indian curries from the Old Town and the Tandoori Grill is Park Balluchi. They serve the best traditional curries and sweetmeats. The Dilli Haat street market is the equivalent of Mombasa's Biashara Street in Mwembe Kuku. Aunt has turned me into an expert at bargaining on silver jewellery and silk fabrics.

Driving in India is complete madness. You drive against traffic chaos, cars, carts, elephants, bicycles, camels, trucks, motorcycles and the inevitable rickshaw. Everyone hoots! Bumper-to-bumper madness. If you want to pass, you hoot. And since everyone is trying to pass, everyone is hooting! Cows and camels mingle in between the vehicles. Motorcycles with four to five people riding side-saddles is a common sight and makes me feel at home.

Jaipur on the other hand is a calm city. They call it the Pink City. It is one of the most beautiful places in modern India. It is peaceful unlike the chaos in Delhi. The Chokhni Dhani Village is another architectural marvel, and of course I was captivated. Aunt knows my obsession with architecture so she indulged me a few times. Another place she took me sightseeing was The City Palace. Although home to the present day Maharaja, some rooms have been opened to the general public.

The Jantar Mantar observatory displays the incredible abilities of medieval Indian astronomy.

I fell in love with the Amer Fort, eleven kilometres outside of Jaipur, an ancient citadel blending ancient Hindi and Islamic architecture. It is a breathtaking and impressive construction made out of white and red sandstone. The walls are covered with murals, frescos and minute mirror work. The outer boundary resembles the Great Wall of China from pictures I have seen.

After sightseeing, aunt treated me to a curry dinner of chicken tikka with garlic naan at the

Sheraton Hotel in Jaipur but it did not rival Veraswamy's, our favourite in Mombasa's Old Town!

You girls would love Mumbai because it is India's powerhouse and the hub of Indian nightlife and fashion. It is the centre of the thriving Bollywood film industry. The skyscrapers and modern architecture captivated and mesmerised me. It is the most populous city in India. It also has the largest slums in the world; the poor descend on it everyday hoping to better their lives – the spectacle reminds me of home and our informal settlements inhabitants.

Mumbai Trident Hotel is another marvel. I loved the Bandra market where I bought some Nag Champra incense.

By the way girls, if I might digress just a little bit and make you laugh. Every time I bite myself accidentally on the inside of my cheeks, inner lips or tongue I remember you three because of the way Kemu and Myra's mama both believed that if you bite yourself while talking or chewing someone somewhere is talking about you – remembering these African myths is so wonderful when one is as lonely as I am. I pray I keep biting myself so that I am reminded that you're thinking of me! The same happens whenever I stumble on my right foot and remember that the old ladies would say it was good luck and bad luck if you stumble on your left. Do you remember the one where, if your right hand itches you will get a fortune, and you should not scratch it because you will be wishing away your fortune? Myra really loved that one! And that if your left hand itches you will lose a fortune and you should scratch it thoroughly to wish away the bad luck? Even when I hear an owl hooting, I take *it as a bad omen. Just like when I dream of a meaty dish and remember that Myra's ma would say that such a dream signifies a death that will occur soon! Oh -- how I miss you girls!*

I have to stop here for now. I will write you more about incredible India some other time. I have a knitting lesson from aunt in an hour's time. She is teaching me how to weave a quilt using old cotton saris, an old Indian tradition. These quilts last for years because they are hand-made. I have cut out four shapes of people, three to represent you three girls and the other a male figure of Victor, so that I shall never forget my friends. Aunt refuses to use shortcuts of modern technologies and insists on hand-woven quilts. She is teaching me to stitch by hand using the stem stitch. She insists on this particular stitch because it doubles up on itself and will never unravel, just the way you guys will never unravel from my heart! I hope that Myra's health has improved. Please take care of her and make sure she eats well balanced meals and takes her ARVs. You both know she is terrible with meds!

Sometimes I think that despite my sadness, I am better off. The other day I met a Jogini. *The Hindi word literally means 'servant of god.' She is a young girl of barely fourteen. I met her by the Tista river when I went with aunt for one of her spiritual sacrifices. The girl told me that she lives in a tiny one room shack in Narayanpet, a rural village in the southern Indian state of Andhra Prudesh. She told me that she became a Jogini when she was only twelve-years-old! Aunt explained to me that* Joginis *are dedicated annually before puberty to the goddess Yellamma, a compassionate smiling deity who protects*

213

villages, wards off natural disasters and cures illness. Once you are dedicated as a Jogini, you have to sleep with any man who wants to sleep *with you! And if one wants to marry you, you have to accept and if you try to refuse you are forcefully married off and have to stay with the man as long as he wants you! Aunt says it is a two-thousand-year-old tradition that cannot just be wished away.* Joginis *are accorded a semi-holy status and worshipped! The girl explained to me that she did not even understand what marriage entailed when she was married off. All she remembers is that her whole body was covered in turmeric and the blood of a sacrificial sheep. A thali, a sort of necklace, was tied around her neck and her fate was sealed because she was the only child of poor parents.*

Girls, though I know that I am better off than the Jogini, *sometimes I think of revenge on my parents for doing this to me. But then I remember that revenge is like the spicy coconut chutney and mango pickles we make in Mombasa to eat with samosas, kebabs and* daal bhajias *which leave explosions of flavour on your tongue; delicious at first and then they leave a stinging aftertaste in your mouth!*

Maybe that is why some say that revenge is a dish best served cold, but I have decided that it is a dish best not served at all, though my family expects me to marry someone I do not know and do not love! How can I detach myself from my past? Even if I were to manage it, I will still agonise over too many bygones.

Together with this letter is another parcel that will be posted to you by my aunt. It contains some saris for all of you. I have chosen the best Regal

Benarasis stiff with Zari thread and sprays of gold flowers on royal red. You will love them. Aunty chaperones and supervises me at every turn and she will read this letter before she posts it to make sure I have not written anything untoward for you to pass on to Vic. She will then seal the envelope herself. She told me to forget about Vic and said that a person comes into your life for a reason, a season or a lifetime. Papaji and mamadi ordered her to make sure I have no access to a cell phone or internet service until I am married to a man of their choice! Grandma says that one cannot marry someone without knowing their root. She said that they are going to find me a nice Indian guy with no stains, whose generation they will investigate to their second generation! When mamadi calls to say hello I can always hear papaji breathing by her side. Grandma says they have prepared a substantial dowry and are seeking a conservative Indian bridegroom for me. I wonder, my friends, is there anything worse than a conservative Indian male? Between me and you, I could not care less what colour, creed, caste or race my husband comes from so long as I am in love. Girls, I am so surprised that it is not only in Kenya that mixed racial relationships are difficult to maintain. I realise that my parents' attitude towards Vic is from their old-school traditional upbringing in India. Here, I have found out that there even exists a silent thumb kind of rule. The upper caste Indian fathers forbid their daughters from marrying certain kinds of people referred to as BMW, which stands for Black, Muslim and White! Can you believe that? They will accept anything but BMW, so you can understand where papaji and mamadi are coming from.

I feel sad that someone is going to come into my life in the form of a husband I do not love when I only have space for Vic in my heart. But when I think of auntie's words, I feel that what I had with Vic was for a season, even though he lives on in my heart. Kemu, you were sort of in love once with Maxi and might understand, but not Myra, who even if love knocked her on the head and gave her a concussion, she would not recognise it unless it came bearing monetary gifts -- just saying this to make you laugh a little bit as I remember how Myra always told us that love is mercurial and sooner or later it disappears! In hindsight, I now feel that she had a point as there seems to be no need in having certainties in life. Aunty says that love can either make someone weaker or stronger. I think that between me and Vic, I am the one who went bankrupt because our love transformed into an injury for me.

Please girls, tell Vic that we did love one another but it is gone now. It was good and true. I thank him for that experience which I will always treasure. But what is love? I have discovered that love is a code we sketched on the sand at our favourite shore at the Pirates and Sea Waves beach pubs in Mombasa. We wrote so many of our dreams and secrets on that fine sand. We would look away for a second and the wind would blow our makeshift letters away so easily. And with the sun peeping over the horizon like those overripe pregnant oranges from South Africa ready to explode forth their juices, the time would pass. The hours would rise and fall like the waves of the Indian Ocean. The patterns would shift, and when we looked again the words we had sketched on the sand barely minutes ago said something else;

our pure love drowned in the shallow waters of the ocean of societal expectations. Even though I did not know it then, my life had also sunk in that ocean of expectations. That is the shifting sands in our lives. For Victor and me, tradition cut away the frayed rope of a hopeless love that tied us together. Now, I am here waiting to get married, dressed in my symbolic peach silk sari like the morning sky, the colour of innocence in India. Were my dearest papaji and mamadi to know that I lost my innocence to Victor months ago, they would burn me alive! I am just so lucky that I am not pregnant. I will sit here a while longer and stare at the eastern sky as if to retrieve my lost innocence. I will try to write to you more often. I miss you. Love always,

Shilpa.

PS: Girls, I forgot to mention that grandma and aunty have insisted that I let my hair, which you remember I had cut to a fashionable bob, grow long, the way it used to be. They say that the sacred books like the Bhagavad Gita, Ramayana, Mahabharata, Kama Sutra and Ananga Ranga among others indicate that short hair is not auspicious. They say that if a woman cuts her hair short then she is cutting off her husband's strength. Duh? Mamadi never told me this!

* * * * *

As I put the letter aside, feeling so depressed and sorry for Shilpa, I did not for the life of me imagine that the next person to disappear from my life would be Latifah, first physically and later on psychologically. Her arranged and forced marriage had resulted in a cute little boy, Osman, now almost four-years-old. I prayed that her son would give her the *amal* and *farah* that she had been longing for.

THE SERENITY PRAYER

...reasonably happy in this life...

...furaha maishani...

The Devil is in the Detail

Something was seriously wrong with Latifah. Where was she? I could sense it in my bones because I had been unable to get in touch with her for several weeks and their house was locked. Finally, one of their neighbours told me that she had been arrested by anti-terrror detectives and taken to Nairobi with her husband and young son, Osman, who was barely four-years-old.

We could not do much except wait for her to show up.

One day, a month later, I heard that she was back. I dragged Myra early one morning even though she was not feeling well so that we could go and see Latifah. Her narration was like a thriller movie or a best-selling novel. We found that she had opened a Swahili dishes restaurant to make ends meet, and as we settled down to help her prepare the days specialty of mutton biryani and chicken pilau, Latifah commenced her story. We lit the large charcoal *jiko* as we listened to her.

"...Girls, I could smell fear the way one would smell imminent rain in tropical Africa. I was in the custody of our own anti-terror detectives from the ATPU[i], American FBI[ii], Britain's MI[iii] and Israel's MOSSAD[iv]. The blindfold was dragged from my face. I opened my eyes and took a minute or so to adjust to the sudden sunshine. Petrified, I almost fainted when I realised that I was atop a skyscraper. Mist and fog, despite the sunshine, floated hazily over our heads. We seemed to be almost twenty storeys up. Goose bumps riddled my arms and I trembled

---

i Anti-Terrorism Police Unit

ii FBI – Federal Bureau of Investigations

iii MI – Military Intelligence

iv MOSSAD – HaMossad leModi'in v'leTafkidim Meyuhadim (Hebrew) -- Institute for Intelligence and Special Operations

when I espied the KICC[i], the Times Tower and the I & M[ii] Bank Tower in the distance.

"The fact then dawned on me that we had been flown from Mombasa to Nairobi, Kemu. The Kenyan detectives stood in the background and it was re-affirmed in my consciousness once again that it was the American, Israelis and Britons who were truly and firmly in charge. But it was what I had suspected these past couple of days.

"I could not feel the bullet lodged in my spine, Myra. The numbness set in three days ago and the surgeons said that in the meantime nothing risky should be tried as long as I was out of danger.

"Anyway, I did not have time to think of myself as I started wondering where they had taken my son, Osman. The last I remembered seeing him was in the aeroplane. We were both blindfolded. The tears seeped out and trickled down my cheeks. I was handcuffed, helpless and at the mercy of these operatives.

"One of the well-built white American's voice brought me back to earth, "welcome to Nairobi Al Qaeda!" He was the one who kept insisting that beautiful Arab women were right now in vogue and were being used by terrorists as suicide bombers. The detective kept staring meaningfully at my slender build and almost white Caucasian skin. He had asked me about my eyes with the oriental tilt at the edges. I told him it was a result of intermarriage between Arab settlers and a Chinese lineage. I was surprised that a lady was among the American detectives. She kept in the background and did not talk. The only giveaway as to her gender was the blond hair peeking from below her service cap and the outline of her bust and slightly feminine figure. She was holding in her hand the black hood and blindfold that had been removed from my head and eyes."

---

i Kenyatta International Conference Centre
ii I & M – Investments & Mortgages

We are familiar with Latifah's kitchen, so together with Myra, though stupefied, we went around the kitchen collecting the ingredients for the chicken pilau. The sack of catering *Mwea Pishori* rice, water, strands of saffron, sticks of cinnamon, vegetable cooking oil, *ghee*, garlic and ginger paste, *garam masala*, onions which we sliced into thin rings, cloves which we crushed absentmindedly, yoghurt, chilli powder, chicken which we cut into quarters, cardamom pods which we crushed, sultanas, blanched almonds, salt, the large fifty kilogramme catering *sufuria*, a large frying pan and large wooden spoons for stirring. Latifah continued talking almost like a robot...

"I had wondered to myself silently why they were insisting on that line of questioning? They had almost killed me with the bullet in my spine. Couldn't they see that I knew nothing of my husband's supposed double life as a terrorist? The operative pointed to the sky and continued, "we know that you believe that Allāh is up there but we need you to also know that we are the FBI and we are on the same level. As you can see, neither Allāh nor Osama bin Laden are here to save you and your son, but I am, so you better start talking to me!"

"I trembled at the blasphemy, Myra. The eerie feeling like I was standing before Jack Bauer in a re-enactment of the American anti-terrorism TV hit thriller 24 permeated my being, and I remembered that Jack Bauer did not take or process your fingerprints but actually separates your fingers from your hands!

"My mind slipped back to the genesis of this nightmare. You girls remember that having been married off by my ba and unable to pursue my dentistry course, I had opened my small beauty salon. I had then started going on frequent business trips to the Middle East and Dubai to source for beauty products for the additional spa I wanted to try out. Intuition to me is the essence of a woman. A couple of trips each month and I realised that I was under surveillance. A Comoran national who is a family friend and a detective attached to Interpol alerted us and confirmed my suspicions. But I still wondered why my family was under surveillance.

"Mombasa, as you girls well know, is considered a narcotics conduit and a hotbed of international terrorism. To the natives and inhabitants of our port city, the FBI, MI and MOSSAD crawling and snooping in every conceivable corner is a common day occurrence. As you well know, my husband Abdel and I, despite whatever conclusions the FBI and other investigative busy bodies come to, are Kenyans born and bred in Mombasa. My husband's brother is a Kenyan citizen and a naturalized Yemeni. I had long suspected that my brother-in-law was either peddling cocaine and heroin for one of the coastal drug barons or smuggling contraband through the old port near the ancient fish market. But then again, on the other hand, everybody has illegal deals going on the side to supplement his or her legal income due to the flagging economy.

"The bustle of the sea-front fish market in the Old Town always makes me feel like I am starring in a Bond movie shot on location in Timbuktu. That day in the sleepy alleys near the old port and ancient fish market, we had just had a thrilling day at the open sea swimming gala held annually at the historic Fort Jesus. The sound of the sea was soothing. The huge Fort looked imposing. Remembering our history lessons in high school, I always imagine how it had looked in the fourteenth century with the Portuguese barricading themselves from invaders."

We washed the rice with warm water until the water was running clear. We heated the light vegetable cooking oil and added the spices. We heated half of the *ghee* in the large saucepan and fried the onions until they turned golden. We added the cinnamon, cloves, and cardamom pods and mixed them together. We added the rice, ginger and garlic paste to the onion and *ghee* mixture and stirred until the rice grains were well coated with *ghee*. We added boiling water and covered the *sufuria* on the *jiko* to come to a boil for thirty minutes.

"Osman, who is going onto four-years-old, is turning into a champion as his tiny legs propelled him across the channel in the freestyle. Later, as the crowds dispersed, Osman, as always fascinated by crowds, followed them along the narrow alleys of the old town. We bought *cassava* crisps powdered with red *masala* chilli powder in the narrow lanes full of people with their wares.

"You know the bustle of Mombasa's old town with a magnetic pulse of its very own. Indian shops selling sweetmeats opposite the Makinnon market, which the locals call Markiti, long corrupted from the word Market. The hawkers make the alleys seem even tinier. The old town is a kaleidoscope of colour with Swahili and Arab women dressed in *bui buis*, Indian women in flowing saris and *bohra* dresses, Giriama women in *lesos* and men in *khanzus*, and ancient buildings now gazetted by the government as national monuments. Most of the houses are relics of the nineteenth century but with tenants who are goldsmiths with thriving businesses mostly serving Swahili and Arab clientele with intricate jewellery. We pushed and shoved and mingled with shoppers buying perfumes, meat, vegetables, spices and thin vermicelli. Women with sewing machines also lined the alleys offering cheap labour for urgent repairs. Rowdy youths with spray cans decorated the walls with graffiti. The *Muezzin* called for evening prayers and the faithful started closing shop hurriedly.

"We trekked through the old buildings on Kibokoni road. The hot noon sun had passed over into the afternoon. Women from the storied houses lowered down baskets, which had money, on ropes to hawkers with handcarts on the street. They shouted to the hawkers in Swahili or in Cutchi (for the Indians) what they wanted to purchase and the hawkers put the vegetables and their change mostly in coins in the baskets. The women pulled the baskets back up. The spectacle amuses curious first-time visitors.

"As usual our sun-baked island smelled of sex, sun, sea and salt. We had neared the oceans furthest beach and water was trickling down some open drainage system into the ocean. Arab men with large brass urns on hot charcoal *jikos* were selling their *kahawa thungu*, the very strong yet sweet and scented coffee in tiny delicate china cups.

"The crowd swelled into what used to be the Old Government Square, now the Treasury Square, the location of several modern banks like Barclays and Standard Chartered, overlooking the old port and harbour. I love my Old Town hood. Despite some buildings looking decrepit, it still remains a place not to miss for holiday seekers because it teems with history.

"As the large crowds dispersed, we parted ways with my husband at the fish market, where he had gone to join his friends for a cup of *kahawa thungu* and a board game of *karam* or *dumna*. As you well know, our house is just around the corner, and I was looking forward to a quiet evening as I contemplated on whether to prepare chicken pilau or mutton biryani for my family. But as fate would have it, it was not to be.

"Girls, I had hardly settled in the kitchen when my son's screams and the sound of splintering wood had me bustling into the living room. My unease tripled when I came upon our broken Lamu carved front door and police in civilian attire in our living room. The only startled exclamation that came to my lips was 'Yaa Allah!' I thought it a normal raid for narcotics but

I shivered and could not put my finger on the source of my disquiet. Then a sort of sixth sense or karma permeated my being. Soon I found out the source of my uneasiness. American FBI operatives, British MI detectives and Israeli MOSSAD had accompanied the Kenyan detectives to our home. 'Bismillah!' I invoked the name of God under my breath to calm myself. I took Osman to his room quickly and asked him to recite the *Kalemah* and names of the *Panjatan*. Despite his stammer and stuttering condition, or in Swahili as we say *kigugumizi* or *ulimi mzito* that is heavy tongue, I knew the recitation would help him calm down. He soon fell asleep. The detectives ordered me to switch off the stereo that was blasting Arabic tunes of 'Habibi' and 'Halwa ya Baba'.

"In eerie re-enactments of American TV thriller 'Threat Matrix,' they questioned me about my husband's connections with Al-Qaeda cells. They showed me copies of multiple passports with Abdel's face on them and asked me why he had different names. I was bewildered because the discrepancies were shocking. The different passports had my husband Abdel's photo on them but with different names. Aliases, the detectives called the different names. Different passport numbers, different dates of birth and different places of birth. And even different places of issuance. Some had 'Passport Control Nairobi' as the source and some had stamped on them, 'Passport Control Mombasa.'

"The cops had misgivings over my father-in-law's vocation as an *Imam*. They said that my husband was a wanted man in the United States of America by the ICE, that is the Bureau of Immigration and Customs Enforcement, over violation of immigration laws from his last visit there that lasted two months a year ago. I was not aware of my husband visiting America. For those two months he had told me that he was meeting some acquaintances in Tanzania in relation to a *madrassa* tutor's vacancy! The FBI had gone on to inform me that they had cause to believe that my husband helped in the training of Al-Qaeda suicide bombers who killed seventeen American sailors on the USS Cole some years back.

"They had then asked me if one Fazul Abdullah was hiding in our house. They said he was East Africa's Al-Qaeda mastermind and a fugitive from justice. The name rang a bell though. Then I remembered a 'Most Wanted' poster I had seen at the central police station when I had gone to get an abstract for my lost National Identity Card and at various shops in the old town. The poster said 'Have You Seen This Man, Fazul Abdullah? He Is A Terror Suspect Most Wanted In Connection With The 1998 Bomb Attack At The US Embassies In Nairobi And Dar-Es-Salaam And The 2001 Bombing Of Paradise Hotel In Kikambala. The Reward For His Arrest Is 325 Million Kenya Shillings.'

"I was so shocked that I ran to the bathroom and threw up. The police, nevertheless, went ahead to turn our home upside down. In a couple of minutes anything breakable was in smithereens. I was shocked and fainted for a couple of minutes. When I came to, they did not believe that I knew nothing. There was pain in my heart at what I saw as a betrayal. Could Abdel be involved in this international vice? Weren't the copies of his fake passports proof enough?"

We heated the remaining *ghee* in a separate frying pan, added the sultanas, almonds and yoghurt, stirring often though stupefied by Latifah's narration. We let the mixture cook until the cardamom pods puffed up and started to split, releasing oil. We watched, like when we were kids, as the melted *ghee* separated slightly from the yogurt. We then added the chicken portions, the *garam masala* and chilli powder to the frying pan and cooked for a further twenty minutes until the chicken was slightly cooked through. Afterwards we poured the mixture into the already cooking rice and mixed thoroughly. After that, we took a large *sinia* and covered the pilau mixture. We heaped burning charcoal on top to create an oven of sorts to let the rice cook slowly. The chicken pilau was done.

"I still insisted that I was only a wife, mother, daughter, sister-in-law and daughter-in-law. My husband, a *madrassa* teacher, his brother a businessman, and his father an *Imam*. The FBI did not care about my convictions. They woke up Osman and handcuffed us both. I know it is against procedure and against the law to handcuff a child – they ignored me when I protested. We sat down to wait for my husband to show up. Abdel came home and stumbled upon the scenario. Obviously he resisted arrest and tried to help us. Instead a bullet ended up being lodged in my spine.

"Later, we came to learn that my brother-in-law and my father-in-law had been alerted to the situation in the house and had boarded a *dhow* at the old port that was bound for Somalia laden with sugar, rice and other exports.

"I wondered silently why they did not rush to the airport or take one of the cargo or cruise ships docked at the main Kenyan port. The FBI operatives answered my unasked query by telling me that my husband, brother-in-law and father-in-law's pictures had already been posted on the internet and were in circulation at all major outlets worldwide, including airports, as possible terror suspects and that they could not possibly get safe passageway on any legal route!

"In later days, I was to ask myself questions in the police holding cells. It was ironic. Somalis are fleeing to Kenya as war refugees and my brother-in-law and father-in-law go into self-exile to Somalia! My husband was not even denying the allegations and yet he was also not telling the detectives that I knew nothing of his subversion. I wondered. Is that how he had been able to finance our annual holidays at five-star beach resorts in Malindi? I remembered the day, a week or so ago, when I stumbled on books about terrorism in his study. When I had asked him about them, he had insisted that he was studying the phenomenon that the threat had become and its impact on Islam as a religion!

"In police custody, I realised that I had to be subservient to Western forces to survive this ordeal for my son's sake. That is if human rights activists petitioned successfully for our release. I knew deep down that we were going to be under surveillance for the rest of our lives.

"On the day of our arrest, I had wondered why our Lamu door hadn't protected us. I remember my late grandfather, who was a *mganga*[i], teaching us that in ancient times all modern doors in Lamu had prominent shining brass studs. The wooden doors were carved with motifs of chains and ropes to chase away djinns and evil spirits. Djinns are believed to prefer dwelling in the sea but they occasionally inhabit houses and human bodies.

"The belief was and still is that the main door being auspicious and the entrance to the main courtyard it protects the house from evil intruders. It is believed that brass studs warn the djinns and evil spirits that they will be pierced and the ropes and chains will tie them up. It is thought that the djinns get so scared they immediately turn away, knowing that this is a protected house. Our Lamu door has the brass studs, chain and rope carvings, but it did not protect us from the FBI, MOSSAD, MI and Kenyan ATPU!

---

i Kiswahili -- Medicineman

"The police initially indicated that they were holding us for irregularities in our immigration documents. All I know is that my husband is a *madrassa* teacher at Masjid Toba Mosque in the Guraya neighbourhood in central Mombasa. He graduated here in Mombasa at the Coast Islamic Institute. He later went for higher studies at Madina University in Saudi Arabia and then on to the African university in Khartoum. Interestingly, Saudi Arabia and Khartoum seem to pose a problem in the minds of the Americans. Otherwise, why would they have my husband's history and itinerary down pat for the last five years or so? I find it strange that the Americans seem to have a problem with jet-setting Muslim intellectuals."

As we waited for the chicken pilau to cook we started to prepare the mutton masala for the mutton biryani. First, we washed the rice and soaked it in warm water for half an hour. We took a little cooking oil, some cumin and saffron, and left those soaking in a little warm water. We cut the mutton into two inch cubes. We then gathered the ingredients for the biryani. A cup of *maziwa mala,* the fermented curdled milk, grated ginger, crushed cloves of garlic, several chopped green chillies, teaspoons of saffron, several large blanched and peeled tomatoes ready for crushing in the blender, several small potatoes, light vegetable cooking oil for deep frying, sticks of cinnamon, cardamom pods, cloves, cumin seeds, several medium-sized onions which we crushed finely in the food processor, coriander, cumin powder, turmeric, *garam masala*, yellow food colouring for portioning the rice, and salt to taste.

"My spine had gone numb and I did not even feel the pain; my thoughts were on my son and the live bullets that were flying all over our home! Neighbours did not come to our aid despite being aware of our predicament and hearing the commotion. They are wary of the

ATPU, FBI, MI and MOSSAD incursions and missions in Mombasa's Old Town, and no one wants to be branded a terror suspect or a sympathiser to the cause! The detectives are even known to enter mosques with their shoes still on, a sacrilege to the Muslim faith. You girls know that along our ten mile strip that is Kenya's coast, once you are branded a *'ghaidi,'* that is Swahili for terrorist, you are a goner and so is peace for your family. No one wants to be associated with *'ughaidi,'* that is terrorism! The Americans believe in *'E Pluribus Unum'* which means 'In God We Trust.' They seem to forget that we also have Allāh in whom we place our trust.

"Deep into the night we were taken to the Mombasa Port Police post to apparently pick up other terror suspects who had also been arrested and locked up. And then we went to a secluded airstrip where we were driven to in a flurry of activities. I was not given a chance to make any telephone calls or let my family members know of what had befallen us. The Americans and Kenyan police did not hide the fact that we were headed towards Mombasa West via the Kibarani Flyover. I, together with my husband and son Osman, were blind-folded and hoods put over our heads. My husband, apart from the handcuffs, was also put in leg irons and shackles.

"Osman was so excited. To him, we were playing a game. He thought we were playing Blind Man's Bluff or Hide and Seek. He called out to me in the darkness saying *'Kibe?'* (Have you hidden yet?). And I replied back in a child-like manner *'Bado!'* (Not yet!).

"His four-year-old mind was even more delighted when we were handcuffed! It seemed we were deemed extremely dangerous, but Osman thought we were playing cops and robbers with real handcuffs and guns on display!

"My husband, being a *madrassa* teacher and his father an *Imam*, attracted all sorts of characters to our home. I remembered the time my father-in-law was taken in for questioning because he was suspected of knowing one of the men believed to be a mastermind behind the 1998 bombings of the American embassies in Nairobi and Dar es Salaam, as well as the Paradise Hotel in Kikambala in the north coast of Mombasa targeting the Israelis. This fact only seemed to have marked us out as possible terror suspects.

"I sensed that there were other 'prisoners' in the plane with us. I could smell the almost palpable fear. I heard the Americans mentioning Baidoa and Mogadishu in Somalia often. I had only heard on prime time news and read of these 'extraordinary secret renditions' of terror suspects in the newspapers. Never had I thought that I would be a victim."

"'Ma! Ma!' my son insistently called me, tugging at my *bui bui* cloak. "*Paukwa*?" he asked innocently in the traditional way, maybe seeking re-assurance that I was still with him as we were blindfolded and handcuffed.

"'*Pakawa!*' I replied inviting him to tell me a story.

"'*Sahani?*' (Plate?)

"'*Ya Mchele!*' (For rice!)

"'*Hapo zamani za kale...*' (Once upon a time...)

"I started remembering how a close friend of my husband, who is an Omani national, was recently ejected out of the country on claims that he was a terrorist. Though I was blindfolded and I knew it was pitch dark, I sensed a flurry of activities around us. I wondered who our pilots were. To the crew of the flight it seemed this was an important government-sanctioned mission to accomplish and it was all in a day's work. Were they from the Kenya army or Kenya police? Didn't they have a conscience or misgivings about transporting blindfolded and firmly handcuffed passengers? In case of an emergency we would be totally helpless. But the FBI believe they are a super power above emergencies! They have forgotten 9/11.

"We were in the custody of American agents and yet they could not tell us what federal law we had violated. I questioned the sovereignty of my country, Kenya, as before. Under my breath, I muttered *'Yaa Allah, Yaa Rahmaan, Yaa Raheem.'* The rhythmic quality of Arabic soothed my soul and the words as usual had a stabilizing effect on my mind.

"As the plane bumped around I remembered what I had been taught about Islam. Uppermost in my mind was that Islam is not meant to be a misogynous religion. But then isn't that what it had become? I thought of my son. The next day we were supposed to go to Haller Park, Mombasa's award winning ecosystem that turned the fairy tale love story of Mzee the tortoise and Owen the hippo into a New York best-selling children's book. It was the school holidays and I had promised him that after visiting the nature trail we would go to Wild Waters, Mombasa's newest and most extravagant amusement park. But it was not to be. Instead, we were on an aeroplane on a secret rendition to an unknown destination! That is what negative US travel advisories about Kenya have done to my family. Despite American marines and the super power's sub-marines keeping vigil off and on Kenyan waters, the fact remains that poverty has contributed to the proliferation of international terrorism.

"The KPA slogan over the years says, 'Gateway to East and Central Africa.' My foot! Only for the select few. The elite. That is why people in coastal Mombasa believe in *juju* and *voodoo* and will go to any length and make nocturnal visits to the most notorious *'wachawis,'* that is witch doctors, They even murder people who stand in their way of gainful employment at the port. It doesn't matter that their offspring and maybe siblings secure employment in the blue collar section as *vibaruas* (casual labourers) to earn three-hundred shillings a day.

"Poverty. An incapacitating penury that makes it possible for bombs assembled in Somalia to be slipped into Kenya under noses of military personnel despite exchange of security intelligence. No matter what CIPK[i] and SUPKEM[ii] say, this impasse and persecution of innocents will continue and Islam will also continue getting an ugly polish when we continue to fight back. This persecution will be worse if the Americans manage to convince our government to grant them permission to set up a naval base on our waters. I do not know about that. Grant is a nebulous term.

"Down to earth again. In the plane the FBI, MI and MOSSAD operatives guffawed as they watched the latest Osama Bin Laden video forwarded to them via the internet. Osama calling for martyrdom. They turned to me and asked me why I named my son Osman. They asked why the name sounds like Osama. They asked if Osama is his God-father. I shivered at the innuendo and insinuation. The Kenyan detectives, as before at our house, remained silent in the background.

"Girls, a lot of crime goes down in Mombasa, but our Kenyan detectives hardly follow that up, intent only on harassing innocent civilians like me and my son. How many mafia-like Italian criminal gangs operate as investors in Malindi and Watamu? Yet they are not on Kenya's most wanted list."

"Most people do not appreciate the fact that international terrorism is as complex as it is hydra-headed. Crude as it is sophisticated. It always mutates but the common denominator remains the trail of

---

i Council of Imams and Preachers of Kenya
ii Supreme Council of Kenya Muslims

devastation and the rivers of innocent blood which flows. Innocent blood of our children. I wonder. Does the Western world think that the blood that runs in our children's veins is blue? Different from their children's? Isn't it all red? Don't our children all feel pain?

"The plane had dipped into another turbulent air pocket and I was startled out of my reverie. The detectives had not bothered to pick up the *Tasbih* prayer beads that had dropped from the pockets of the hand-cuffed prisoners and even stepped on them unfazed with their huge military boots! Regardless, the male prisoners continued chanting the *Tasbih*, albeit softly. Some murmured the *SubhannAllāh* thirty-three times under their breath, and some coherently chanted *AlHamudu Lillah* and *Allāhu Akbar*.

"All of us on the flight were by then thoroughly terrified not knowing exactly where we were headed or what our eventual fate would be! The bulge of my Qur'an in my handbag on my lap had given me a calm re-assurance."

We marinated the mutton in the curdled milk, garlic, ginger, green chillies, half the tomatoes and saffron. Though the marinating should be overnight, one can marinate with a minimum of two hours. We marinated for the almost three hours it took to prepare the chicken pilau, which needed no marinating. We deep-fried the potatoes, which did not have to be cooked through, as long as the surface was sealed. We then boiled the marinated mutton for half an hour until it was tender.

We heated the oil in another large pan, added the cinnamon, cardamom, cloves, cumin seeds, cooked for about ten minutes, until the cloves and cardamom puffed up. We added the onions and fried them until they were a rich golden brown, which is the most important part of preparing the biryani masala. We added the other half of tomatoes, cooked for another ten minutes, added the turmeric, cumin and coriander powders. We then cooked the mutton and potatoes, mixing them to make sure that the meat and potatoes were coated with the tomato and onion sauce. Our mutton biryani masala was done and we left it to cook for another half hour.

"...In Nairobi, after the ominous threats aimed at me atop the skyscraper by the FBI. My son and I were moved from police station to police station so that the media and human rights activists petitioning for our release would not be able to track us down. They never did! Of course the FBI could not take us to the central police station in downtown Nairobi as it was the first place any novice would check!

"We were all over Nairobi. From the dusty Industrial area police post to the Hardy police post which was situated in the leafy affluent Karen suburb. We even had a night's stint at the decrepit Capitol Hill Post in Upper Hill!

"A night later we were off to the JKIA[i] and our extraordinary secret rendition's phase two had begun! Arriving in Mogadishu we could only believe that our fate was nigh, that no action against us was a mistake. We found ourselves being shipped off to two different underground detention facilities in Addis Ababa. One of the American interrogators had several flight passenger manifests that I had travelled on recently. From conversations aboard the plane it emerged that a holidaying Omani prince had recently been mistakenly arrested! I was questioned about the July 2005 London bombings.

"For the life of me I could not understand why they kept going on and on. After being holed up in an unlit underground cell for two days of further questioning without seeing the face of my interrogators, I was flown back to Nairobi. On the second day of my incarceration

---

i Jomo Kenyatta International Airport

in a Nairobi police station, I found myself joined by four US uniformed personnel. They asked me about one AbdulMalik Mohamed. They said he was my husband's friend and that he was wanted in connection with intelligence they had received that he is part of the East African Al-Qaeda cell planning an attack on the IAAF World Cross Country Championships slated for later this month in Mombasa! I had stared at them in shock. For the umpteenth time, didn't they seem to understand that I knew nothing of my husband's other life?

"They asked me if I knew another terrorist on their most wanted list called Harun Fazul. I replied in the negative and I started shivering at the thought of what the police were going to do with me. One Kenyan official tried to absolve himself of any harmful eventuality to me and my son saying, '*Chochote upitiacho kuwa mvumilivu, jaribu kuelewa ya kwamba ni lazima upitie haya. Tuna linda maisha ya wa Kenya.*[i]'

"Which lives? What about my son's? What of the bullet lodged in my spine? Did they care that in any eventuality of an operation to remove it I might end up paralyzed or a vegetable?

"I thought of the Loyalty Pledge we would chant every Monday and Friday morning in our primary school assembly and wondered if these Kenyan detectives ever memorised it. 'I pledge my loyalty to the President and Nation of Kenya. My readiness and duty to defend the flag of our Republic. My life, strength and service in the task of nation building, in the living spirit embodied in our national motto *Harambee* and perpetuated in the Nyayo philosophy of peace, love and unity.' If they did memorise it, how could they accuse me of being a terrorist?

"All this time, for the few days we had been under

---

[i] Kiswahili -- 'Whatever you go through, be strong and understand why you must go through this. We are protecting Kenyan's lives.'

arrest, we had not been given any food or water to drink, apart from my son. Some of the men in the plane had stood all the way, even though they were blindfolded, handcuffed and shackled together by leg irons!

"We filed into dingy underground cells and were given Coca Cola bottles to pee into. To some of the men taking a leak into Fanta bottles seemed to come naturally to them as if they had been here before. It was stinking, dirty and dusty, with rats all over.

"In the meantime, CIPK petitioned the authorities to release my husband. He was not released, but I was set free together with my son, with no explanation and no apologies. A judge ordered the anti-terrorism police to produce the purported terror suspect (my husband) in court, but they ignored his summons. Contempt of court? Your guess is as good as mine girls, but I knew for sure then that as Kenyans we do not have an independent judiciary. We are just mere pawns in a game of chess. I was simply told we had been released with no charge and that it seemed it was a case of mistaken identity. But for how long will this go on?

"I wondered. Mombasa, after all, is regarded as a hotbed of international terrorism. It has been weeks now and my husband has sent word through the 'network' that he and a motley group of fellow terror suspects, including male children, were headed to a dangerous war zone after being detained at several black site detention facilities run by the FBI, MI and MOSSAD.

"They were then flown to Baidoa. My husband later sent word that there were over twenty military personnel with them on the plane with explicit instructions to ensure that my husband's group was transported from Ethiopia to Mogadishu overnight and handed over to the authorities there.

"He later said that at the detention facility he was put on an aluminium seat with electric wires attached to it, tortured and forced to sign a document claiming responsibility for Allāh alone knows which terrorist action.

"I was worried about the war in Somalia and rebels who have moved into the capital city. Some ambassadors at several foreign missions have tried in vain to have my husband released to no avail. I fear for Abdel. After a painful week of waiting in limbo for word on Abdel I realised that I was waiting for Godot! The next I heard was that he had been transferred to the dreaded Guantánamo Bay detention camp in Cuba by the Americans. I have been told that the prison houses suspected terrorists and the 9/11 plotters. US officials say that the Guantánamo prison meets all the standards of humane treatment as laid out in the Geneva Convention. From what we hear from the prison, it is worse than what the Americans turned the Abu Ghraib prison in Iraq into."

Meanwhile, with the mutton masala simmering, we started to cook the biryani rice. We heated oil in a large *sufuria* and poured the oil and cumin mixture on the rice. We added enough boiling hot water to cook the rice. We also poured the saffron and water mixture that had been soaking on the rice and put in a little of the yellow food colouring on portioned sections of the rice. We covered the *sufuria* of rice with a *sinia* heaped with charcoal as with the chicken pilau to create an oven to cook slowly. Our biryani rice was done.

Latifah continued.

"...Deep down, I now understand why some people get gratification out of calling Americans 'Infidels.' They have justification. The Honourable Minister of State of Immigration is busy deporting people left, right and centre without investigating the genesis of the proliferation of terrorism in our region. Neither he nor his counterparts in Internal Security are helpful. The devil is surely in the detail.

"The government spokesman, on the other hand, regarding my predicament said, '*Afadhali tusumbue wachache, lakini tuepuke kulipuliwa tuhakikishe waKenya wako salama*,' (which loosely translated means, "It is better we inconvenience a few, rather than be bombed and lose many Kenyan lives.")

"Are the Americans and Israelis in charge here? Mass secret renditions have become the order of the day. Commissioners from the KNCHR[i] have tried to have my husband released in vain. *MUHURI*, which is Kiswahili and translates to "stamp" in English, is an acronym for "Muslims For Human Rights."

"They have filed a suit in the high court on my behalf. Now, I am being told that we are waiting for the ever smiling Attorney General to file a replying affidavit. I am a beautician and dentist-in-waiting, so when they start talking about the aim of the affidavit being out to prove that the people who have been handed over to Somalia and Ethiopia were actually out of the jurisdiction of the Kenya government, I do not really understand most of these shenanigans.

"Some of our sympathizers just go along and turn a peaceful demo into a fracas by shouting "*Takbir! Takbir!*" which translates to "Praise God" and somehow make matters worse. The UK-based Reprieve and Cage Prisoners were onto our case too.

"Personally, I think that the terrorism bill should not be passed in our parliament. The August House should guard against such harmful bills sneaking their way into parliament and becoming law. Innocents like me will rue the day that such a bill sails through. Other nationals with links with the Islamic Courts Union and who seem to be on the receiving end of America's short stick are Syria, Lebanon, Yemen and Tunisia. Of course, there is no sovereignty in Kenya, otherwise would my husband

---

i Kenya National Commission on Human Rights

have been extradited to the notorious Guantánamo prison by the Americans? If we were sovereign would these secret renditions be taking place? Of course not girls! Aren't Kenyan judges competent? My prayer is that Allāh will never again let me fall into the hands of Kenyan, British, Israeli, American and Ethiopian or Somali agents.

"Kenyan Muslim leaders will continue to be up in arms against what they term as gross mistreatment and blatant abuse of Kenyan Muslim citizens' basic human rights by security agents, but that is as much as they can do. That is, be up in arms against the odds. Our people will continue to be arrested on terrorism charges and then be turned over in so-called renditions to directionless, lawless and sometimes stateless regimes which specialize in torture tactics. It is time we realised that instead of healing, playing religion is now hurting people. Case in point is my husband's Guantánamo prison transfer. The American Ambassador knows nothing of my family but there he was on prime time live television describing my husband, not in so many words, as the devil re-incarnate. He said that my husband is a dangerous man, an international terrorist and a man of dubious nationality. Dubious nationality my foot! We have witnesses who grew up with him in Majengo, the Swahili *mtaa*[i] where he was born and grew up! Even the ageing *mkunga*[ii] who assisted his mother at childbirth is shocked and scandalised at the allegations of dubious nationality!

"Kemu, Myra, I tell you girls, words are binding and can surely never be taken back. Statements reading, 'Pursuant to a common understanding between Kenya and the Transitional Federal Government of Somalia, some of those who have been captured have been...' are

---

i Kiswahili -- Neighbourhood

ii Kiswahili -- midwife

a disgrace. This is especially so when a document is embossed on Kenyan Government paper with our coat of arms are. They give America, Israel and Britain a carte blanche to destroy our lives and kill our children's spirits. Do the FBI, MI and MOSSAD think that your husband wakes up one morning, cheerily smiles at you and says, "you know what honey? I am a terrorist and I bomb Americans and their allies for fun.

"It has now turned into months. My family has been destroyed. I have not heard of what happened to my husband, nor have I heard from my brother-in-law and father-in-law.

"Tears well in my eyes and flow over when I watch CNN and hear of bombings in Central Baghdad, the stronghold of returned-from-exile Iraqi Shiite cleric Moqtada Al-Sadr and in Peshawar in Iran. I flinch when I read of a young girl willing to die a shahīd so that her family can benefit from the payment and thus shed the cloak that is the poverty her family wallows in. I shiver with trepidation when I hear the US military blaming renegade Shiite militia. I cringe with pain when I hear of anything to do with the Gaza Strip. I tremble with indignation when I hear Hamas officials commenting on the same and blaming Israel. I cry at the sounds of ground-to-air missiles and rockets falling into Palestinian homesteads. I am saddened because I am a mother and I feel the pain of the mothers in those regions; innocent civilians who have been labelled collateral damage of a pitilessly selective war not of their making.

"The last news I received was that one most-wanted terror suspect, AbdulMalik, had been finally arrested by Interpol a couple of weeks ago and extradited to America where he had been charged with hijacking and hazarding an aircraft. My husband, still at Guantánamo, was charged with one-hundred-twenty overt acts allegedly committed in furtherance of the September 11 attacks. His lawyers told us that all defendants would be given military and civilian defence lawyers and have the right of appeal. That was it. I have not heard a thing in months.

"Girls, I do not know what hope to offer my son who asks for his father every day. My neighbours are scared of being branded terrorists and they shun me. They have stopped coming to my beauty salon and they do not come to our home to visit with us. I have no income now. That is why I am trying this restaurant business. I am already developing complications with my spine. The bullet is still lodged there and the doctors fear to tamper with its location though a tentative date has been set and a delicate surgery scheduled. Will the American government compensate me for disability and loss of income? Are my son and I going to starve to death? Should I now actively involve myself in terrorism or peddle drugs to survive? I now understand why CNN reports that there is an increase in female suicide bombers.

"My life has become a nightmare. You both know my younger sister Jamila, who works in the front office of a hotel in Dubai. She sent me money last week for the operation that will relieve the stress on my spine. As I went to pick up the money which was in American dollars at a Forex bureau near Fort Jesus, the FBI pounced on me. They wanted to know who had sent me the seven-thousand American dollars and what it was for. They wanted to know why I needed an equivalent of half a million Kenya shillings. They insisted on asking me if the money was from a terrorism contact. I asked them why they did not use Interpol to track the money. I cannot even receive money through Western Union or Money Gram without the police snooping around me!

"That is why I think I will now start using the

Hawala[i] system which is more private. It pains me that the FBI can think that I can have anything to do with murder most foul, and help in causing pain to families and maiming of innocent civilians. Today is the tenth anniversary of that dastardly bomb attack in Nairobi. Kenya's own black and bloody Friday. I remember how Kenyans' lives came to a standstill as we mourned collectively. How we huddled in groups and cried at the hundreds of lives lost. The simultaneous bombs that targeted the American embassies in Nairobi and Dar es Salaam were a probable condemnation of our country's intelligence network. To me, as a mother, these terrorist outrages had no rhyme or reason.

"Yet four years later, the 1998 attack was followed by another that destroyed the Paradise Beach Hotel in Kikambala, North Coast of Mombasa. A hotel which had Israeli connections. More than a dozen Kenyans lost their lives. I shivered when I pictured the cold-blooded simultaneous bomb attacks, with one aiming a missile at a civilian aircraft that had just taken off from Mombasa's Moi International Airport for Israel. Luckily, it missed. It would have been a catastrophic tragedy. The launched missile was found miles away by villagers in Jomvu in Mombasa West. Do you remember how we had watched the prime time news in the evening in shock, horror and awe; wondering how such a missile had been smuggled into Mombasa?

"Girls, I think that travel advisories from the American government notwithstanding, my community must stop knee-jerk reactions whenever a bomb detonates, coming out to protest against affronts on 'our people,' 'our kinsmen,' and 'our religion.' We forget that we are all vulnerable to the evil machinations of these merchants of global terror.

i Arabic -- An informal money transfer service, which may be doing so without licence.

"Girls, the Qur'an has become my constant companion and select verses are ingrained in my heart.

'Allah loves those who turn to Him constantly.'

'Shall I seek for my cherisher other than Allah, when He is the cherisher of all things?'

'Allah does not place a greater burden on a soul than it can bear.'

'After a difficulty, Allah will soon grant relief.'

'Whoever believes in Allah, He guides his heart.'

'This is but a trial, most of them do not understand.'

'Put your trust in Allah, He is sufficient as a trustee.'

"Nowadays, Myra, the only time I get to interact freely with other Muslim women is during Ramadan, when I force myself to share food with them in the evenings during *futar* as we break our fast. As we await the Chief Kadhi to announce that the moon has been sighted, I hurriedly whisper '*Saum Maqbul*' or '*Ramadan Kareem*' and rush off. Of course I miss my husband terribly, especially when I see other husbands and fathers carrying out the ritual of *zakat-ul-fitr* during this holy month. It is given out by the head of the household on behalf of himself, his wife and children. It is unlike *zakah*, the alms for the poor that is carried out at the end of Ramadan. The next time I will interact with other women is during *Eid-ul-fitr* or the *Lailat Al Miraj* where we celebrate the night journey and ascent of Prophet Muhammad, peace be upon him. This is where the revelation of *salat*[i] was given to him when he travelled from Mecca to Jerusalem in a single night on a strange winged creature called Buraq.

"He ascended to Heaven, met earlier prophets and eventually God told him of the duty of Muslims to recite the salat five times a day.

---

[i] Ritual Prayer

"I am so broken, girlfriends, that even as I try to run this restaurant, I hardly get any customers. They are scared of being branded terrorists or sympathisers of subversion. All I know is that despite the shifting sands in the patterns of our lives, and as surely as the devil is in the detail, as women we have this amazing capacity to maintain our equilibrium even in the face of life's brutality and mutability, its incessant and unforeseeable vicissitudes, ever forgiving and implacably cognizant. Though you might not understand entirely what I am going through, I promise to write a book on this experience. I pray that you will get to read it. And please pass my greetings and love to Shilpa if you reply to her letter or if she calls you from India. Inshallâh."

Later, as I left the Old Town with Myra, I could not help but feel that we had lost Latifah psychologically. I was proven right months later when she became withdrawn, disappeared to Lamu and forgot all about pursuing her dentistry course. Now that Shilpa had also been shipped off to India, the only friend I had left was Myra. I prayed to God that He heal her, for she had been sickly of late.

THE SERENITY PRAYER

...and supremely...

...na sana...

From Shifting Sands to Deeper Dimensions

Malindi, Kenya.

Retracing Ernest Hemingway's imaginary footsteps on the pristine white beach, I recall his novel which clinched him the Nobel prize in the fifties, 'The Old Man and the Sea,' a truly intriguing Parisian saga. Though the tale of an old man, a young boy and a big fish is set in the Gulf Stream off the coast of Havana, Hemingway loved escapades in Malindi. Nelson Mandela's words also resound in my head saying, 'There is nothing like returning to a place that remains unchanged, to find the ways in which you yourself have changed.'

But as usual no quote beats my papa's mantra as we grew up warning, '*Kila mtu atabeba msalaba wake.*' He would never come out with it in so many words, as I have told you before, but like talking drums going kabum, kadum, kabum, he would always repeat himself.

How I have changed since the three years that I was on this beach. It was a happier though temporarily out-of-money occasion and not to scatter my friend Myra's ashes to the Indian Ocean's four winds like we have done today. The mundane thought of how few Kenyans have the privilege of strolling on a private beach, which is part turtle nesting conservation, entered my mind.

The onset of the receding harmattan across from the Sahara seemed to be a week ahead of schedule. The ripping sensation of the wind slapped my face as we got out of the speedboat. Myra's mama clutched possessively the now empty urn that had kept her daughter's ashes safe; minute granules that have now been scattered to sea near her girl's favourite dolphin territory to fulfill her last wishes. I remember her lamenting last week that she had carried Myra in her womb for nine months and coincidentally nursed her on her death bed for nine months before she passed on. I had silently thought that this proximity of birth and death was an enigma us mortals could not explain.

Myra, my friend, God has called you. The call of the Almighty is like the call of the sea. No one hears it but the one who has the nature of the sea in her or him. And you did love the ocean. That is why you chose its waters as your final resting place.

My attention was drawn to Myra's German husband as he pointed out that Brad Pitt and Angelina Jolie, Hollywood stars, were on vacation up the beach. Strange how fickle human nature dictates that we suffer collective amnesia in the wake of celebrity tidbits, forgetting the noble fact that Jolie was in Kenya as UN Goodwill Ambassador with Professor Jeffrey Sachs, UN Special Advisor on the Millennium Development Goals. It was a small wonder then that when people come from sojourns along the Kenyan north and south coasts, they asked us mere mortals how the rest of Kenya was doing! Maybe that was why wise Swahili sages said, '*Mombasa raha. Kuingia harusi, kutoka matanga.*[i]'

My memory shifts back a couple of months ago.

It was on one of my visits since Myra's health started failing due to the onset of full-blown AIDS. That day, I had gone alone because Latifah had disappeared to Lamu, or so she said, and Shilpa appeared set to stay on in India. I told Myra that I was a proper Christian now. One who read her Bible daily and practiced Christianity. She told me I was just switching from one flight of fancy, my insanity of writing, to another form of insanity saying, 'is it this new contemporary charismatic Christianity complete with prosperity preachers I am hearing about?

i 'Getting onto Mombasa is fun (like a wedding); leaving is a sad affair (like a funeral).'

252

As I had watched her lying in her large ornate Lamu carved bed, her slight frame wasted, a chill feathered up and down my spine. I remembered how as small girls we would rub chicken droppings on our gums to make our permanent teeth grow faster when we lost our milk teeth, as my Magokoro told us. Goosebumps pushed through my clammy skin as I remembered how on one of our numerous holidays in the Kisii highlands, we were taught how to make strong ropes for tethering the cattle.

Myra had woken up suddenly and our eyes had met and locked fiercely in a time-warp like embrace. We were trying hard not to talk of her impending death yet she was on her deathbed and too far gone. I shivered at my morbid thoughts. Why do people avoid reminiscing when death beckons? I wondered if it was because life expectancy in our country, according to latest development statistics, has been cut down to thirty eight. I longed for my formative years when we were growing up. We would be taken upcountry every holiday and death in our village was very rare. It was a momentous event talked about in whispers. Funerals were stupendous and awesome occasions.

Then came the advent of technology. We were told that technology would enhance our lives. It did not. Instead, death became commonplace. People we knew died every day of cancer, tuberculosis, hypertension, AIDS, cardiac arrests, road accidents, plane accidents, ship accidents, botched hospital operations, thyroid growths and fibroids. For all these deaths, we blamed everything from the materials used to manufacture sanitary towels and tampons, antiperspirants, deodorants to vacuum packed ready-to-eat cured meats, bacon and ham we buy at the super markets. And even witchcraft!

...As I had looked at Myra, our eyes filled with tears. A somber mood engulfed us and we started talking about our youth. An innocence lost and never to be recaptured. We could see ourselves happy-go-lucky in our school bus on an educational tour with Latifah, Shilpa and other students to the game reserve. We were ten years old in the same primary school and belting out our croaky renditions of Pollyanna's song. *'If you're happy and you know it clap your hands, If you're happy and you know it clap your hands, If you're happy and you know it and you really want to show it, If you're happy and you know clap your hands. If you're happy and you know it click your fingers... stamp your feet... shout hurray...say we are...do them all...'*

We became closer friends courtesy of our country's schools admission criteria that saw us selected to the same semi-private cum semi-public high school with a mixture of poor and wealthy students. We remembered how the other student's flashy rides made Myra vow to get herself out of the poverty she had been brought up in.

We were four girlfriends who looked odd because our childhood Indian friend Shilpa always tagged along. Right from nursery school through to primary. First we met as Brownie Cadets in lower primary school, then we moved on to become Girl Guides in upper primary and later Ranger Guides in high school. Only in high school did Myra and I continue together, but Shilpa and Latifah went to different schools, yet all four of us still maintained our tight friendship.

Always at the back of my mind papa's voice whispered *'Kila mtu atabeba msalaba wake,'* echoing subconsciously near like a cross between a watchful African king vulture and an albatross hovering protectively.

We remembered how I talked to Myra, Latifah and Shilpa on my circumcision when I was eleven. FGM. Infibulation. Whatever. This was a rite I barely understood but which changed my life, leaving an indelible mark. How back from that memorable and gruesome December holiday we took mirrors, removed our knickers and squatted so that we could see the difference. I was cut and they weren't.

We reminisced on our youth in high school. On an incident that broke her heart. How one day when she had been expelled for lack of tuition fees, she had locked herself in her boyfriend's apartment to catch up on revision while he was at work, only for the door to be opened by another lady who also had a key. The woman claimed to be her boyfriend's wife from Nairobi with their two children in tow. It became an ugly scene when Myra discovered that her man, who worked at the port and was a centre-forward on the national basketball team, had been playing her.

Our friendship was a journey fraught with mishaps, including my obsession with anything in print.

In high school, hiding novels in between huge chemistry tomes to appease my insatiable thirst was my pastime. Teachers having to call my parents to school to make me promise that I would pay attention in class was the order of the day for me.

We reminisced on how my dad thoroughly spanked me when he found me reading *After 4.30* by David Mailu. He said it was pornography of the highest order!

I recalled sitting in papa's rickety Fiat in the late seventies and hearing my district commissioner dad swearing "Bloody Fucking!" at a jay walker. My seven-year-old mind was immensely fascinated by the 'F' word and wondered what it meant. It was the second time to hear those swear words from papa. I prayed that we would almost run down jay walkers every day, so that I could catch a glimpse of that side of papa which he rarely revealed.

...I was startled out of my reverie and we continued to reminisce.

On parents who never wanted to discuss matters pertaining to sexuality because it was considered *mwiko* (taboo). We were left to our own devices. My daughter, who just turned twelve, and was about to enter teenage-hood -- wow! -- had a guiding and counselling teacher and Sunday school teachers who were no longer conservative but held boot camps on girl-boy talks.

We laughed over our many broken hearts. How I would run to Myra when I lost a boyfriend because I had refused to have sex with him. I remember in her formative years, before her family moved into our hood in Mbaraki, Myra had grown up in a hostile hood and casual sex was no big deal.

As we reminisced, we moved on to escapades, including our first disco, without permission from our folks. How one of our friends was raped, and the next morning cops were at our doorstep because I was the last one seen with her. I was lucky it was the school holidays and my parents were at work. Our friend was traumatised. She could not talk and was hospitalised. Eventually, our parents found out and we got a terrible beating, tongue-lashing and more than a grounding!

As we grew older and came home from a nightclub in the wee hours of the morning, Myra's mama would lament, suck her teeth to show disdain and warn us saying, '*Nyungu ya gana ndimerega*[i].' I had wondered at the time if she was a psychic or trying her hand at being a clairvoyant. Time proved her right though; Myra never did bear any children!

Our minds switched back to how another prominent rich schoolmate had a safe abortion.

It was illegal but there she was at a prominent

---

i Kikuyu proverb -- 'A rotten gourd seed does not germinate;' -- veiled reference that immoral people seldom get offspring.

hospital, the operation done by an equally prominent doctor courtesy of her equally prominent wealthy mother. We learned early that in Kenya, anything goes if you have the prominent quid.

'*Kila mtu atabeba msalaba wake,*' papa's voice would shout in warning, always so subtle yet so powerful, keeping me out of trouble. The paradoxes of our motherland's rich versus poor policy. The haves and have-nots.

Against our advice, a prominently poor friend went to a prominent back street quack for an abortion. The pretender botched the operation using crude methods in spite of the promise that it would be a safe abortion using traditional herbs. Foreign bodies remained in her womb. We did not know it and thought she was lucky to be alive. Weeks later she developed complications and died. Her uterus had "rotted" because she was scared of seeking proper medical attention. I remember her dying and telling us never to undertake such a risk. I remember being so mad because this would not have been the case had her pastor father not stopped talking to her. I am not surprised that she decided to have an abortion so late into her second trimester. I was horrified when I saw that the six-month old foetus was a fully-developed baby boy albeit a bit premature!

I remember how her clergy papa would not even look at her when he found out she was paged or PG as we called it, let alone smile at her and wish her good morning. His Blessed Church of God congregation followed suit. The youth group dissed her behind her back. Fingers pointed and mouths snickered. At least her mama would try to act normal and sometimes cry into the bosoms of the other Mother's Guild members when she needed to express her emotions. Elderly Christian neighbours let our friend know without uttering a word that it was a grievous error she had made and that abortion would have been an easier option, discreetly wiping her 'sin' from the public book of insult and condemnation. She had made a mistake and the consequences, by the time she had the fateful abortion, protruded grotesquely on her once slender figure and weighed three kilos on the outside and a ton on her heart, a load she could hardly bear.

But I asked myself, how had the condemning tongues helped her in the end? Her pregnancy was too advanced and she would have been better off having the baby. Now she was dead and her pastor papa had lost a daughter and grandchild. I just wished that she could have gone in earlier for the operation but second-guessing was not going to help us. She was gone and we let her soul rest in peace.

As I talked to Myra we remembered another friend who died immediately after high school. Her death was as a result of wanting to get married to her high school sweetheart. Their parents refused to bless their relationship over a long-standing family feud coupled with dynamics of coming from different ethnic backgrounds -- something I later went through with my papa concerning my relationship with Maxi. She roasted herself like a bonfire by pouring kerosene on her body from head to toe and lighting the matchstick. She died a week later -- an agonizingly painful demise. On her deathbed she held the hands of both mothers and told them that she had died to reconcile them, and that the two families should henceforth stop the grudges.

My mama had sucked her teeth in sadness at the tragedy and told us to be strong saying, '*chinguru chia abanto, nchogu egwatia mbara.*[i]'

Sisters always stick together. We remembered how through our teen years my parents were always fighting,

---

i Kisii proverb -- 'The strength of human beings [together] is like an elephant splitting wood.'

and I would sometimes seek solace and refuge at Myra's home. We went to college together and through more drama.

Another sister's fiancé, threatened with bankruptcy, committed suicide by drowning himself. He drove his car off the ferry ramp at the Likoni channel and into the Indian Ocean. We had to be there for her. The shock caused her to miscarry.

Myra, Shilpa, Latifah and I were always together though, even on our subsequent entry into the job market and encounters with amorous bosses. Enter the HIV and AIDS era and another sister's husband died. He never told her he had been diagnosed with HIV. He hid his status. Callous doctors revealed it to her a couple of days after the funeral; early 1990s style with no counselling sessions. She collapsed and died from the resultant shock. Their two children suffered an unceremonious paradigm shift from chauffeurs and exclusive private schools, to being shipped off to live with grandparents and assimilated into rural public schools. They had no savings; hence no food. Their father had squandered the family wealth treating himself well in disregard of family needs and the future.

We reminisced on how excited Myra, Shilpa and Latifah were when I was pregnant with my baby Nehema. The three ladies had run up and down, whenever they spent the day with me, pandering to my demands of insatiable cravings for fried and sometimes roasted cashew nuts, or the House of Manji chocolate cookies; and the chocolate chip cookies from Paul's Cookie Man in Eldoret, which were sometimes out of stock in Mombasa supermarkets! One would be forgiven to think that it was Myra expecting a baby, yet she had decided not to have children. She could not risk exposing her baby to the HIV virus because by then there was no Nevirapine.

We remembered how Myra still spent her holidays with me and Nehema when she was on a break from the university and would help me to teach her how to read and write. How she was there for me when I broke up with Nehema's father. How Myra constantly castigated me, whenever I was broke, for sitting on my ATM[i], and not using the Barclays Bank[ii], as she fondly referred to using one's sex appeal to get favours.

Kabum, kadum, kabum, papa's voice would cry. '*Kila mtu atabeba msalaba wake.*'

As we reminisced we remembered how Myra once told me that before she met her husband, she had been using her Barclays Bank efficiently and had seen so many penises that were she to attach them end to end, she would be able to supply piped water to her father thousands of miles away at their village in the highlands. But finally it was this one German man that brought her the elusive happiness, inclusive of a Lamborghini in the driveway of her own ten-bedroom beach mansion.

"...Now here we are my friend Myra. It is almost twenty years since you tested HIV positive; proof of what the power of love, a positive outlook on life, good nutrition, healthy eating habits and a cocktail of anti-retrovirals can do."

As we reminisced I suddenly blurted, "look where your Barclays Bank has landed you Myra!"

We laughed so hard until tears rolled down our cheeks and you started coughing uncontrollably in pain. Your mama, smelling of incense and carrying a tray of cups with the aroma of fresh *kahawa thungu*

---

i Automated Teller Machine -- euphemism for vagina.

ii No offence meant to Barclays Bank -- young ladies use it as a code to refer to wealth and prestige.

with whiffs of crushed *mdalasini*[i], and *iliki*[ii], just the way you liked it, had come in to check on you. She could not understand how we could be laughing so hard yet you were dying. I had said, 'Ma, we're talking about certain Barclays Banks and ATMs. You would not understand!'

As we burst out laughing more uproariously she went out puzzled, shaking her head but with a smile on her lips and a look in her eyes that seemed to say, 'At least you're making her laugh.'

At that moment, instead of dwelling on death I had picked up Myra's memory box from her bedside drawer. She had decided that because she did not have children she did not want to leave a memory book behind. Instead, she would have a memory box with our childhood mementoes that she would bequeath me once she passed on. We had both eagerly dipped our fingers into the soapstone box and dug out her old photo album. We flipped through faded photos of our childhood. The 1980s black and white photos. Whoever said that 'a picture is worth a thousand words' was spot on. In one almost decaying photo we were playing Gogo-Simo! And, shouting *'Tapo!'* Is that us with wobbly sisal ropes trying so hard to skip Double Dutch when we could not afford proper skipping ropes? There we were playing hop, skip and jump. And another playing *Kati* and *Mama na Baba* with Shilpa. Her long hair in silky ponytails dangling all the way down her back to her buttocks, looking odd as the only Indian girl in our all-African neighbourhood. We reminisced on how once Shilpa's long silky hair had to be shaved because it had been infested by lice when we were in the fourth grade!

In one nursery school photo we were performing 'Skip to my Lou.' In Myra's bedroom I could almost hear the children's chants echoing,

---

i Kiswahili -- Cardamom
ii Cinnamon

'I lost my partner what shall I do? I lost my partner what shall I do? I lost my partner what shall I do? Skip to my lou my darling.'

In another photo we were splashing about in the rain and I could tell we were singing, 'Rain, rain go away come again another day, little children want to play.'

There was Latifah with her curly Arabic hair bunched atop her head like a halo. The thought of angelic halos suddenly reminded me that what Latifah has gone through lately, in the hands of anti-terror detectives, was not saintly at all!

Unbelievable what photos preserve! God should have let us be and immortalised our now grown-up bones, just as my papa had done when he snapped the lens of his camera and captured us on Polaroid for posterity. There we were as precocious teens with tiny yet gangly limbs. Huge, dimpled and infectious grins, oblivious of tomorrow and how we would be treated with contempt and opprobrium. Each photo was like a ticket to the past; each revealing a moment, not only the faces, but the furniture and any other object in the background. Like the framed words above the wall adjacent the dining table. Gold lettering on a red background. Stern and forbidding like papa's face across the table. 'Christ Is The Head Of This House. The Silent Listener To Every Conversation. The Unseen Guest At Every Meal.' The photo snapped by papa when Shilpa had joined us for dinner once. Her eyes were animatedly staring at the framed words, not comprehending but bewildered. As bewildered as I had been when I went to their house for the first time and saw her greet her papaji by joining her hands together and bowing in a brief namaskar of respect.

Another childhood chant leapt to life from another photo '...in and out the bamboo forest, in and out the bamboo forest, in and out the bamboo forest you are my partner. Tapi, tapi, tapi on my shoulders, tapi, tapi, tapi on my shoulders, tapi, tapi, tapi on my shoulders, you are my partner...' I glanced at another photo. I remembered that ancient mvule bookshelf from where I had borrowed papa's first edition books. Jomo Kenyatta's *Facing Mount Kenya* and *Suffering Without Bitterness*, Jaramogi Oginga Odinga's *Not yet Uhuru*, Ngugi's *Secret Lives*, Ochieng and Karimi's *The Kenyatta Succession* and even Muammar Gaddafi's *The Green Book*. I remembered with nostalgia those Akamba carvings of the big five -- the lion, hippo, elephant, leopard and buffalo.

...I continued staring at the photos. I knew that even though Myra was here with me, the photos could not be re-enacted. They could not be reposed and snapped again. Not without reaching through time. Everything was present but untouchable. This melancholy stayed with me even as we placed the photos back into her memory box. I loved being held in the grip of this melancholy, but could not figure out why these photos were so powerful beyond their obviously nostalgic tug.

"Kemu, we were so giggly then, but like the shifting sands of the beach we love so much, our lives are about to change again." Myra had interjected my thoughts with a probing voice waiting for an answer.

"Umm. Yeah Myra. It certainly looks like we were having lots of fun!" I had replied, evading her larger invitation to discuss her imminent death. As we had shut the memory box, I had cringed at the disconnection from the events in the photos to the present and my sick girlfriend. I suddenly knew why the photos had such a powerful effect on me. I wanted to be there again. To be in the photographs. To be in the past. A child with no cares or responsibilities. In love with my girlfriends.

To be in a time warp. Before the 'other woman' came into my family's fold. I wanted papa to be a young DC again reserving us seats near the presidential podium on national festivities at the stadium, or hoisting five-year-old me onto his shoulders at the Mama Ngina drive sea front. I wanted mama to be a well-positioned senior state counsel and not bitter with papa's extra-marital affairs. I wanted Myra to be healthy again. I wanted Shilpa and Latifah to be here with us. For us to be a team again – a tight sisterhood.

Instead of voicing my thoughts out aloud I had stood up and slipped into the music system's CD player Jay-Z and Mr. Hudson's current hit song, 'Young Forever.' The song always brings tears to my eyes because it is so emotional.

As we had finished reminiscing, I had stared at Myra's body riddled with fading scars and falling scabs caused by Karposi Sarcoma sores as a result of HIV and full-blown AIDS, and I knew that just like the shifting sands in our lives, the last grains of sand in her hourglass were telling me that the sunset on her colourful life had finally arrived.

Inevitably though, we read and re-read Shilpa's letter to us. Pain has changed our lives. Shilpa left us for India and we remained the three of us. And then we lost Latifah psychologically to alleged terrorism and she has now become a recluse. And Shilpa does not even know about Latifah's troubles. Now it is the two of us. Me and you Myra, and now you are about to leave me. And I will be left all alone. There will be no more cooking of mutton biryani served with yoghurt and lemon pickle or chicken pilau served with *kachumbari*. No more visits to the Tandoori Grill, Club Rio, Bella Vista or Yul's Aquadrome for extreme water sports.

A week later, you were dead Myra. Along with your magnanimous heart, and inherent generosity. *Life slipping away from someone you love is so incomprehensible.* Death is such a baffling phenomenon and the swiftness, boldness and permanence of yours had served to create a sense of trepidation in my heart. I remember many years ago at paternal Sokoro's wake, Magokoro told the mourners that at one time or severally in our lives, death touches us and everything begins to make sense. And that death with its finality is painful to accept and to deal with. Magokoro was so wise.

...Myra my friend, now I stare at the setting dusk. The blue glittering sea is a peaceful embrace draping me like one of Shilpa's soft silk emerald saris. The setting sun with its golden glance thrown my way and angled hard on the receding waves like the start of the evening fire on Magokoro's hearth. I miss you already as I marvel at the beauty of the sunset. I stand alone hushed by the flaming sky as the sun moves towards the western horizon, seeming to hesitate a moment the glowing orb slipping out of sight, leaving the sky ablaze with brilliant shades of orange, fuchsia and red. It seems like my frustrations of the day of losing and letting you go to sea are silenced by the majestic yet soothing embrace of this glorious sunset – a befitting farewell to you. I'm overwhelmed by the milestones we've covered. Remember our five cartwheels and five somersaults, an almost religious routine on the beach at Tudor Creek and Madubaa years ago? It was part of our exercise regimen. No expensive gymnasiums with imported treadmills for us as we could not afford them. It is sad that now one cannot go to public beaches anymore for some quiet time. The minute you sit down with a book, beach-boys hit on you. It is even worse for our young ones. I cannot let my Nehema go to the easy access ones, like Pirates or Jomo Kenyatta, with her friends without fear of molestation, or hard drugs like cocaine and heroin being introduced to the girls.

It is sunset and the sun has finally slid into the horizon. I am alone on the beach. The others have gone to the mansion and left me alone to my grief. I sit down on the wet sand and start sobbing. I howl until there are no more tears left. I have not cried so much in many years. I never do seem to have time to cry.

I recall Nehema's voice a few days ago saying plaintively, 'mummy, has aunt Myra died and gone to Jesus in Heaven? Won't we be going to her beach house no more?'

I cannot believe you are gone. Not you, Myra. I still love you and need you so much, even if I am thirty-secret years young, as we put it. You were almost the last of my remaining few friends. No wonder I have been experiencing what my doctor calls panic attacks, but to me it is a sudden overwhelming and overpowering feeling of anxiety, tension headaches, heart palpitations and night sweats. Irregular heartbeats and suffocation engulfs me at night, the ceiling seems to swoop down hard on my chest. I pray I do not go into cardiac arrest!

I thank God for grandma though, who never relied on conventional medicine, but introduced us to alternative cures like herbs that added more years to your life. And *muarubaini* mixed with basil and eucalyptus. Many of our girlfriends have died in rapid succession -- Celine, Lorna, Nduku, Maria, Lorraine, Achieng.

When will we be honest about AIDS? When will we stop reading in obituaries about 'cancer' and 'long illnesses bravely borne'? When will some parents from my village stop blaming *ebibiriria*[i] for every HIV infection?

You acquired all the wealth you accumulated because you had learned to forget the means and enjoy the ends, but you left it behind to your relatives because you did not have children. I give your people credit though, for

---

i Kisii -- "Evil eyes" believed to bewitch others.

not insisting on their full traditional burial rites, maybe because you left them well provided for; bungalows, high-rise apartments and other investments. Even when your maternal *guka* insisted that he be given a banana stem to signify your body, which he said your mama was throwing away to evil spirits at sea when he heard of your cremation, an event he still cannot comprehend, your mama stood her ground to protect your wishes. Your maternal *cucu*, whom whenever we saw over the holidays seemed to always be thinking of you -- weaving her loving wishes for your afterlife into her tapestry as she weaved her ciondo baskets – was also baffled.

It was as if she knew your escapades which we narrated to her would soon cut your life short.

By stating in your final will and testament that you wished to be cremated and your ashes scattered at sea, you hurled back at your paternal relatives their cruel words which they had uttered when they found out your HIV status. You made them eat humble pie, wishing they'd never spoken those words, those years back. Whoever said that 'words can never be taken back' was dead right -- pardon the pun.

I find myself thinking that ashes are so light and just as it is said that dead men tell no tales, neither will your light ashes. They will keep your secret of your loneliness despite being rich because you craved for children – your ashes will not be there like a grave and an epitaph which would have served as a constant reminder to the guilt of your relatives of not being there for you.

Weirdly, albeit sadly, I remember that among the seventeen curses proclaimed by Taban Lo Liyong is one reserved for misfits, a short life and death without funeral rites. Today, as your papa's *Meru* patriarchal society, who were used to confining you to the periphery of the community and denying you a social identity, watched your German husband let go your ashes, their words, '*muka gati kwao*[i]' and '*muka gati mwiriga*[ii]' must have come back to haunt them. I remember how years back, some had even added shamelessly 'especially if she has AIDS.'

Yet here they were today, scattering their daughter to the winds instead of laying her to rest with her ancestors back at the village. It is a worthwhile lesson for my Gusii people who tell women '*Mokungu tabwati sobo*[iii]'

I saw unveiled relief in their eyes as your secret-carrying ashes, that could not tell any tales, floated away and quickly disappeared as your mama whispered farewell '*Arokoma kuuraga*[iv].'

I tried to understand your wish for cremation. I would have preferred a grave where I could visit you with your favourite blooms of Lily of the Valley. I went to Google and Wikipedia to try and demystify the origins of cremation.

> *"The word 'cremation' comes from the Latin word 'cremo,' which means 'to burn,' particularly the burning of the dead. Cremation was the norm with ancient Greeks and Romans. They believed in immortality of the soul and saw no reason to give special attention to the body, which they looked at as a prison. Cremation is the process where the body is incinerated by intense heat and flame. All substances are consumed and vaporised except bone fragments and any non-combustible materials, which usually weigh approximately two to four kilogrammes. The bone fragments are pulverised after cooling into finely*

---

i Meru proverb -- 'A woman has no permanent abode,' -- used in context of subjugation of women.

ii Meru proverb -- 'A woman has no clan,' -- used in context of subjugation of women.

iii Kisii proverb -- 'A woman has no home," -- used in context of subjugation of women.

iv Kikuyu expression -- 'May you sleep well where it rains,'- blessing/ Godspeed.

ground granules. The remains or 'cremains' as some prefer to call them, are commonly known as ashes."

It seemed to me a cold (pardon the pun, Myra) impersonal way to send off a loved one.

A few days after my research there I was, tears stinging my eyes as I watched you being laid on the pyre. Followed by your cremation and then smoke billowing from the chimney of the crematorium.

At the funeral home a few days earlier, I remember finding it hard to believe you were dead as I lovingly un-plaited your now unkempt human hair weave which you'd lately been using to cover your thinning, once healthy, dreadlocks. For days, as you lay reposed at the funeral home, every evening I came to 'visit' you to ensure that the mortuary attendants were preserving your body well, before attending your *matanga*[i] at your parents' home. I would look at you and remember Unoka's (Okwonkwo's father in Chinua Achebe's 'Things Fall Apart') words: 'Whenever I see the mouth of a dead man, it reminds me of the folly of not eating well while one is alive.' Later I would have this incorrigible nightmare that, like Sophie Mol in Arundhati Roy's *The God of Small Things*, you would suddenly turn and flip into a couple of our beach cartwheels and come back to us alive. But it was not to be.

I remembered too how a day earlier at your wake, I had thought how uniquely technology had changed our world. People used to travel from abroad to attend their relative's funerals. This is no longer the case as people now use technology to convey their condolences. Take the example of Njeri, your cousin who lives in America. She called via her cell phone to express her sorrow. At your wake your mama's cell phone was propped near the microphone when Njeri called to talk to the mourners.

We heard her wailing and lamenting your passing, all the way across the Atlantic! It nowadays seems easier

i Kiswahili -- wake/funeral vigil ceremony.

for relatives abroad to lament down the cell phone wires and then swiftly Pay Pal, Money Gram or Western Union the money they would have used for an air ticket to the departed soul's family to help in burial arrangements. It is not the same as the warmth of a person travelling physically to come and offer condolences. Your *cucu* had looked on in horror and utmost condemnation at the enfolding spectacle when the MC had propped your mama's cell phone near the speaker, for Njeri to lament from Boston and then later announced how much Njeri had Western-Unioned. Your *guka* had disgustingly termed the modernity an abomination.

On the same day, I found it scary when I heard some young ladies discuss how nowadays, jobless and desperate people buy or borrow newspapers just to have a look at the obituary and find out who has died. They religiously go through the 'National Album' as they call the obituaries and note where the deceased was working and if it was a good position in the firm. They then take, post or email their applications for the vacant posts! This must be as a result of the sickening state of our economy. The ladies went on discussing how some desperate women look for wives who have died. If the caption in the obituary suggests or hints at a wealthy family, maybe by the firms the children were working for, or if the widower is owner of a brand company or even the deceased herself, they note the deceased husband's names and then go after the rich 'widower.' They said that such women are called gold diggers. I wondered, duh? What of the young men who behaved in the same way and searched the 'Album', and then went for the rich bereft 'widows' -- these men were the so-called gigolos of society, I reminded them.

* * * * *

In the enfolding darkness, the encroaching African dusk creeps in by surprise as usual like a huge dark blanket. As I stand up a gigantic wave slaps into my slight frame and sweeps me off my feet. Dazed, I land on the hard wet sand with a thud. A pinch on my bottom from a scurrying crab and a sting on my big toe from a sea urchin brings me abruptly back to my senses. I am soaked from head to toe and my bare-back halter top and flimsy string shorts are no help against the chill. A piece of red floating a few meters away catches my eye. It is Milan Kundera's novel *Identity*, which I had been reading in the speed boat. Strangely, I think of the 'I' in *Identity* as my persona. My alter ego floating away with your ashes. My split personality lost at sea. My writing comes to mind. My salvation. My saving grace.

My friend, the scars on our bodies are heliographs of pain, so that humanity and mankind, blind as they all come, can read us like Braille. I will never forget your encouragement, even as you studied hard to graduate as a marine biologist. Telling me to keep writing even if I am never published. I wish I could have embers of a bonfire to signify mourning just like my people in the highlands of Kisii do. I would keep vigil beside your *ekeroba* for weeks but as always you have chosen the unconventional, and decided your resting place should be the waters off Sardinia Two.

That wondrous isle near where your husband bought you your beach mansion as a fifth wedding anniversary gift, the millions of shillings he spent seeming to him like a few coins. You loved that isle which enhances its mystery by remaining visible for eight hours in the daytime during low tide and becoming completely submerged during the high tide. Few locals know of its existence. It is not marked on the Kenyan map due to its minuscule size. I remember our mud baths with high sulphur content from the mud of the isle believed to clear blemishes. Italian tourists who were said to have taken an intense interest in the small spit of sand about three decades ago named it Sardinia Two after the Italian island of the same name.

Now, I have to accept that you are gone and move on with life, but I cannot stop missing you.

Everywhere I go I feel your ethereal presence. We were practically co-joined at the hip like Siamese twins! Sometimes I would act like the Pope of Fools in Victor Hugo's *Hunchback of Notre Dame*, yet like the inimitable Melchizedek in Paul Coelho's *The Alchemist*, you, Myra, always knew with your subtle innuendoes how to nudge me gently in the direction of my dreams, and like the shepherd boy Santiago, I have listened to all sorts of voices where my writing is concerned. If I were to read out each entry from my diary of scars etched on my body, it would be like reading an almanac of nightmares. I cannot let all be lost in the ashes of my dreams. Before you died you reminded me that the greatest enemy to my dreams is Kemunto, that is myself. I am the most lethal weapon that can be used against my dreams. I must conquer my fears first before conquering my dreams. '*Kila mtu atabeba msalaba wake.*' Indeed papa's warning has proven to be prophetic.

My friend. This is an ode to you.

I lower my head in pain. In your obituary in the local newspapers, the caption above your smiling, beautiful face read 'celebrating a life well lived.' I will miss you. I thought we would grow old together but it was not meant to be. I stroll towards the mansion as my mind slips back three years ago to how happy and carefree you were, because despite being HIV positive you had found someone to love you.

We have lost many friends and most of their deaths have had to do with poverty. An incapacitating drudgery that makes one yearn for more than they have. And that yearning is not a sin, or is it? We share a history. Just the way history can be spelled without the letter 'o' and still be pronounceable – histry. The letter 'o' is a big zero in our histories. A cervical circle of nothingness and a shared history of continued want.

You have come a long way, Myra. From tending your paternal *guka's miraa*[i] bushes in Meru or washing coffee beans at your maternal *cucu's* plantations and picking tea leaves as we chanted 'two leaves and a bud,' to remind ourselves how the tea leaves were supposed to be carefully picked, with two mature leaves and a bud. To owning beach apartment blocks and four-wheel drive vehicles and finally succumbing to your death.

I think back six years. Indeed, we all have our personal crosses to bear.

Six years ago...

I strolled on the deserted beach, my shadow a solitary silhouette. Gazing at the sun shrouded by dark clouds, I willed my fortitude and serenity to control my fears and frustrations. An indecent proposal had come my way. I wondered if it would turn out to be another fiasco so soon after the casino job that had almost landed me in jail. But how could I be thinking of that proposition?

'*Kila mtu atabeba msalaba wake*' my papa's voice had echoed in my mind.

Cross-legged, I sat down on the beach and scooped the fine sand, letting it slip through my fingers to be blown away by the wind. I loved it there. A secret rendezvous for my thoughts when looking for an escape route from my immediate troubles.

Oh Myra! How could you tempt me in that way, with such a proposition? I remembered our many shared

---

i Khat

holidays, when I could be allowed to join you in Kiambu, the Kikuyu highlands. Always just the two of us because Shilpa and Latifah's parents would never allow their children to spend holidays in the African highlands.

You seemed to favour holidays at your mother's maternal home than in Meru, your papa's paternal one.

I sighed again as my mind slipped back to the present and my reminiscing.

My daughter was almost through kindergarten. I needed a substantial amount of money to cover tuition and admission fees for first grade at primary school. Some people said that I had too much pride. I could not bring myself to borrow money.

The cold water seeping into my jeans jerked me back to reality. The tide was coming in.

I stood up when I heard the barking of dogs. Myra had sent them to look for me. I had told her that I wanted to be back in Mombasa by ten and it must be almost nine now. The friendly Dobermans rushed at me. I bent down to pat Bibi and Bwana's heads. It was my last day here. Soon, I was in deep meditation reflecting on my host's proposal. You probably think I am digressing. Let me take you back to how it all began.

Last week on Wednesday, 12.30 p.m.

It was a humid July morning and fumes of heat were rising from the hot tarmac of the road. Walking along the asphalt of the pavement deep in thought, my subconscious registered that a car seemed to be following me. You know what I mean, that deep hum of SUVs that convey how expensive they are by the near-silence of the engine.

Whoever was behind the wheel hooted several times. I stopped when I realised that the driver was trying to attract my attention. The metallic gray Lexus glided to a stop.

The tinted window on the passenger side whirred down automatically. I stooped to see who was driving. I managed to inaudibly say, 'hi Myra,' as I looked at my friend.

I had not seen her since January and we were then past mid-year.

She opened the door for me. She explained that she had been trying to get my attention all the way from the CBD but it had been difficult in the lunch-hour traffic.

She had managed to end her pursuit and caught up with me on Nyerere Avenue. She ended her explanation with expletives and exasperatedly saying, "Where the hell are you walking to, anyway?"

I replied that I was walking to Mama Ngina drive. It had become my haven in turbulent times.

I would go there to meditate, gazing at cruise and cargo ships entering Kenyan waters to drop anchor and dock as others lifted anchor, the passenger and vehicle ferries moving to and from the Likoni channel, and the occasional speed boats, ski-jets, gliders and sail boats.

Myra sensed that something was not right. Maybe it was a look in my eyes.

"Hey girl. What's wrong? Is Nehema ok?" she asked after my now six-year-old daughter.

"First of all, come here and give me some love!" she exclaimed, giving me a tight hug. We started talking nineteen to the dozen. We had changed jobs and lost contact. She asked if she could buy me lunch at the Nyali Beach Hotel. I told her the North Coast was too far away as I only had an hour to spare, and suggested Dorman's, the popular coffee outlet in town. She turned and headed downtown.

We were soon having our meal as I explained the financial constraints I was facing.

Since leaving the hotel industry, and following my parents misfortunes following the 1997 clashes in Likoni and my short stint at the bank, my current salary at another temp job hardly met basic needs or provided enough to pay for my daughter's tuition fees. I asked what she had been up to. I remembered that she had quit her last job and literally disappeared off the face of the earth. She told me that she was now residing in Malindi and was in business.

A warning bell went off in my head when she said that the wheels she was driving were hers, fully paid for. *'Kila mtu atabeba msalaba wake.'* I remembered papa's words. I asked her what sort of business could pay for such a car in just eight months.

"Oh. This and that," she vaguely replied.

I insisted on an explanation because I knew before she quit her last job she hadn't saved a single Kenyan cent!

"I have linked up with some foreign investors and we have cottages we rent to tourists. Sort of holiday homes. You know what I mean."

The warning bell in my head turned to a siren. Her tone of voice was not convincing and had a fake ring to it.

"No Myra, I do not know what you mean!' I said emphatically. "Where did you get your share of the capital?"

I was skeptical about her explanation and I told her so to her face. We started laughing. We could share anything. The last time we had been together we had been snorkelling and frolicking with dolphins off Wasini Island, famous for two twin Islands, *Mpunguti wa juu*[i] and *Mpunguti wa chini*[ii] and Kisite Marine Park, a renowned reserve of dolphin territory. I remember disembarking from our favourite dhow Mv Taisiri and wading in knee-deep water to reach the shore. Another

---

   i Swahili – Upper Islet
   ii Swahili – Lower Islet

time it had been the Mv Ashraf. We had played with the groups of females with their calves. The hump back and spotted dolphins looked awesome as they kissed each other on their snouts and leapt into the air in synchronised pairs. They would swim close, almost touching us, and glide under and away in a jesting manner, only to return again and again. Our guide told us that the dolphins liked the protected reef with unique corals which rivalled Australia's Great Barrier. The mammals normally swam up the Shimoni channel around the eastern edge of the Island. That day there were more than ten, tame and absolutely fascinating.

Few people know that Wasini, an awesome archipelago, was once loved by the Chinese and bombed by the Germans. Arab conquerors had called the island Wasini because of the Chinese traders who had frequented it for ivory and mangrove poles in exchange for porcelain and cloth.

History has it that Sheikh Mohamed Issa bin El-Mandry built the island's first water tank in 1885, but the Germans, who had colonized what is now Tanzania, had bombed the water tank during the First World War.

Such a rich history. There is also a one-thousand metre boardwalk with sea birds and marine turtles, and jutting fossil coral outcrops with Swahili names for their shapes -*Jiwe la Simba* -- shaped like a lion, *Jiwe la Jahazi* -- shaped like a dhow, *Jiwe la Ndovu* -- shaped like an elephant, and *Jiwe la Mtu* -- shaped like a human being.

Later we would have dinner at Charlie Claw's restaurant where we witnessed a mosaic of international cultures.

I remember how we'd pretend we were Tin Tin from our favourite comic book, or mimic Captain Haddock screaming, *"Thousands of blue bilious blistering thundering typhoons!"* and their companion, the eccentric absent-minded Professor Calculus, who kept begging everyone's pardon and asking them to repeat what they had just said!

"Hellooo? Are you there? You seem to have wandered into your own world." Myra's disembodied voice intruded on my memories.

I came back to earth. "Sorry, I did wander off. I was reminiscing about the last time we were together at Wasini," I replied dreamily.

"Well you don't have to dream, Kemu," Myra said. "Why don't you do something about it?"

"Like what?" I countered.

"Like come visit," she said. "Malindi isn't exactly Wasini but we can re-enact a bit, can't we?"

In the end, I reluctantly let her know that I had a free weekend coming up starting the very next day but that I was flat broke.

"Finances are not very favourable at the moment," I told her.

"Nonsense!" was her very prompt reply.

She fished out her credit card and in a couple of minutes we were driving to the Air Kenya offices.

It was like I was in a whirlwind.

The time jump too swiftly whispered into my head. This is not my friend but a different person.

In a thud I came back to the present and fifteen minutes later I had my plane ticket to Malindi for the following day in my hand.

I remembered an email Myra had written recently to me boasting that she continued to 'eat fire in Malindi[i]!'

I stared at the ticket bemusedly. Little did I know that the week-long hiatus in Malindi was going to be a defining moment of my life, shifting to new perspectives and deeper dimensions.

---

i A colloquialism directly transliterated from Bantu dialects meaning to have a good time.

Thursday 2.00 pm

Myra picked me up at Malindi airstrip. She introduced me to her two friends who were also her partners. One was Italian and the other German. As I tried to strike up a conversation with the foreigners, they seemed wary. Their monosyllabic answers to my questions irritated me. I found myself thinking internally, 'These white people perplex me! Don't they know that it is un-African, rude and insulting to have one-word answers to rhetorical questions?'

Later, I was to find out why they shunned strangers.

We drove to their cottages at Watamu, a beach resort, ten kilometres from Malindi.

Their compound's electronic gates opened to allow us in. The spacious grounds were impressive. Maisionettes and bungalows, some unoccupied, dotted the grounds at intervals.

Was that why indigenous beach hotel owners were complaining that foreigners given tax concessions by the government were poaching their clientele by offering cheaper rates?

I was given a cottage all to myself. The grounds were located on the strip of a private beach plot. On site was a large, free-form swimming pool, jacuzzis, saunas and satellite dishes hosting cable Mnet-Dstv. I was going to start by spoiling myself silly on Movie Magic!

After a while I started wondering. What had Myra gotten herself into?

We went down to the beach for a swim and later to the market.

One of Myra's partners, Antonio, the Italian, insisted that he wanted to buy *Kungu Manga*[i] to try it out later. The coastal people consider the nut to be an aphrodisiac. <u>I wondered why</u> he kept looking pointedly at me. Was

i Kiswahili -- Nutmeg

this a taste of things to come for the few days I was going to be here? I knew I would have to put him in his place sooner rather than later and set the record straight.

That evening we went out for dinner at the Lion in the Sun where the menus did not list prices, and for exclusive use of the resort for a week one needed to fork out five-million shillings. The beach resort was owned by Flavio Braitore, who also owned the Formula 1 Renault team and also used to date super model Naomi Campbell. Myra told me that the millionaire was a frequent visitor to the country and that she had rubbed shoulders with him and his wife Elizabeth Gregoraci, the Wonderbra model. Myra did not see it amazing as she name-dropped. She reeled off names of the world's who is who frequenting the Malindi tourist circuit -- Naomi Campbell, Formula 1 champion Fernando Alonso, Microsoft boss Bill Gates, former Chelsea coach now with Real Madrid Jose Mourinho and his family, and actress Angelina Jolie with partner Brad Pitt.

We sat down for a quiet dinner and got into a lively discussion.

The topic turned to the thousands of educated Kenyans who were jobless, while illegal immigrants in a lucrative crooked scheme were getting work permits in our country and were then referred to as 'expatriates' when some could hardly spell their names. Some more often than not turned out to be suave con men, especially in the banking industry! Myra's partners Antonio and Kahn the German, came across as jaded cynics.

Back at their place I excused myself and went to rest in my cottage for half an hour. I then decided to go down to the beach again. As I passed by the mansion I heard shouting and wondered what was happening. I did not mean to eavesdrop but I could not avoid hearing some of Myra's screamed words which reached my ears. "How could you?" she shouted, "I thought we agreed. No ex-spouses! No ex-lovers and certainly no excuses!"

I heard Kahn's muted voice in the background. "Do not start blowing hot and cold with me!"

A door slammed followed by sounds of breaking glass.

I covered my ears, walking hurriedly away, memories crowding my mind. Memories of my papa and mama's fights and the day I broke up with Maxi, Nehema's dad.

Though Maxi had been jobless for close to two years and I paid for everything including the rent, my younger sister's college tuition and our daughter's baby class fees, his disappearing and reappearing acts were nerve-wracking. I remember refusing to sleep with him after a particularly bad disappearing stint of three months. I did not know where he had been. He refused to go for HIV testing and tried to forcefully make love to me and I had refused. I remember holding the knife that night. "Are you going to stab me?" he had demanded.

"It is your prerogative. You rape me, I stab you. You don't rape me, I don't stab you,"

I answered, clutching the knife in my puny hand. "I do not want to be another AIDS statistic. You have seen the demographics on HIV. I have to take care of my baby. Try and force me into having sex with you and you will regret it because tomorrow you'll be in the newspaper headlines as another tragic victim of domestic violence!" When he looked into my eyes and realised that I meant it, he had left me alone.

...I shook my head trying to clear the cobwebs from my mind and strolled down to the beach.

I stayed there till late night when Myra came looking for me.

"You had a fight with Kahn. What happened earlier? I thought you two were tight?" I paused then said, "I heard snippets of your shouting match with him, though I did not mean to eavesdrop."

"I was mad because when you left the house, Antonio's girlfriend came over with one of Kahn's ex's and I was pissed off. I was not amused," Myra explained.

"I have noticed that you stay up at the main house with him. So you're now shacking up with your partner?" I asked.

"Please do not use that derogatory term and tone with Kahn. I love him and he loves me."

"Ok. Ok. Sorry Myra," I replied. "But you are my friend and I am concerned. I have noticed you're really tight with this *jamaa*[i] *Kwani*[ii] you have decided to hook up with this dude for real? I don't want you to get hurt and I don't want to be a spoilsport or *katsia*[iii] you, but why not legalise it? Get married or something." I had tried to shake off the habit of mixing Swahili slang with English but it had become a sort of Kenyan culture. "Kahn won't hear of marriage but he will come around. I am working on it." she said dejectedly.

"Myra, doesn't that tell you something? HIV positive or not?" I insisted.

"Please!' she interjected. "Why parry with semantics? Me. Him. Hurting me. Hurting him. Does it really matter? You're here so we can have some fun. Let us just drop it."

"If you say so." I had agreed.

We ran down to the water's edge like the two little girls we used to be ages ago. Little did I know that tonight and the day after was going to bring forth more drama and shenanigans.

* * * * *

Later, we decided to join the two men and have a night cap before calling it quits. We were soon into dissecting

---

i Kiswahili slang -- Dude
ii Kiswahili slang -- denotes as in 'so you have ...'
iii Kiswahili slang – 'To cut short/spoilsport.'

Kenyan banks and how influential personalities acquired loans by only a shake of the hand across a bank's chairperson's desk. Antonio and Kahn shifted to discussing how the resort was getting exaggerated electricity bills of a million Kenya shillings.

They had refused to settle them and the KPLC[i] was threatening them with disconnection.

I knew there had to be a clincher somewhere, and then it came.

A former councillor from the district had offered to help if they parted with two-hundred fifty-thousand shillings. He claimed that it was possible for him to see to it that the high billing stopped and the million shilling bills disappeared. I was mortified.

We were in the new millennium and I thought Kenyans were rising to the occasion of collective responsibility.

I asked Myra if what I was hearing was true. She said it was and that the quarter of a million was ready for the councillor to pick up the following afternoon.

I wondered what happened to patriotism. The others were looking at me as if I had gone crazy. It appeared as if they'd taken bribing, commonly referred to as TKK[ii], for granted. They were used to greasing any outstretched palms with money to get favours like doing away with protocol, bureaucracy and red tape or landing a government contract. The two investors argued that they found the culture entrenched in the country. I told them that it takes two to tango. If they stopped offering bribes there would be no takers. I wondered aloud if they knew that a charge existed in our laws about bribing government officials. Laughing cynically, they told me to wait for tomorrow and see for myself! I

---

i Kenya Power and Lighting Company

ii Kiswahili -- 'Toa Kitu Kidogo -- Euphemism to bribe (Give out something small.)

asked Myra what happened to her belief in her people's saying that, '*Kagutui ka mucii gatiha kagwo ageni*.' For all I could and see and hear, the lamentations of the righteous are all but echoes.

Friday, 1.00 p.m.

The councillor arrived.

We all had lunch together. The show began thereafter. I had been praying that the councillor would not compromise his dignity and integrity by taking the money. After lunch they did not even retire to the day room, as if Kahn and Antonio wanted me to witness the unfolding scenario first hand. Amidst the discussions on government rhetoric on various socioeconomic issues, Antonio brought out an attaché case. The money was counted and given to the councillor. I almost threw up in disgust at the gleeful look in his eyes.

Kahn impaled me with his gloating eyes, as if to say, "We told you he'd take it."

I wondered. If leaders we elected to the frontline using the ballot and our vote betrayed us, then it really was true that the corruption culture was deeply embedded in our social makeup like an appendage.

I pushed back my chair, almost stumbling on the carpet. Myra looked at me with eyes, which spoke volumes, albeit silently. 'Woman-up girl and get real! Stop being so naïve and grow up,' she seemed to be saying.

Later

While changing for dinner, I was determined to thrash it out with Myra concerning her financial situation. She was my childhood friend and I would not let her

---

i Kikuyu- The oil of the homestead is not for rubbing onto palms of strangers.

browbeat me. These cottages could not be the source of all this money. Kabum. Kadum. Kabum. Papa's voice echoed.

In the dining room, the aroma of soup wafted from the kitchen. I teased Kahn and Antonio saying that I hoped tonight we were having *ugali*[i] because I was missing it and my favourite fried *sukumawiki*[ii]. Kahn and Antonio just laughed and told me to go to the kitchen and cook what I wanted. I wondered if they could be having some maize-meal flour and the greens I craved?

In the kitchen I donned an apron and started rummaging in the cabinets and deep freezers. God knew why he took me to that kitchen. Maybe it was to touch someone's life and He used my love of *sukumawiki* to do it! I interact well with all types of characters, so naturally the cook, a Giriama from the Mijikenda[iii] community, a girl of around seventeen named Rehema, instantly took to me.

She was surprised. She seemed to be wondering silently what a guest of the high and mighty was doing in the kitchen. And wonders of wonders, I was speaking Swahili! That meant immediate affinity with the locals. I find it a shame that many Kenyans have sunk to an all-time low. So-called elitist groups hardly speak Swahili and frown upon those who converse in their tribal dialects. A good example was Myra who spoke fluent German and Italian and only spoke English and some Swahili when the likes of us were around. Her paternal and maternal mother tongues of Meru and Kikuyu were strictly reserved for only when her mama or grandma was visiting from their rural home.

I had gathered from her that Rehema's family were squatters they'd employed so as to help them make a

i Kiswahili -- Staple dish made from maize flour into hardened cake.

ii Kiswahili -- Green kale or collard greens. Named thus, which translates to "push the week" because it is cheap and affordable.

iii Nine sub-tribes of coastal Kenya

living. She had also taught the girl how to cook. As I engaged the girl in small talk she introduced a whole new perspective to Myra's version; small talk indeed it turned out to be!

I got a chicken from the freezer. There was no *sukumawiki* but at least they had spinach which could do as a substitute. No maize-meal flour either, but the girl told me that we could go up to the road side kiosk and get a packet as the shopping centre was now closed. I think she was also secretly craving our staple food *ugali*. I went back to the dining room and told Myra that I was going out for maize-meal flour. She told me to borrow her BMW. The wheels housed in their garage left me agape!

The Maasai Moran night guard and Bibi the Doberman accompanied us. As we drove up the road, Rehema showed me where they lived. The slums were squalid, dilapidated clusters of mud and coconut thatch huts. No proper sanitation, no tapped water and no electricity! No wonder for the days I had been here she appeared downcast.

She started explaining their circumstances as a by-the-way conversation, that the beach plot where the investors had built cottages was grabbed from her father. (The ugly monster that is land grabbed by fat cats rears its head again.) I thought I heard wrong but she continued.

Her narration was heart-wrenching. Her family had been helpless with no steady source of income and had stood by, hapless onlookers, as the local chief colluded with land surveyors to ensure their ancestral land was grabbed. To add salt to the injury, the two foreign investors then employed Rehema and her siblings for one-thousand Kenya shillings per month doing manual labour on the grounds and as house-helps. Her brothers and male relatives spent the little money they earned drinking *Mnazi*, the local coconut palm wine, in obscure and nondescript dinghy drinking dens.

Back at the house over dinner, I discussed the land issue with Myra and we got into a heated argument. My view was that the issue should be settled soon as it was highly volatile. Even now, Kenyans are like sitting ducks! Examples abound of how during the Kenyatta era, the first family grabbed large tracts of prime land and beach plots in the Coast and country wide. They had then used the land for political patronage and leverage, rendering indigenous owners squatters to wallow in abject penury. No wonder people say generations of the Kenyatta family will never identify with the word poverty. The volatile issue evokes bitter memories and fingers are still pointed at the family.

Antonio and Kahn did not want to hear anything about it. All they could say was that Rehema's family had been unable to clear a debt on land rates they owed the local council and their land had been sold because it had been allocated to them by the government. And that since they failed to develop it within the government's deadline it had been re-possessed and sold off. To the highest bidder, perhaps?

I wondered how much of their millions had ended up in the pockets of the local chief and his cronies? Where could people like Rehema go to for help if people meant to help them colluded to rob them? Never mind that, Rehema told me her family had a land title deed. A tattered and yellowed piece of paper dated 1920 and which reads in part:

'Colony And Protectorate Of Kenya. The Registration Of Titles Ordinance 1920'

My heart bled. Historical injustices and land alienation issues are a ticking time bomb waiting to explode in our country.

Sunday morning

This is where I started my narration to you of six years back. I was back at the mansion from my morning stroll on the beach.

"Kemu, why do you want to leave so soon? I thought you had two more days?" Myra asked.

"I miss my baby, Myra. I cannot wait to get back." I replied. "Have you thought about my proposal?" she continued.

I still could not believe it. Such a wild proposition!

I had tried to blank out the conversation from my head, though I had been the instigator. I had wanted to know where all the money came from.

To be a drug mule? I could not traffic narcotics!

I remembered our conversation of last night...

"Myra, I cannot. We've heard of people dying when these pellets burst in their stomachs." I said.

"I will promise you one thing, Kemu. You do not have to swallow any pellets. We can arrange for you to have a suitcase with a false bottom. You do not have to worry about getting caught. We have our network and your luggage won't have to go through security checks." She countered.

"I won't exactly be FedEx!" I replied sarcastically. I came to my senses and continued, "Myra, do you ever stop to think of what these drugs have done to the Kenyan youth?" I tried again.

"Listen to you, Kemu! Will you please stop being silly? Stop focusing on other people and start thinking about yourself and your child for a change. You do not have a job. How are you going to pay your rent? Whatever you call it, bakes, quid, dollars, chapaa, bread, shillings, pesa or colour! Money makes the world go round! And you do not have any! How are you going to survive? You'll earn lots of bakes, more than a million shillings just for this single run. You better think twice, and please do not start on me with that guilt-trip stuff! If you continue behaving this way you'll remain poor in Kenya for the rest of your life, when you can enrol Nehema at those pricey private elementary schools where you pay a quarter of a million shillings per term!" she added melodramatically.

I stared at her incredulously. I was transfixed as if watching scenes from American TV thrillers 24 and Alias. My dad's voice chose that moment to intervene. '*Kila mtu atabeba msalaba wake.*'

Who was this stranger in my friend's body?

My mind wandered back. I saw us under my Magokoro's watchful eyes pounding millet in the pestle and mortar before grinding it finely using the hollow mother stone and baby stone. The songs of the stones and songs of grains lulling us almost to sleep. Collecting firewood and later storing it in the ceiling store made of rafters.

I was jerked back abruptly...

"It is dangerous, Myra. My baby needs me. I cannot risk jail. And do not re-assure me that like Michael Schofield you'll re-enact Prison Break and get me out!" I retorted.

"You aren't listening, my friend. You are a beautiful, young, smart, talented and ingenious Kenyan. No one will suspect you. You'll look like a sales executive when you walk through that airport security, Kemu."

I could not believe this was the Myra I knew talking! With her first class honours degree in Marine Biology. Was her preferred major coming in handy? Or a case of a country's desperate jobless graduates? "Anyway what's your take on this, Myra?" I asked her. "You know I have always been against anything dishonest to a fault. Maybe that is my undoing, but I cannot start now."

She didn't respond.

I was not really surprised by this development in Myra's life; statistics indicated that drug dealing had become a multi-billion dollar 'industry' and that Kenya was a main transit point.

"I have to leave, Myra. Please drop me at the bus station," I requested shakily before temptation got the better of me.

"No need to take the bus Kemu. I will drive you to the airport. One of our friends owns a private charter. He'll fly you to Mombasa. He owes us a big foreign currency favour."

I smiled indulgently saying, "Do not tell me that Kahn and Antonio are also into money laundering?"

I was joking, but when she dropped her eyes without answering it made me wonder.

Sighing listlessly, I ran a hand through my hair. "No thanks. Today I don't wanna fly. I need the forty minute ride so I can think."

Kahn and Antonio were not there. I had already told them I was leaving this morning.

At the terminus Myra offered me an envelope. "Open it," she urged.

When I did I could not believe my eyes.

The money was going to pay my rent and Nehema's tuition ten times over. Was she tightening the noose around my neck in a last ditch effort to change my mind?

"I cannot take this. It's too much. I have a question though. When you met me on Nyerere Avenue, it was not a coincidence, was it? Had you been targeting me, Myra?"

I had this leaden heavy weight in my chest. It was pushing its way into my throat. I thought it was my breaking heart. I tried to swallow it back into its rightful place but realised it was tears as they spilled over.

I remembered my mama. She always told me that, '*Noita omonto botuko, getutu 'nkere maiso.*'[i]

At that moment I felt a subtle shift in my resolve not to get involved. It was blood money. Drug money that was destroying many families. Was I at a crossroads? Where was I going to get the rent and Nehema's admission, and tuition fee for the new term in primary school? Was I cutting my nose to spite my face?

"My dear Kemu, to be honest I knew of your problems and this was my way of bailing you out. We've come a long way together. Please, just take it. Otherwise what are you going to do about the tuition?" Myra asked.

"I don't know Myra. Maybe, if I could just have one-hundred shillings for my fare?" I had instilled much faith in my strength of character. I was not going to start compromising that judgement now.

This much I knew. My honesty, integrity, dignity and pride, no matter what else you take from me, that much remains intact. At that moment, I felt that at least once in a lifetime, one gets to a point where one encounters episodes where our doubts surrender to convictions. This was such a moment for me.

Soon, I was on my way. I always enjoyed the scenery of the Arabuko Sokoke[ii], but that day I did not seem to notice it. I was preoccupied with my own thoughts.

I reached Mombasa at half past ten. I passed by the college where my sister was studying and told her that I would pick up her niece as I was back in town. I saw the questions lingering in her eyes and weighing on her young mind. It had been that way for a while. She had been suspecting something was amiss but could not come right out with it and ask me.

---

i Kisii proverb -- 'Commit a cold blooded murder in the night, but the thicket has seen you.'

ii Tropical Rain Forests in Malindi and Kilifi districts along Kenya's coast.

Maybe it was time I explained to her that I was going to take drastic steps which may seem draconian to her, to cut down on finances -- like her college tuition for one. Once home, I locked myself in my room. I had five hours before I could pick my baby from kindergarten. I stayed on my knees, seeking divine intervention. Otherwise, how could I pull through this dire financial situation? Tears streamed down my cheeks. Was I going to be able to move from shifting sands of doubt and insecurity to deeper dimensions of Kenyan's known incredible resilience? I guessed I had rather be at peace with myself than risk repercussions. After all, Swahili sages said that, *'dunia duara[i]'*

* * * * *

...I tumble down the years from the time-warp and into the present like in a sci-fi movie. I am shivering and I am on the beach.

Myra, we've just scattered your ashes abroad. You turned out to be a marine biologist who decided to pursue the pleasures of life, and discard your science degree instead of using it to find a cure for this disease that has taken you to your destiny.

God-speed my dear. No more talks and walks with you on sandy beaches at Casuarina's Deck or Italian Gellati ice cream at Yul's Aquadrome, no sumptuous lobsters above The Mooring's floating boat or the Tamarind Dhow. Certainly no more water-skiing and scuba diving. No dancing at Yama's, the Reef Hotel's beach pub, the feel of the fine warm golden sand on our naked feet and different changing colours of the ocean reflecting our moods. No more Mombasa Sports Club's manicured lawns and a book to read as we await the live band's strains of Malaika, Jambo Kenya and Hakuna Matata. Nothing could ever replace the magic of a starlit

---

i Roughly transliterated means ,'The world is round and what goes round comes around.'

African skyline as we made silent wishes on a shooting star.

* * * * *

A month later, I stare at your death certificate number and see that now you have become another statistic for researchers. Just as we are statistics many times over from our birth certificate number, our KCPE[i] national exams index number, our KCSE[ii] index number, our national identity card number, our voters card number, our KRA[iii] PIN number, our passport number, and the latest, our KNBS[iv] number handed out during the recently concluded national census. I wonder when I will have my own death certificate number.

Myra, I know that life is transient but death is more universal than life. Everyone dies but not everyone lives. And Myra, you did live. I should know that and what a colourful life! What I did not know is that sadness, pain and loneliness could be so claustrophobic. Sometimes I oscillate between several emotions all at the same time. But as I said earlier, there is a place where my doubts surrender to convictions and my coldness to warmth. That place is in the solitude of my heart. In that solitude I am embarking on a journey without you for once, where I am to discover the emptiness of grief and the slow process of recovery. You will forever live in my heart.

...Weeks later I tremble when I read this entry in my journal. It sounds like a rhapsody of realities for now I am truly alone. All my friends are gone.

---

i Kenya Certificate of Primary Education.
ii Kenya Certificate of Secondary Education
iii Kenya Revenue Authority
iv Kenya National Bureau of Statistics.

THE SERENITY PRAYER

…happy with Him…

…kufurahika na Mwenyezi Mungu…

Coming Into My Own

It is usually said that the road to hell is paved with good intentions, and my analysis of my situation certainly seemed to be turning to paralysis. Should I have taken up Myra's offer to traffic narcotics? Had I miscalculated my confidence? The confidence of trusting in my character, that I would not be corrupted due to meager salaries that hardly met our daily needs.

Nehema's school fees for a full school term were outstanding, and so was the house rent for two months.

We were living hand-to-mouth and literally swimming against the tide. Was I being penny-wise or pound-foolish as Britons would say?

I suddenly thought of my late paternal Magokoro.

'*Kana goseboka nyasaye abarende*' is a statement that is close to my heart and late Magokoro's favourite goodbye. As Malidoma Soma says, I simply used to go home to her to be. God rest her soul in eternal peace. To be within her simple peace used to be a sort of heaven. When she would tell me and Nehema, '*Kemunto omochokoro oone na Nehema omochokororia oone,*' (Kemunto my grandchild and Nehema my great-grand child) '*kana goseboka Nyasae abarende.*' She simply meant 'As you grow older, may The Almighty be with you.' Though if translated directly it is like a riddle and means 'continue growing taller, God guard you.' Whenever she told us that, I always felt like she handed me the rainbow!

Another of her favourite parting shots was, '*genda enchera endabu etari nebigocha, Nyasae abasesenie.*' A long sentence that, simply transliterated, means 'may you have a smooth path with no stumbling blocks (meaning troubles) and God bless you.' She had a way with words that always reminded me of what beautiful people Africans are. As usual in our African way, she laced it with juicy anecdotes and allegories that told me that she wished me and Nehema a smooth and safe journey devoid of misfortunes on the way. Magokoro would tell me that unpredictable events were like spokes poked into one's donkey cart's wheels, and that was why life was filled with human ingenuity, to overcome these spokes. I learned from her that one needed to learn how to handle these spokes.

It was as if she knew I would constantly be met with buyer beware! along the way. The age old Latin doctrine reminds me of Taban Lo Liyong's famous blank poem. A blank page that was sort of letting you wonder what the writer was going through or thinking as he left the paper blank.

The past couple of months I had been relieving our church secretary who had gone on her annual leave. She came back last week and I started job seeking again. Every time I walked into offices and my CV was perused, I had to explain the one year gap when I had been on probation and could not get a job. I could not bring myself to lie when asked about what happened at my former working place. How could I explain the one year gap? Should I tell prospective employers about my year-long court case and near conviction when I ended up being placed on probation? The minute I opened my mouth and honestly talked about the court case and probation, shutters fell over long faces and I lost a chance at being gainfully employed. I felt downtrodden, like I was a good-for-nothing. I became bitter and had low self-esteem. I felt like I was a part of what some older self-righteous Kenyans in our society consider 'a lost generation.' A generation with no university degree through no fault of our own. I only had a diploma because I had to take care of my daughter single-handedly and also pay her school fees. In addition, a court case had rendered me 'damaged goods' and had almost turned me into an ex-convict. To make matters worse, without money in Kenya one is like a criminal -- the dregs of society.

I talked to a few people who advised me to start lying. They asked me to resort to fibs and white lies with a straight face and employ the services of a professional CV writer who would cover up the gap effectively, because 'CAVEAT EMPTOR' was certainly inscribed on my forehead and society had added 'DAMAGED GOODS!'

I suddenly thought of Magokoro again. Though she was no longer around, anytime I encounter Mahatma Gandhi's words, 'To forget how to dig the earth and tend the soil is to forget ourselves,' I remember her because she would always come to my rescue with her wisdom. She would tell me that I was pre-destined by God for greater things. I recall watching her as she weaved her baskets for picking tea leaves. I remember feeling like she was weaving her loving purpose for me and my daughter Nehema into the tapestry of time, especially when she would ask us to stop using spoons to eat. She insisted that it was un-African and one would never be satisfied and would remain thin! So she would insist on us using our fingers to dig into the succulent chinsaga greens and mounds of steaming *ugali*. She would also advise Nehema against scrapping at remains of food in the *sufuria* in which it had been cooked, saying that was inviting hunger to the homestead!

I wish too that paternal Sokoro was here to read my future for me from grandma's gourds filled with cowrie shells and his Ouija board which he had inherited from a colonial master for whom he had worked as a cook. To strum a traditional tune for me on his *obokano*[i] in his *akala* tyre sandals, munching hot *ugali* from

i Kisii – 8-stringed harp.

his ever present traditional bowl, *ekee*[i]. I missed my grandparents' African wisdom and way of solving problems. This is why I was thinking of the departed old souls. I had finally landed a job, but I was openly being asked to cook up figures that would convince external auditors that my boss's firm was clean. Yet, it was not. Figures were fiddled to evade the tax man. Accounting books were set on fire to conceal evidence. The excuse would be that when the night club's offices had burnt down in a minor fire the documents perished too. My boss was not scared of committing arson. Whenever I refused to cook figures other staff would do the boss' bidding. As a result they would get salary increments.

Even the cops investigating the suspected arson were involved in the cover-up.

Another time the boss ordered me to make sure that a high flying international dance hall star, whose album was topping the charts globally and was due to perform at the club one night, should be provided with the weed and champagne he had requested. First of all, I knew it was illegal to smoke weed in Kenya so I refused the weed request but complied with the champagne. The boss hit the roof and ordered one of the security details to look for the weed. Later in the club, I was shocked to see the star defiantly smoking the weed in the presence of policemen and I wondered if, when some foreign superstars perform, smoking weed becomes legal for a short while to law enforcers who turn a blind eye.

I was too scared to do anything underhanded. I had once almost gone to jail for an offence I did not commit, a.k.a the casino and probation. I dared not do anything illegal. But then, on the other hand, I was not getting any increments.

---

[i] A traditional hotpot made from sorghum fibre /dry millet stalks and cow hide that keeps food hot.

Because I was in the administration department, other times the boss would ask me to fire employees like waitresses and hostesses from the nightclub or restaurant because they had refused his amorous advances. He would then refuse to pay them their gratuity and service pay without any reason. He did not seem to have the words gratuity or service pay in his vocabulary but he loved the word Pro-rata!

I saw cabinet ministers and Members of Parliament (MPs) coming to my multi-millionaire Swedish boss for handouts when they knew he needed a favour. I soon realised that the powers that be were adopting a fatalistic attitude, yet in many countries bureaucracy was fast turning out to be a phenomenon of the past! I would think to myself 'someone ought to reprimand the old reprobates!' No wonder the other day one lady added a post script to her lonely hearts advert in the papers, proclaiming 'Ministers and MPs need not apply.'

I continued earning half the salary others were earning. On enquiring, I was told that increments were awarded on 'merit' and 'improvement.' What was left unsaid was that if I did not start cooking figures of the energy drinks he imported for sale in the country, and go to the warehouse to replace genuine bin cards with the 'cooked' ones, I would never get my increment. I continued refusing to cook the figures and falsifying the amounts of imported goods, and by doing so I was deemed as an undeserving case for an increment, forever. I went on swimming against the tide and being pound-foolish as others would call it. I prayed that I would get a job that was straight forward for once. I was finally on the home stretch to coming into my own and relying on my own convictions. Even today, I can't see a Pirelli advert and the slogan 'Power Is Nothing Without Control' and not think of this control freak boss who loved this advert to death, and would madly shout at employees that black represents power. Even all his wheels and company vehicles were painted black. In all his rides he had blaring from loudspeakers *he ain't hanging with a broke gold digger,* lyrics of Kanye West's track, "Gold Digger".

THE SERENITY PRAYER

...forever in the next...

...milele hata milele...

Turning Rages into Pages

It was already turning into a public lynching. There was mob justice from the least likely of sources even before the case was mentioned and a date fixed for court hearing.

"Are you serious? Can you dare?"

All these questions were posed to me by many people, even before the court papers were processed.

I know for most women self-preservation is a strong motivator. For me it is to stand up for truth and justice, though sometimes it may lead to self-destruction. I had let sexual harassment pass at the bank where I worked previously and at the casino where I had almost ended up in jail. This time I was not going to let it go. So, I had dared to go to court with a leading law organization that fought for women's rights. They filed a sexual harassment and wrong dismissal case. It dragged on for a year and no hearing date was fixed yet. 'The man eventually slept' as my people say – that is, he died! And I remembered that Magokoro used to say that 'it is only the foolish sand fly that gets buried with the corpse.' I decided to withdraw the court case and lay some ghosts to rest!

* * * * *

From asking me to cook figures, my boss had degenerated into a worse pastime of pestering me to become his woman. His habit of talking in the third person should have alerted me that he was a man used to having multiple women. Working at the casino and now the night club and energy drink firm for my current boss, I had learned that most unfaithful and promiscuous men cultivate this habit. He always talked in the third person when referring to himself or replying to any question posed to him. 'One needs to work hard.' 'We shall call you later.' 'One needs to be careful these days.' 'If Schmid wants a woman, Schmid gets a woman.' 'We've missed you baby. Why haven't you called us?' He used this one when on the phone to one of his mistresses.

The day I walked out of his office for good was the day I believe I finally came into my own.

I remember that day as clearly as if it were today.

...I was sitting cross-legged on a bedroom balcony overlooking the English Point across the Nyali Creek. The picturesque Old Town beckoned captivatingly. I was at the boss's house waiting for the driver to pick me up. The boss had given me an assignment, which I had initially refused to carry out. That was when he showed me the part of my appointment letter that read in part, 'management can change your duties and timings at their discretion.' I had, after all, read my contract and signed on the dotted line when accepting this job!

I still needed this job so I had agreed to go and do it. He had wanted me to come and take an inventory of his household electronics for insurance purposes. I saw it as improper to go to his residence because he had propositioned me sexually several times and I had turned him down. His bedrooms had ceiling to floor mirrors. As I recorded the electronics I came to a halt when I entered the master bedroom. I did not understand why the man had so many expensive cameras in the bedroom. Some were concealed while others were on tripod stands. I had heard the rumours about him, that he liked to watch himself on the mirrors while having sex and also would record his love-making sessions. But I always give people the benefit of the doubt until they are proven guilty. I then decided to call the office so that I could be picked up and tell the boss that I was unable to record the cameras in his room. I would tell him that I could not figure out where the serial numbers for the sophisticated cameras were situated.

As I sat on the bedroom balcony waiting, I did not hear the verandah door opening. I suddenly felt a hand on my shoulder. Startled, I jumped up. It was the boss.

He said, "Kemu, do you know how vulnerable you look sitting there?"

His charisma always pulls one like a magnet. I suddenly understood now why ladies fell over themselves to get and keep his attention. I felt a peculiar loneliness sneaking up on me and I squashed it. Sometimes we never want to be candid about our vulnerability and admit that we need someone to take care of us.

"I am sorry sir. I didn't hear you come in. I called the office so I could be picked up, but I have not finished here. I do not think I will manage alone to turn the cameras around for the serial numbers. I was expecting the driver to come and help me."

"I know. I told him I will pick you up. You know my feelings for you, Kemu. I want you."

I stared at him and replied as always. "And I have told you time and time again that I do not want you,"' infuriating him further.

"Kemu, what makes you think you're so special?"

Why was he so angry?

He made as if to hold my hand but I slipped out of his range and picked up my cell phone from the floor where I had been sitting. I calmly called for a cab, but before I could walk past him he had already switched on one of the cameras. I was shocked and ashamed at what was showing on one of the plasma screen on one wall. I felt like I was transfixed and rooted to the spot; ashamed on behalf of some young ladies of Mombasa. I was staring at some people whom I knew. I saw some familiar faces from the night club circuits. They were in bed with him. In one close-up video shooting they were in twos, threes and even fours. He had captured the models in Polaroid in orgies with him. I noticed a current reigning beauty queen. Some were former pageant winners. There were also men in the groups. I saw some naked little boys and girls who looked like they were only ten-years-old! The man certainly qualified to be certified as a pedophile. I knew pornography and videotaping such scenes was illegal but what was I to do?

I saw a more mature but familiar face. She was a prominent personality's wife. I trembled, pitying the younger girls. Did they know what damage such exposure could cause? This is especially so if they won an international crown? Why do our girls let these foreigners do this to them? A silent voice whispered in my ear, 'because of the money they splash around.'

Such is the tragedy of young girls; most of whom have grown up in poor families. I brushed past him as he stared at me enigmatically. I wondered why he had shown me the footage. Is it a case of a territorial male boasting of his conquests? I made up my mind there and then to get out of his life and group of companies. I had rather stay without a job. Wealth is a relative thing. It seemed that in his establishment, sexual harassment comes with the territory and is a sort of occupational hazard! There was also no point of me going to the police to report what I had seen in his videos, especially with the young children. There would be no point because he always tells us that he has the entire police force in his pocket.

* * * * *

Once back at the office he fired me. Maybe to show who was in power, he had gone to one wall on which he hung photos and caressed one where he was with the president. In that photo the occasion had been contributions to the president's bursary fund and he had contributed a million shillings. He was showing me that whatever we did nothing could be done to him. Next, he had fingered his Berretta pistol maybe in a show of might of who wields power and control. He reminded me that there was no point of going to the police. We had even heard that people who crossed him ended up dead and whenever relatives initiated investigations, the police said that there was no sufficient evidence to prosecute him. In his office on that last day, he had looked at me and said he would give me a hard time with the labour officials if I dared take him to court and charge him with wrongful dismissal. He said that he would claim that I had absconded duty. My foot! I told him that I wouldn't go to the labour union officials because it was a waste of time and I knew that was what he wanted. I further told him that the law would catch up with him one day because many of us had seen him summon the officials to his office and bribe them with white envelopes full of money. He countered by telling me that he might be a foreigner and holder of an alien's identity card, but he had been in Kenya more than twenty years and knew the Kenyan psyche like the back of his hand. He said that he was just about to become a citizen and that I had dare not ruin that chance for him. He told me that my intelligence would not get me anywhere in Kenya and ordered me to leave the premises. I answered him that I was going to walk out with my two legs as I did not own a personal jet like he did!

He gave me my summary dismissal letter. Barely two hours later, he went to the bank to withdraw his millions. He usually kept the money in a safe in his office to use as bribes on the police, customs officers and government officials seeking handouts. As usual, he went to the golf club with his briefcase in the trunk of his four-wheel guzzler. Gangsters struck at the club brandishing guns. They commanded patrons at the exclusive country club to lie down. They only targeted him and took his keys from him. They drove off with his car, the briefcase containing the money and his original documents.

Despite it appearing like an inside job from his employees who knew he had gone to the bank, it looked like God's hand at play. Earlier on he had fired me, did not pay me my dues but lost much more in the robbery. He later told his other employees that he had never been robbed in the twenty years he had been in Kenya and that it was like God was telling him that he had been unfair to me. He called me and asked me go back to work for him but I refused. What a pervert!

His car and money were never recovered. We never heard of the incident in the media because exclusive clubs had prior arrangement with media houses not to report on adverse incidents that occurred at their establishments.

As I reminisced later, I wondered what step to take.

We knew that cabinet ministers making 'courtesy calls' to his office were not there to discuss policy, democracy or good governance. They were there for freebies. The same applied to the white-suited industrial court officials and NGO[i] executives who wallowed in per diem allowances who came to solicit for funds from him for fictitious good causes. The ministers and others never knew but they were captured on hidden surveillance CCTV cameras in the Swede's office. Maybe that was his security in case one of them tried to blackmail him one day. Had I dared to report to KACC[ii] I knew I would be dead in a day.

In coming years I waited with bated breath for real

---

i Non-Governmental Organization

ii Kenya Anti-Corruption Commission

men to kick his white ass out of our country, but for many years no real men were standing up. Kudos to the African he-man who finally came up and bought him out of his own discotheque and energy drink company. He dared to be a lone ranger and it helped because he was also a multi-millionaire with connections in the right places.

My former boss, who had investments in almost every industry, later told some of his former employees that he now had no friends in the present government and political dispensation. I felt happy because everyone knew that he used to bribe members of the previous regime. Now he was being sued left, right and centre by aggrieved parties of years ago, businesses and individuals alike, because he always used to look for reasons not to pay for services rendered. I also sued him for sexual harassment and unlawful dismissal but he died a year later, before the case could get a mention in court, as I mentioned at the beginning of this chapter. Some people said he died of a cocaine overdose and others said it was a heart attack. Yet others said that it was AIDS – I sure was glad that I had not slept with him! Many court cases had to be withdrawn, including mine.

To give credit where it is due though, and this time it is to the government, at least now the Employment Act of 2007 requires employers with more than 20 employees to formulate a policy on sexual harassment. Among the provisions of the Act is the definition of sexual harassment, assurance of a sexual harassment-free environment and an assurance that action will be taken to ensure such harassment does not occur.

* * * * *

I was so used to running to Shilpa, Myra and Latifah to cry on their shoulders. Now that I was alone, it felt odd that they were not here to share my troubles. I can still hear God whispering to me and talking to me during that first Aha! moment at the police holding cell, ten years ago. That still, small voice saying, 'Write. Write. Write. Do not give up on your dream of becoming a writer. Give it your best shot. Do not just try. Do not believe in almost because almost does not count. Give it your all and your best and I will do the rest. I will open those hitherto closed doors for you.'

And the same urging at my second Aha! moment when on my knees in our sanctuary at church. I believe I have come full circle. I have clung on with a tenacious grip even when I could not see God's doors! Even when all I saw were strips of cracks I squeezed through stubbornly.

Coming into my own? You bet! All sorted out? Of course!

I now definitely know what I want, don't I? Just to write and write and write some more. Sometimes all you do have is a prayer. I have moved to Nairobi, our capital city. I am older and wiser now. I interact with other writers. I do not miss a *Kwani*, Litfest, or a Story Moja Hay festival. I do not miss a *Kwani*? Sunday Salon Reading at Kengeles or a mic session on poetry nights at Club Sound. Nor do I miss a Story Moja Sunday reading at the Ethiopian Das Restaurant. I attend all Kikao and Utenzi nights at the Wasanii restaurant at the Kenya National Theatre and every Amka literary session, the open space for women writers at the Goethe Institute. I also never miss the annual Nairobi International Book Fair. All these interactions have paid off. Girlfriends, I hope this story of ours, which I have taken the liberty to write, will be my debut into the literary world!

I have finally found peace in my writing, maybe to try and understand the scars etched upon my body like a heliograph of pain. One on my vagina, another on my arm and many other hidden ones. A braille letter to be read by humanity, blind as they all are. I will not self-destruct by not writing of my experiences, now that we have more open spaces as writers for expressing ourselves.

I am happy that editors from publishing houses are getting back to me and I gobble up their notes and advice to me: 'Your prose style is strong.'

'Often the shift in narrative needs to be clearer.'

'I like the voice and originality, though in some instances one hears the authors' voice and not the characters.'

'The paragraph structure is somewhat unorthodox.'

'I notice a number of fragments in the drafts. Please re-work a little bit more.'

'The various strands of narratives in the manuscript can be made into a more forceful narrative, though some readers may view the subject matters as unconventional.'

'The images you use are strong and evoke emotions successfully.'

'You have an original and powerful writing style.'

* * * * *

Girlfriends, if we could find justice then we would scream at the top of our voices. Speak, we can; converse, we do; give speeches, we have; yet still we are unable to scream for help. We sometimes long for a helping hand. We crave justice and our hearts plead for mercy, but scream? We cannot. If we could, we would, but since we all cannot, then we won't. But with pen in hand, paper underneath and sometimes with fingers flying over my laptop keyboard (which I finally bought) I will let my writings scream for all of us. Despite the shifting sands under my feet, in my short life I have tried to separate the selfless from the self-absorbed. Stopping short of self-destructing just to maintain my self-preservation, but it has not been in vain. I thank God that I have finally come into my own. I promise myself never to look back knowing that I want to write for a purpose; to stop hoarding letters of silence in my heart. Instead, turn my rages into pages. Even if they are painful papers, they will encourage other young ladies to hold on to their dignity no matter what. I have learned that no one can take your dignity away from you unless you give it to them willingly. No longer will walking away from challenges be a pattern of defiance in my life. No longer will my life seem like a series of orchestrated miscalculations or a series of addictive missteps.

With tears in my eyes, I fondly remember that Magokoro would tell me that a body of work is never finished. That it is cumulative. It deepens and expands with patience each day that you give your best, give back and contribute to the betterment of our country. Not in so many words, but she would say that slowly but surely does it. '*Binto mbia ng'ora, nsaga nsaga mbwango bikwanga,*' that is Kisii for what the English would say is, 'Hurry hurry has no blessing,' the Swahili '*Haraka haraka haina baraka*' or '*Mvumilivu hula mbivu*', Myra's mama in Gikuyu, '*Ihenye inene riunaga gikwa ihatha,*' and the French '*La patience est un chemin d'or.*'

We take so many things for granted, like the tantalizing aromas of turmeric and cardamom spices at dinner time as we gorge ourselves on delicious mutton biryani. We do not question the shifting sands of the beach on our Kenyan coast or the blueness of our ocean. We take for granted the sudden gifts of golden glances the sun throws our way. We even take for granted our destinies. But Myra, Shilpa and Latifah, we all know that we cannot deceive destiny, and this is my destiny. To fill sheets of papers with words created at first only for me,

Kemunto, as a form of self-therapy, as I wonder at what became of our ambitious visions. Myra, God rest your soul. You finished your Marine Biologist degree but put it to the wrong use. Latifah, society made you to discard your dentistry course. Shilpa, will you ever get around to pursuing your ambition of becoming an architect? It seems that it is left to me to at least accomplish my dream of becoming a writer. I promise you I will turn all our rages into pages – it is called 'girl power.' The sky is literally only the lower limit for my writing. I will indulge in it and leave behind a lasting literary legacy because to me writing is to tie time and space in chains. We have gone through so much together. Sometimes it was as if we were in a space with no options. I see it as providence and serendipity that the four of us met. This much our voyages together have taught me, that the beauty and tragedy of life is in the shifting sands of its fleeting nature. In moments we hold briefly but are forever etched in memory.

THE SERENITY PRAYER

…AMEN.'

…AMINA.'

GLOSSARY

Amal – (Arabic) – Hope

Farah – (Arabic) – Happiness

Jelebi – (Urdu) – Indian sweetmeat made from white flour and yoghurt, dipped in syrup of different colors and then deep fried in round swirls until it stiffens.

Laddoo – (Urdu) – Indian sweet balls served at most weddings and celebrations. Made of ghee, gram flour, nuts and sugar.

Paan – (Urdu) – Betel leaves stuffed with condiments like lime paste, areca nuts, grated coconut, crushed pistachio nut powder, sweet cherry jam and chutney.

Pbuh – Peace be Upon Him

Penda or Pera – (Urdu) – Sweetmeats made from khoya (dried powder milk), seasoned with cardamom and decorated with pistachio nut slivers.

Panjatan – (Persian) – Refers to the five members in the event of the cloak, i.e.: Prophet Mohammed, his daughter Fatima el Zahra, his son-in-law Ali ibn Abi Talib and his grandsons Hassan and Husayn (Peace be upon them all) in Arabic 'Hadith-e-Kissa' (A tradition from the daughter of the Prophet (Pbuh) and quoted in all authentic books of Hadith.

Kalemah – (Arabic) – Formula recited by all Muslims and converts / reverts to proclaim belief in Allah as One Absolute God and Muhammad as His messenger.

Shahīd – (Arabic) – Martyr

Yaa Allâh – (Arabic) – 'O God!'

Yaa Rahmaan -- (Arabic) – 'O most kind!'

Yaa Raheem -- (Arabic) – 'O most merciful!'